Carl Nixon is an award-winning short story writer, novelist and playwright. His first book, *Fish 'n' Chip Shop Song and other stories* went to number one on the New Zealand bestselling fiction list and was shortlisted for the Commonwealth Writers' Prize for Best First Book. In 2007 he won the Bank of New Zealand Katherine Mansfield Short Story Competition.

Nixon completed his first novel while he was the Ursula Bethell/ Creative New Zealand Writer in Residence at Canterbury University in 2006. *Rocking Horse Road* saw him identified as 'a major talent' by *North & South*, and was long-listed for the International IMPAC Dublin Literary Awards 2009. His second novel, *Settlers' Creek*, was also long-listed for the IMPAC in 2012. Both novels have also been published in Germany.

His writing for theatre includes *The Birthday Boy* and *The Raft*, numerous plays for children, and he has adapted for the stage Lloyd Jones's novel *The Book of Fame* and JM Coetzee's *Disgrace*.

The Virgin & the Whale

A LOVE STORY

CARL NIXON

VINTAGE

A VINTAGE BOOK published by Random House New Zealand
18 Poland Road, Glenfield, Auckland, New Zealand

For more information about our titles go to www.randomhouse.co.nz

A catalogue record for this book is available from the National Library of New Zealand

Random House New Zealand is part of the Random House Group
New York London Sydney Auckland Delhi Johannesburg

First published 2013

ISBN 978 1 77553 375 7
eISBN 978 1 77553 376 4

Design and internal illustrations: Carla Sy
Cover design: Kate Barraclough
Cover illustration: Jochen Schlenker/Getty Images
Author photograph: Stephanie Nixon

Printed in New Zealand by Printlink

This publication is printed on paper pulp sourced from sustainably grown and managed forests, using Elemental Chlorine Free (ECF) bleaching, and printed with 100% vegetable-based inks.

The assistance of Creative New Zealand is gratefully acknowledged by the author and the publisher

creative nz
Arts Council of New Zealand Toi Aotearoa

For Rebecca, Alice and Fenton.
And for MN, of course.

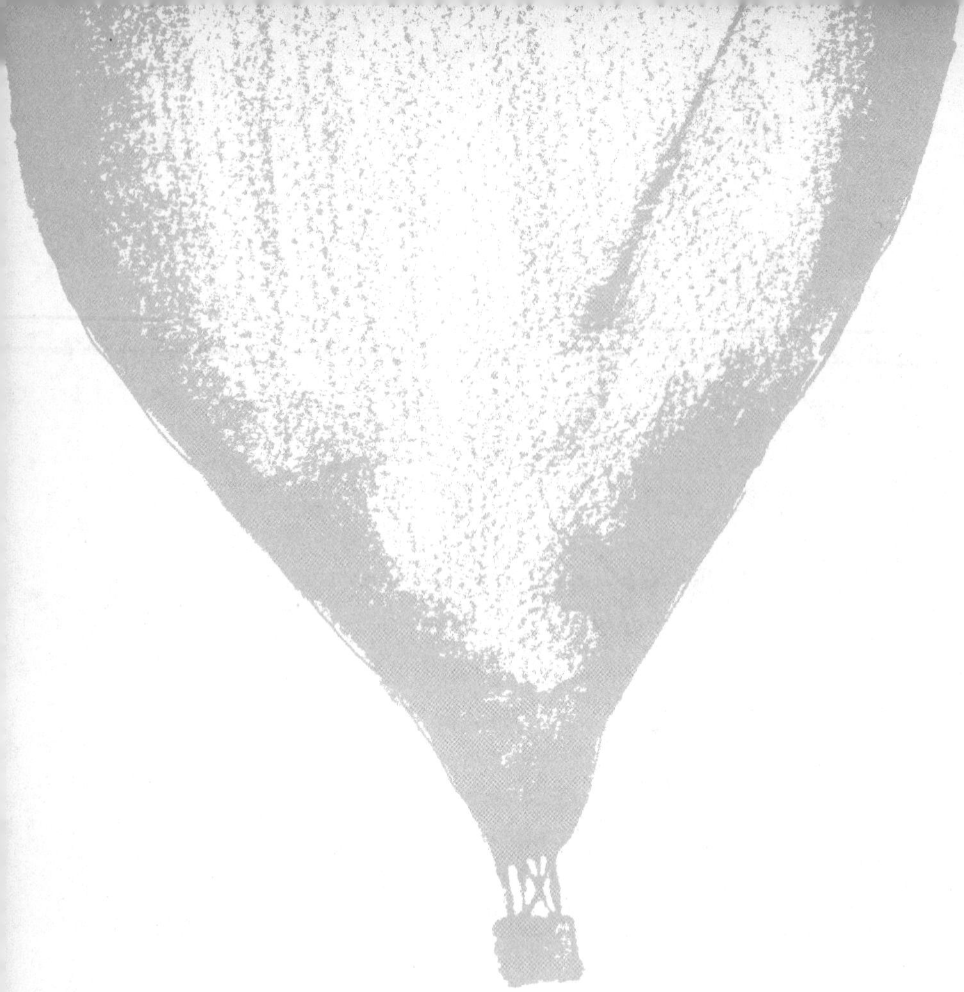

Stories, we all have stories. Nature does not tell stories, we do. We find ourselves in them, make ourselves in them, choose ourselves in them. If we are the stories we tell ourselves, we had better choose them well.

– JAMES ORBINSKI

We have, each of us, a life-story, an inner narrative — whose continuity, whose sense is our lives . . . If we wish to know about a man, we ask 'what is his story — his real inmost story?'

– OLIVER SACKS

You have to begin to lose your memory, if only in bits and pieces, to realise that memory is what makes our lives. Life without memory is no life at all.

– LUIS BUÑUEL

the beginning

In early May 2008 I received a telephone call from a softly spoken man. I will refer to him here as MN. He introduced himself and explained that he had recently read and enjoyed my first novel, *Rocking Horse Road* and thought that I might be interested in writing about his family's history. Being accosted by strangers armed with their life stories is a hazard of the writing profession. Some people are convinced that theirs will be an instant bestseller if only they had someone who could 'just write it down'. MN was very polite and outlined his story for me succinctly. I was particularly taken by one thing that he told me. I remember it clearly. He said, 'My mother fell deeply in love with a man who had no memory.'

Although I was still apprehensive, I agreed to meet him a few days later at a café in the centre of the city. I arrived early and sat at a table by the window facing the door. MN turned out to be a tall, slightly stooped man with a tanned face and white hair growing in tufts above his ears. He wore a navy-blue jacket and striped tie. I guessed he was in his early eighties (in fact he was ninety at the time).

After he insisted on buying us both a cup of coffee, he explained that he and his wife had retired to what used to be their holiday home by the beach, an hour's drive north of where we sat, although she now worried about global warming causing the ocean to rise. Personally, he didn't think it would happen in his lifetime. He had been a civil engineer for most of his career — forty-five years with the city council — and had contributed to the design of many of the city's bridges and roads.

I immediately liked MN. He impressed me with his old-fashioned manners and the thoughtful way he formed his replies to my questions. He elaborated on the story he had told me over the phone and I jotted down a few notes while he spoke. It is fair to say that by the time we had both finished our coffee, twenty minutes at the most, I was firmly hooked.

I arranged to meet MN again on several occasions over the following months. He and his wife regularly came to town to spend time with their three grown children, seven grandchildren and the most recent arrival to their extended family, a great-granddaughter. MN could usually spare me an hour or two during the course of a day when they were visiting. By this time *I* was the one who was keen to talk to him, often ringing to seek answers to the questions I formulated between our meetings.

Any doubts I had about the veracity of his story had evaporated at our second meeting — at my house this time — when MN produced a small bundle of documents, some of which dated back to the First World War. There were a dozen photographs, copies of hospital and army records, as well as the first two handwritten pages of a manuscript for an unpublished children's book. Most significantly for me, there was also a long letter from his mother written to MN in the year she died, 1969, when she was seventy-nine. All this became the basis for the story that you are about to read.

At MN's request I have changed the names of everyone involved.

He insisted on there being absolutely no publicity for himself, his wife or their wider family. To a certain extent I have fictionalised the setting, although the city of Mansfield, and perhaps the stately home, Woodbridge, may be recognisable to those who know them by their true names. Although I have been obliged to extrapolate and embellish to fill gaps in the story, the bones of the tale and a truly surprising number of the details were all there on the day that MN first spoke to me on the telephone.

Regrettably this book has taken longer to complete than I first imagined. Finding a suitable voice and then the structure took experimentation and numerous false starts. On three separate occasions I put the story aside, sure that I had come to a dead end, that I did not have the talent or the patience to complete it. Each time, however, I was drawn back by the promise MN's story showed. The delays were also due to a more pragmatic reason: I needed to complete other writing projects with more immediate financial returns. However, as any novelist will tell you, false starts, delays, interruptions and procrastination are all normal parts of a book's gestation.

MN read the early drafts of my manuscript and gave his blessing to the idiosyncratic way that I have dealt with his family's tale. Right from the start he said that he wanted it to be told as a story, rather than a piece of non-fiction. That is why he approached me, a playwright and novelist, and not a historian.

Sadly, both MN and his wife died in the winter of 2011, within weeks of each other. My only regret is that he was not able to see the published version of what has become the book you are now holding, *The Virgin and the Whale*. I trust that he would have approved.

I hope that you are as captivated by MN's story as I was when I first heard it.

Carl Nixon
March 2013

one

How to begin?

It is a perennial problem. Ever since the first campfires struggled to keep the clawed shadows of the forest at bay, storytellers have grappled with what combination of sound and meaning to set loose among the dancing firelight. Which words should be cast towards the expectant faces?

Or, in a relatively recent development: what inky scratchings will lead the argosy of dark shapes on their way, bobbing in military rows across the calm pale oceans bordered by these covers?

Spoken or written, either way the first words must be strong enough to carry the burden of everything that follows.

Once upon a time. It has certainly stood the test. But I think not; not on this occasion.

In the beginning was. That is undeniably one of the most ancient and powerful openings of all.

Let me tell you a story. No, far too generic.

A man walks into a bar. Unlikely.

But wait. For our purpose, perhaps that last *will* do. Conventional wisdom holds that when trying to get an audience's attention it's a good idea to begin with something light-hearted; an icebreaker to draw people in, to get them on side.

So here is the joke: *Balaenoptera musculus.*

Admittedly it's not the rib-tickler it was when first told by Carl Linnaeus back in 1758. That's the year the diminutive Swiss botanist, one of the first to practise rigorous scientific thought, classified the blue whale into: order (Cetacea), suborder (Mysticeti), family (Balaenopteridae), genus (*Balaenoptera*) and species (*B. musculus*).

The funny ha-ha part is that, while the Latin *musculus* is generally translated from the Latin as 'muscular', it can also mean 'mouse'. The biggest creature ever to exist on the face of the Earth is given a name synonymous with all things small.

Starting with a straightforward explanation may be best after all. It's not flashy, but it will suffice.

This story takes place in the year 1919 in a small city. It is the third largest metropolitan area of a country, which is a former colony and still a dominion of Great Britain. For the purpose of our story let us call this city Mansfield.

The city was named by one of its founding fathers in tribute to his hometown in the English county of Nottinghamshire. As was nearly always the case, the area on which Mansfield was built already had a name. In the language of the tribe of dark-skinned and tattooed people who had lived there for countless generations the name spoke of an abundance of food, combined with the word for a basket woven from flax. The wet lowlands and estuary teemed with flounder, herring and eels. It was a cornucopia of shellfish and waterfowl. *Place-of-the-overflowing-food-basket* is a rough translation, although even then some of the subtleties of meaning and cultural significance are lost.

This name went unnoticed by the vast majority of the colonists.

On the day of its (re)naming, Mansfield, to the pale newcomers, was just a collection of temporary huts located near the coast at a swampy meeting of two rivers. Unproductive. Wasteland. Some settlers thought it *so* unpromising that upon arriving at the port after a voyage of many weeks they immediately upped sticks and set out for other provinces.

By 1919, however, the swamp has been drained and the twin rivers contained between narrow banks. Mansfield has risen to become a thriving city. Its port is the busiest in the country. Wheat, barley, wool, frozen lamb and mutton, all grown and raised on the fertile plain that stretches away from the city to the west as far as the mountains, are shipped from the port as fast as they can be produced, destined for Mother England.

The city's inhabitants are overwhelmingly of good British stock: English on the whole and some Scottish. (Blessedly, from the point of view of the other settlers, the Irish have largely stayed away.) Most of the citizens are either immigrants or the children of immigrants. They still refer to the United Kingdom as Home (note the capital 'h').

The indigenous tribe was only ever small and exposure to measles and influenza quickly reduced their numbers to almost nothing. By 1919 there is hardly a brown face to be seen in Mansfield. This lack is viewed by most of its citizens as one of the city's most positive attributes, along with a high quality of ground water, well-maintained street surfaces, the lighting of public places and the early and widespread adoption of both electric trams and Mr Bell's telephone system. Mansfield also boasts excellent sewerage. The tidal estuary has proved to be a very convenient depository for the city's effluent; it is flushed twice a day.

It may be enough by way of description to say that Mansfield is sometimes referred to as 'the most English town outside of England'. If this conjures up images of a shallow river lined with willow trees, of Gothic Revival and Neo-Baroque buildings in stone and brick, or men in white playing cricket on summer's emerald lawns, perhaps a central square with an impressively spired Anglican cathedral, well, then you wouldn't be shooting very wide of the mark. Not wide at all. There are similar towns and cities to be found scattered throughout the world: Australia, Canada, New Zealand, South Africa has a few — think of Durban.

One of the most interesting features of Mansfield at this time is its whale. The 'Mansfield Whale', as it is called, is not, unfortunately, a live specimen. (That truly would have been something, perhaps exhibited in a specially constructed pool or fenced-off part of the harbour.) The city possesses the intact skeleton of a *Balaenoptera musculus.*

This had been acquired by the Mansfield Museum just over a decade earlier, in 1908. The government of the day generously contributed £200 towards the cost of acquiring and housing the specimen. Another £300 had been raised by public donation.

The blue whale was already dead when it washed up on a remote beach on the far side of the country. It took four men a month working twelve-hour days to hack, scour and boil away the stinking blubber, the muscle and stubborn ligament from the bones. These were then taken by barge, ship and rail to Mansfield. The bones were later loaded onto carts at the train station and pulled by teams of draught horses to the museum grounds, where they were painstakingly reassembled using metal rods drilled through the calcium.

The skeleton measures 99 feet in length — using the accepted standard method of measuring whales; that is by taking the length of a straight line between the point of the jaw and the notch in the tail, which marks the termination of the backbone.

Head length: 21 feet.

Length of 'hand': 12 feet.

Width of tail: 21 feet.

Not surprisingly, the galleries of the Mansfield Museum were unequal to the task of housing such an exhibit; they were simply far too small. A long corrugated-iron shed was built adjacent to the museum in the grounds of the Botanic Gardens specifically for the job. (Corrugated iron! That most ubiquitous of building materials in the colonies; strong, light, cheap, able to be stacked like playing cards, adaptable to almost any circumstance. It is even pleasing to the eye, given one generation and half a chance.)

The shelter — really just a roof, as it is open on three sides — pushes in against the stone wall on the southern side of the museum close to the main entrance to the Botanic Gardens and is visible from Nelson Avenue. Beneath the iron, the whale — all 9 tons — is suspended above the bare earth by heavy chains.

On the day of the skeleton's official unveiling, 23 March 1909, the *Mansfield Press* reported that 'thousands arrived to pack the whale shelter and overflow into the adjacent galleries'.

The reason for the overwhelming interest was that, at the time, it was the biggest whale skeleton held by any museum in the world. Such a coup sent a surge of civic pride washing through Mansfield. Its ripples lapped against the shores of the entire nation. The 'Mansfield Whale' was even mentioned in such august publications as *The Times* of London and *The Washington Post*. 'Our whale' put Mansfield on the map.

But (there is always one) . . .

Here at the start of our story, in 1919, the time since the end of the Great War can still be counted in months. While the citizens of Mansfield looked away across the oceans to husbands and fiancés, sons and brothers fighting in Europe, rain has blown in under the roof of the corrugated shelter. The crowds have long ago dispersed. The once crisp white bones are faded to grey. The metal rods have rusted, leaving stains the colour of strong tea around the edges of the drilled holes. The damage is most obvious in the multiple joints of the hands. Lichen has found a home along the southernmost jaw (20 feet 8 inches).

Only visitors to the city and young children still stop to marvel at the seemingly impossible scale of the creature's construction. For the rest of the citizens of Mansfield, familiarity and the numbing toll taken by the war have rendered the huge skeleton if not invisible, then very close to that terribly lonely state.

two

Let's choose at random a day in that year — although in a good story nothing, of course, is truly random; every aspect is selected carefully — say, 9 May 1919.

Elizabeth Whitman is walking through York Park. She is still ten minutes away from arriving at the museum and the long shed where the whale is housed. It is a little before eight o'clock in the morning. Elizabeth is wearing a grey and white nurse's uniform with her own heavy woollen coat over the top. Her auburn hair is firmly pulled back, each wisp tamed. She is coming from the small working man's cottage in the north-east of the city where she lives with her mother and father and her four-year-old son, Jack. She is on her way to her job as a sister at the hospital. In your imagination, see her move with brisk steps — nurses' steps; there is always something to do in the wards, someone's needs to attend to.

Elizabeth follows the stretch of gravel path running alongside the Stratford River around the edge of the park where the willow trees lean out over the shallow water. As we watch, she approaches, and crosses, the bridge that marks the eastern entrance to the park. She has arrived at Nelson Avenue, close to the centre of Mansfield. On the other side of the avenue are private homes, a small hotel and the staff club for the nearby university. Bicycles and trams ply the avenue. Leaving the bridge, she turns south. Now, Elizabeth is passing the stone walls of the private boys' college, where two magpies stand guard on the manicured grass. (For reasons of birth and economics she is aware that her son will never attend that particular school.) Slightly later, no more than a hundred of her steps, she is in front of the stone façade and columned entrance of the museum. Twenty feet beyond those she is beside the painted iron fence with the fleur-de-lis spikes that marks the eastern perimeter of the Botanic Gardens. If she turns her head slightly to the right Elizabeth cannot avoid seeing the whale.

But, no, she will not oblige us. She continues to stare straight ahead.

Elizabeth walks this route every working day, rain or blinking sunshine, wind or even hail (it seldom snows in Mansfield), but she habitually fails to so much as glance at the record-breaking skeleton of *Balaenoptera musculus*.

May in this part of the world is autumn. Elizabeth is warm enough in the early morning sunshine, but visibly draws deeper into her coat when walking through the many shadows stretching out across her path. An easterly wind attempts to scalpel through her layers of clothing, although the sky is bright blue and empty, stretched taut above her from horizon to horizon. The plane trees growing along the side of the avenue have already shed most of their leaves. They lie along the bottom of the iron railings, piled by the wind into ochre drifts. She does not notice *any* of this.

Why not? Why is Elizabeth Whitman so distant, so stubbornly unobservant? For the meteorologically minded it would be apt to say that even on such a clear day a cloud hangs over her. Elizabeth's thoughts are far away; literally on the other side of the world. I will leave the reason for her state of mind as a small mystery for the moment. In the interests of good storytelling, I will merely whet your appetite before leaving you — for a short while at least — up in the air.

Much closer than the other side of the world, on the other side of the avenue from Elizabeth, opposite the Botanic Gardens, is the university. As is true with so much in this city — the significance of the place names cannot have escaped you — the University of Mansfield's stony face is modelled on institutions that are also far away. On her way to work, Elizabeth passes Platonic shades of the great universities of Oxford and Cambridge. For those who know them, the original forms come to mind in the stone cloisters and courtyards. A copying from Trinity College here; a dab of Christ Church there. There is further familial resemblance in the arching brows of the Gothic Revival windows, or about the wart-like gargoyles leering from the high shadows. You should, however, picture buildings that are much newer and on a smaller scale. The University of Mansfield was built relatively quickly, over decades rather than centuries, and with the limited resources available to a colonial town.

Imagine an idea that has been boxed and shipped; a kitset that has been reassembled without exactly the right tools; a book imprecisely translated into a new language. Through its narrow cloisters and low spires, its stunted observatory and small quadrangle, the university can really only aspire. The effect is similar to meeting a friend's first cousin. For a moment, you think you know her, but then you realise that it's a case of mistaken identity, and actually she isn't as poised or as pretty as your friend, whom you've always secretly admired.

On this day, a small group of students crosses the avenue in front of Elizabeth. A decade earlier, they would have been out in far greater numbers but the ranks of the university's population have been decimated by the war and there are fewer weekly lectures. At this early hour, the few students who are enrolled move as sluggishly as cold honeybees. They pay Elizabeth no mind.

A nurse walking to work at the nearby hospital is as commonplace in the centre of Mansfield as the levitating skeleton of a blue whale.

three

You are undoubtedly wondering about this story's name — *The Virgin and the Whale*.

Perhaps it is the title that has caused you to dip a figurative toe into these pages? Despite the prurient grin the pairing will raise from some readers as they casually lift this story from the bookshop shelf or toss aside the bright wrapping paper, the pairing of whales and virgins is not unprecedented.

Both, for example, are constellations. A full twelfth of the zodiac is given over to virgins. The world is full of people born between 23 August and 22 September who live their whole lives under the sway of the unsullied stars; practical, reliable people who can also be perfectionists and are prone to being conservative.

The whale is a more obscure grouping of heavenly bodies. Cetus, as it is called, is a constellation of the southern sky, appropriately located in the region known as the Water. It lies near other watery constellations such as Aquarius, Pisces and deep-eddying Eridanus. Cetus has been known since antiquity; in ancient Mesopotamia the constellation was identified with the female sea-monster Tiamat.

If you happen to live below the equator, don't bother stepping outside your back door this evening to look for Cetus. Even seen at its best, the constellation is just a few blurry spots of light in the night sky; nothing at all like a sea-monster, much less a whale. Stay indoors. It is far more satisfying to confine the celestial leviathan's existence to your imagination.

The Bible also contains references to both whales and virgins. Mary was the most famous virgin, of course, although as the mother of Jesus she was a somewhat oxymoronic one. Rebeccah, the future wife of Isaac, is another well-known example. In the Gospel of Matthew, Jesus tells the story of the five wise virgins and the five foolish virgins. Flick back through the pages a bit and it was undoubtedly a whale that swallowed Jonah, although the original Hebrew refers to a 'great fish'.

It is worth noting that Jonah would have been very unlikely to survive the hazardous passage through the jaws of any of the toothed whales. If we are to believe that a man lived inside a whale for any length of time we can eliminate the smaller species of baleen whales; a minke or Bryde's whale simply wouldn't have had the stomach for a fully grown Israelite.

The longest reported specimen of blue whale to date was caught in the 1920s and measured just over 110 feet. The heaviest was a 190-ton female killed by a whaling ship, shortly after the Second World War. At that size the stomach would have been positively roomy. Jonah could have built a bungalow — a bay villa! — within. Perhaps it is not too far-fetched to suggest that it could have been a distant ancestor of Mansfield's own specimen that swallowed that recalcitrant Jewish prophet as he tried to flee from his god.

~

A quick definition: **virgin n. & adj. — n. 1 a person (esp. a woman) who has never had sexual intercourse**

And a clarification:

Elizabeth Whitman is not a virgin. It is important to settle this point right now in case it becomes one of those misunderstandings that drag on indefinitely.

Think of the boss who is introduced to a new worker at the office and for some reason — a wax build-up in one ear, a sudden noise on the other side of the room, a fleeting thought about his dying mother — believes that the man's name is Rupert, when in fact it is Robert. Robert is by temperament slightly shy. After several days of the boss calling him Rupert to his face and receiving no obvious contradiction, Robert effectively becomes Rupert for the duration of his time in that job.

The careful reader will recall that Elizabeth has a four-year-old son. She also has a husband. Or she *had* a husband; there is some doubt here at the start of this story over the correct tense to use. It is time to reveal that the emotional cloud hanging over her as she walks to the hospital on this autumn morning in 1919 is because her husband, Jonathan Whitman, who she calls Johnny, has not returned from fighting in France.

The Great War ended on 11 November 1918; officially, on the eleventh hour of the eleventh day of the eleventh month — a poetic conclusion to four years of slaughter. It has been over for just under five months. Technically Lieutenant Jonathan Edward Whitman is missing in action. On 4 November 1918, he was seen leading a group of three soldiers to look for wounded in a small wood near Le Quesnoy. Shortly after, the area came under heavy artillery fire from the Germans who were holding the town. That was the last anyone saw of the lieutenant or his companions.

The case of Jonathan Whitman and his wife, Elizabeth, is not unique; far from it. Throughout Europe and the British Empire the war has created hundreds of thousands of half-widows and almost-orphans. In some regions the number of missing matches that of the known dead. In times of war, people become small toys, rolling under couches and into the back of drawers. They slip into holes in skirting boards and down drains, never to be seen again.

A full day's train journey north of Mansfield, in the capital city, the words **PRESUMED DEAD** have been stamped on Jonathan Whitman's file at the Army Department. The block capitals and funereal black ink have turned the usual meaning of 'presumed' into a clerk's polite euphemism.

As we continue to watch Elizabeth walking on towards the hospital it is, however, possible to deduce from the set of her shoulders, the tilt of her chin, the purposeful manner of her progress, that she is not a woman who has been made despondent by these circumstances. We may even be able to conjecture that Elizabeth still allows hope to flicker inside her — a lit candle she nurtures against an increasingly bitter wind.

four

A car pulls up with a throaty growl on the side of the road close to Elizabeth. In 1919 cars are only for the very wealthy. Luckily, Mansfield is an obligingly flat town (built on a drained swamp, remember); most of its citizens travel without complaint by bicycle or ride the trams.

Elizabeth observes without any real interest that the car door is the refulgent black of a rain beetle's wings. For a moment she can see herself reflected in its paint and, although by no means a vain woman, she moves her hand reflexively across her hair.

She has already walked on when she hears her name called.

'Mrs Whitman. Mrs Whitman!'

She turns to see the driver still in the act of unfolding himself from behind the wheel. He raises one hand in the air as he calls her name again. A trilling school of half a dozen factory girls on bicycles veers wide of the car door and shoots off up the road.

The driver is tall, his face long and thin — not unlike that of a horse, *Equus ferus caballus* (of which, coincidentally, the Mansfield Museum has a complete skeleton on display in its main hall, barely 100 feet away). With half a dozen strides the man's long legs have covered the distance between them. Elizabeth notes that his trousers and jacket make up a type of uniform, although not a military one.

'Mrs Whitman, sorry to bother you like this. Do you remember me? It's Martin Templeton. I knew Jonathan from the war. I visited him in hospital in London.'

Elizabeth has a vague recollection of the man waiting awkwardly in the day room for Johnny to be wheeled through.

'Yes, I think I do remember. How are you?'

'Can't complain, thanks. I'm sorry to stop you on the street like this, it's very rude, but I've got a message for you from the lady I work for, Mrs Blackwell.'

She frowns. 'I'm sorry, I don't think I know Mrs Blackwell.'

'It's definitely for you, though. I was told to deliver it to you personally at the hospital. I was just on my way there when I saw you walking along. A bit of luck, eh?'

'Yes. What's it about?'

A shrug of his bony shoulders. 'No idea, sorry. The Blackwells don't tell me their business.'

It would be foolish to put this meeting down to anything as portentous as fate (or worse, poor storytelling). Such meetings are commonplace in a city the size of Mansfield. To walk its streets in 1919 is to invite a meeting with a friend, acquaintance or relative. To employ someone who knows someone to whom you wish to be known is nothing.

Martin Templeton fishes in his jacket pocket and hands Elizabeth an envelope. The paper is so heavy and textured that it reminds her of human skin.

'I was sorry to hear about Jonathan.' His eyes flicker across her face and slide down to the footpath.

Elizabeth hears many variations on this sentiment, more so as each week passes with no news. 'Sorry to hear about your husband.' 'What will you do now?' 'Such a pity for your boy. How's he bearing up?' 'The war was terrible but we all have to cope, don't we, dear?'

She nods. 'Thank you, but Jonathan is still only missing.'

His horse's face twitches as though bothered by a fly. 'Yes. Of course.' He is obviously uncertain what to say when confronted by such feminine impracticality.

For the first time, Elizabeth notices that the man is missing three fingers and part of the palm of his left hand. He sees her appraising look and unselfconsciously holds up what remains. 'A trench mortar.'

'I see.'

'Not a really bad wound, though. I've seen a lot worse.'

'Yes, so have I.'

'Leastways it was a decent Blighty. Got me out of there.'

'It's healed nicely,' she says. 'Whoever the surgeon was, he did a good job.'

'That's what the nurses in London reckoned.'

'You were lucky that you didn't have more shrapnel injuries when the shell exploded.'

He grins. 'Actually, I was supposed to be firing the bloody thing. Sorry, pardon my French. What with all the excitement and what-not, I hung onto it for a bit long.'

'At least you've still got your thumb. That makes all the difference.'

'Too right.' He opens and closes his thumb and remaining finger. 'The blokes in hospital used to call me Crab.' (A man with the face of a horse and the hand of a crab. Martin Templeton is a Victorian taxidermist's practical joke.)

Elizabeth smiles. She remembers a young soldier at the hospital in London where she nursed at the start of the war, whom the other men in the ward christened Long John. There was a Hawkeye as well. And later, when she was sent to nurse at Longhurst, she met a Pretty Boy.

'Well, thank you for delivering the letter.'

'Just doing what I'm told. Okay, then, I'd better get going. Nice to see you again.'

'And you.'

She watches as he gets back into the black car, folding himself back down behind the wheel like a ship's deckchair being put away on a rainy day. The car pulls out into the street and drives off. The bicycles scatter before it like lesser fish before a shark.

Elizabeth, left standing on the side of the road holding the envelope, stares blankly into the middle distance. She has been doing that a lot lately. How long she stays there is impossible for her to say. It is not until there is a gust of cold wind and the piled leaves close to her feet shiver and shift that their brittle whispers bring her back to herself.

Slipping the letter into her coat pocket, she turns and continues on to the hospital where her shift is due to begin in ten minutes.

five

Mrs P. Blackwell
Woodbridge House
West Ilam
Mansfield

Dear Mrs Whitman,

I write to request a meeting with you in order to discuss an important matter, which may be of benefit to us both. I will be at home on Saturday, May 17th, at nine in the morning. If you are willing, I will have my driver, Mr Templeton, with whom I believe you are already acquainted, collect you from your home at 8.30 sharp.

Please confirm your attendance by return post.

I look forward to meeting you.

Yours sincerely

The signature is illegible, pressed deep into the heavy paper as though by a tattooist's needle.

Elizabeth folds the letter carefully and slips it back into the envelope, from which comes a faint smell of lavender. She picks up her cup of tea, too hot to drink yet but still a warm comfort in her hand. From the window of the nurses' day room on the second floor of the hospital she can see north across the tops of the trees of York Park. Immediately below her half a dozen patients are out on the river bank enjoying the morning sun. Some are standing, two sit in wheelchairs with blankets draped over their knees.

Another nurse, Kitty Sullivan, a short woman with milk-bottle glasses and 'hips like a draught horse' — her own description — puts her hand on Elizabeth's shoulder.

'What's the matter, Lizzy?'

'Nothing, why?'

'You look worried. I thought it might be bad news?'

'No. Not at all.' Elizabeth has grown used to the other nurses watching her for signs that she has received confirmation of Johnny's death. 'It's an invitation to visit someone, a Mrs Blackwell. Apparently she lives out in Ilam.'

Kitty's eyes grow even bigger behind the thick circles of glass. 'Oh, lah-di-dah! Aren't you mixing in the right circles then.'

'I've never met her. Who is she?'

'You must've heard of the Blackwells?'

'I don't think so.'

'Yes you have. They're one of those old families, came over on the first ships and all that. They're rich as King Midas.'

'Oh, I see. But I've still got no idea what she wants.'

'Maybe you looked after one of her relatives overseas and she wants to thank you in person.'

'I don't remember any patient named Blackwell.'

'It's a mystery then. How exciting.'

Elizabeth puts down her cup next to the sink. 'Yes, I suppose so. Anyway, I'm not going to get too worked up about it.' She glances at her watch. 'I'd better go. And please, Kitty, I'd appreciate it if this was just between us.'

'Of course, you know me.'

She does know Kitty Sullivan. The news of Elizabeth's impending meeting with Mrs P. Blackwell would be all over the hospital before the day was out.

Elizabeth takes the stairs down to the ground floor and walks through the maze of corridors. The hospital is relatively empty. It is hard for her to believe that it was only last November when the Spanish influenza epidemic had been at its height. The number of dead in Mansfield did not reach the same levels as in the capital, where most of the returning soldiers who carried it home on the troopships had disembarked. Even so, all the hospital's beds had been filled. Patients lay on mattresses and gurneys in the corridors. There had been little the nurses could do for the worst cases. They were forced to watch as seemingly strong, healthy men and women died, sometimes within hours. But that had not stopped the entire staff from working until they dropped — quite literally.

Elizabeth herself had become sick during the third week of November. One minute she had been feeling fine; the next, she was unable to stand. She lay at home for five days, delirious and sweating, tended only by her mother. It was testament to Elizabeth's will that only a few days after the fever broke she was back helping the sick. Two of the other sisters and one of the doctors had not been so lucky. Their funerals were solemn but hasty affairs.

When Elizabeth arrives at Ward Six, the usual chorus greets her over the sound of the gramophone.

'Morning, Sister.'

'Hey, look who it is.'

'Got time to chat with an old soldier?'

She moves from bed to bed, asking questions and making mental notes about the dressings that need to be changed, medications administered, who has improved or deteriorated. Private Cooper has lost most of his sight to mustard gas. Elizabeth sits on a chair and reads him a letter from his young wife. She lives on the Coopers' farm at the foot of the mountains, with her mother- and father-in-law. When Elizabeth reaches the end of the letter, she hands it to him. Cooper folds it very carefully.

‘Thanks.’

‘Not at all.’

During the war the entire north wing had been used for the slow tide of wounded and diseased men shipped back from overseas. Most of them, however, have now gone. Ward Six alone has been set aside for the returned servicemen with conditions that have not responded to treatment. Those diagnosed with shell shock have been sent to Sunnyside, the mental asylum in the east of the city. The remaining patients boast complicated wounds or amputations, unexplained seizures or bouts of fever.

The majority of soldiers have already returned to the professions and trades they practised before the war. The government is eager for normality. After years at war, the men are no longer riflemen, artillery gunners, sappers, snipers or stretcher bearers. They are not captains, second lieutenants, sergeants or even lowly privates. They are expected to slip seamlessly back into the roles of husbands and fathers, farmers, electricians, bakers, bankers, high school teachers, tanners, tailors; suddenly all more or less equal. Even some majors and generals are now plain Fred or Rob, just the bloke in the house next door who used to be something or other in the army. After coming down the narrow gangplanks of the troopships they have all been absorbed into the waiting arms of the crowd. They shed their ranks nervously, along with their uniforms. It feels strange to have a choice of what to wear.

Put the war behind you. Look to the future. These are the slogans that they have been sold. And that is what they try to do.

So why do their hands shake? Why is it so hard to slip the bone button into the waiting hole? Why do they wake gasping and sodden in the night, their heart going like a racehorse? Their kids cry when the old man shouts about nothing much.

Hard to explain to their wives how things were — how things still are. They don’t want to burden them. What’s the point in talking about old horrors? Or even the good times, of which there were many.

All the men in Ward Six are in love with Elizabeth. Don’t make the mistake of thinking this is because she is particularly attractive.

There are prettier nurses. Nor is her patients' love bestowed on her because she is kind; quite the opposite, in fact.

Elizabeth sees her patients for what they are, men who are bereft of eyes, arms, legs, lungs, kidneys — in various combinations, both likely and unlikely. They are mutilated, broken, cripples.

You may be thinking that this is a mistake on her part. A nurse should be kind. Shouldn't Elizabeth see her patients for what they *were*: whole complete human beings? And what they *could be*: potentially productive members of a society keen to reconstruct itself?

That is certainly how the mothers and wives express themselves when they visit the patients in Ward Six. When they look at their son or husband, their eyes avoid the stump or the smooth sheets that begin halfway down the bed. They — kindly — pretend that they do not see the rubber tube snaking out from the hospital pyjamas and disappearing under the bed. The visitors always talk about the good years before the war. They talk about a bright future.

Elizabeth, however, lives strictly in the present. She seldom talks to her patients about the past and never makes promises regarding the future. Nursing overseas taught her that. Instead, she massages stumps to restore circulation. She dresses infected wounds without fuss or unnecessary comment. She smooths cream into flesh that is dry and cracked where it has been set on fire. She is practical and caring. But she is not kind.

Elizabeth's matter-of-fact acceptance of how things are proves to be an even greater balm to her patients than her ministrations.

The truth is that the men in Ward Six have come to despise Kind. Every day, they look with far-seeing eyes from the mountaintop of their situation over the kingdom of Kind. They see how it borders on the desert land of Condescension. They understand that Kind has as its capital the crumbled ruins called Pity.

six

Human warfare *could* be studied exclusively through the examination of the evolution of velocity.

In physics, velocity is defined as the rate of change of position. It is generally measured in metres per second. The average velocity (v) of an object moving through a displacement (Δd) in a straight line during a time interval (Δt) is described by the formula:

$$\vec{v} = \frac{\Delta d}{\Delta t}$$

This is a dry definition; obviously unsuited for storytelling. It is only after some consideration that I have included it here, because it proved remarkably pertinent to all those countless protagonists who lay dead and dying at Anzac Cove, on the Somme and at Passchendaele. Seen from a distance, even physics can have a certain poignancy.

The soldiers who fought in the first great conflict of the twentieth century were unfortunate enough to have been born into an era when advancements in science and manufacturing had elevated velocity to an art form. The largest European conflict to precede the Great War had been the Napoleonic Wars, a full hundred years earlier. Then, soldiers on all sides were armed with muskets. These had to be primed by hand; the powder carefully inserted, the bullet tapped into the muzzle. A man fighting at the Battle of Waterloo would have been expected to fire his musket only three times a minute under ideal circumstances. Even then, the weapon was wildly inaccurate over any distance greater than 80 yards.

Compare that with the Vickers machine gun. A single gun with a crew of three men could fire 450 to 500 rounds per minute at a muzzle velocity of 813 yards per second. The gun could fire on positions up to 4500 yards away. During twelve hours in the British attack upon High Wood in August 1916, ten Vickers guns fired a million rounds.

Not to mention artillery. The 3633 6-inch Howitzers built between 1914 and 1918 and used by the British forces fired a total of 22.4 million high explosive rounds. Each shell left the barrel at 1400 feet per second and had a range of 9500 yards. That is just one type of artillery weapon used by one army.

Even the small-bore bolt-action rifle carried by nearly every combatant in the trenches during the First World War could be expected to fire between eight and twelve rounds a minute. It was accurate at 655 yards, but could still kill at more than twice that distance.

The same technology that allowed Henry Ford's motor vehicles to roll off their assembly lines so efficiently allowed these rifles, machine guns, artillery weapons and the bullets and shells they fired — all the modern marvels of velocity — to be manufactured by the millions.

A case in point: Sergeant Paul Ronald Hill, originally from the small English town of Walton. Elizabeth Whitman nursed Sergeant Hill at Longhurst Hospital, just outside London, after he was admitted on 5 March 1915.

The sergeant had been wounded while he was standing in the window of a Catholic church in the remains of a French village, the name of which he did not know. He was lighting a cigarette and wondering where the rest of his company had got to when a German sniper's bullet struck the right side of his jaw.

The bullet that found Sergeant Hill left the sniper's rifle at a truly impressive 2441 feet per second. It slowed only slightly over the distance of 500 yards; certainly not enough to make any tangible difference to Sergeant Hill.

His head was turned slightly in order better to admire a stained-glass window depicting St Sebastian, through which a shaft of sunlight was falling. He thought the window gruesome, but its blue and red and purple panes were beautiful if seen in the right light. The same could be said of the bullet that shattered his lower jawbone on the right side just behind his last molar and carried on, slightly slowed but undeterred, through ligaments and the soft tissue of the mouth, severing most of the sergeant's tongue (he had been captain of his university's debating team and a valued member of the Gilbert and Sullivan Society; of course he had). When the bullet encountered the left side of his face — just doing its job, nothing personal — it punched through that mandible as well before finally leaving the man's body.

It is an interesting historical side note that the bullet had enough energy left to carry on 30 feet to the other side of the church, where it became embedded in an oak beam directly above the choir stalls. The bullet remains there to this day in the fully restored church; a faithful, if ironic, witness to generations of sermons on the nature of brotherly love, to marriages and baptisms, to a century of hymns proclaiming eternal peace.

Sergeant Hill was left clutching what was left of his face. He had to hold his jaw with both hands to prevent much of the lower half falling onto the floor at his feet where the flagstones were already dark and sticky. His mouth was a geyser.

If not for the swift and competent attention of a medic, Sergeant Hill would have lost enough blood to have become just another sacrifice to velocity's progress. The medic had been lying on one of the pews near the altar, trying to catch a few hours' sleep. Sergeant Hill did not feel any pain. Not at first. The medic strapped what was left of his face together with bandages and the sergeant's own leather belt, injected enough morphine to make him comfortable, reassured him that everything was going to be fine — an obvious lie, even to the wounded man — and left to find two stretcher bearers.

After passing through a regimental aid post, a casualty clearing station and a field hospital where they could not do much more than crudely sew together what was left, the sergeant was evacuated to London nine days later and then transferred to Longhurst, where Elizabeth Whitman had recently joined the nursing staff.

The hospital had formerly been a stately home. Before the war the twelfth earl had dined with his guests in Sergeant Hill's ward. On the morning of his arrival, Elizabeth was on duty. She allocated the sergeant to Ward Four, the third bed from the door, on the south side. There were twenty other men in the room. A large fireplace at one end was burning and the patients were glad of its heat.

Over the next eight months, Sergeant Hill underwent four extremely painful and sapping operations. Even then, there was little resemblance between Before and After.

The hospital was within 30 miles of the sergeant's home town. From her room at the end of the ward, Elizabeth watched during his family's visits. Because only a third of the sergeant's tongue remained, talking was almost impossible. His mother wept through her fixed smile. Sergeant Hill's father could not look his son in the eye.

Elizabeth was on duty when his mother broke the news that the sergeant's fiancée, who had made a single shocked, fleeting visit to the hospital, had broken off their engagement. The sound of a man with grafted bones, wire for a jaw and a savaged tongue weeping in the night was not something that Elizabeth would ever forget.

seven

At precisely 8.30 a.m. on Saturday, Martin Templeton pulls his employer's shiny black car up outside the cottage at 22 Sydenham Street. It is a misty morning that promises to clear into a fine day.

Elizabeth grew up in this house and has lived there with her parents and her son, Jack, ever since her return from England. It is a modest cottage — weatherboard, square windows. There are only two small bedrooms. The outhouse is at the back, next to the vegetable patch where her father grows lettuces and carrots and runner beans up lengths of twine fixed to the paling fence.

Elizabeth has been waiting in the shadow of the porch. She steps out through the gate before Martin Templeton is able to come to the front door. It embarrasses her enough that he holds the car door open for her.

'Please, I can manage.'

'Just doing my job,' he says cheerfully.

She knows that her mother will be watching at the kitchen window. Ingrained in both her parents is a profound distrust of the blurred hierarchy of wealth and connection that passes for class in this young country. Those working-class immigrants who sailed out from England and Scotland often did so believing that they would find themselves living in a place where a man is as good as his master. It is a credo they defend, sometimes with an almost religious fervour.

At the moment when Elizabeth is slipping into the leather and walnut comfort of the car, her father sits in front of a coal fire in his cramped living room. He is reading the shipping news in yesterday's newspaper while drinking his second cup of milky tea. Elizabeth's father worked for the port company all his life. He retired five years early as a result of the coal dust that had accumulated in his lungs over a lifetime of loading the black nuggets onto ships. He votes for the Workers' Party and still insists on paying part fees to the union from his invalid's pension, 'to support the cause'.

Elizabeth knows that if her father were to see her stepping into a chauffeur-driven car, the door being held open, he would spit on the ground. His wife has the good sense not to mention it later, when she delivers his third cup of tea.

Martin Templeton drives with both hands on the wheel, the fleshy pincer now in a black glove, three fingers of which are stuffed with tissue paper so that they do not hang limply. He is polite but mostly keeps a professional silence. The car smells of tobacco and leather polish.

Elizabeth is driven along Mansfield's wide, flat streets, past the cottages and factories, and then over roads lined with bungalows and villas. Eventually they cross an indistinct border into a dappled suburb where the houses have grown self-satisfied and fat, and are cloistered behind high fences. At the very edge of the city, the car slows to a near stop and, swinging off the main road like a ship turning against the current, passes between stone gateposts.

She leans forward. 'Are we here?'

'Yes, this is Woodbridge.'

Martin drives slowly along the tree-lined driveway. Elizabeth glimpses a house set among wide lawns, and framed by enough greenery to constitute a small forest. She cranes her neck and gazes at the largest private home she has seen since she left England. Woodbridge boasts wide bay windows, top and bottom, and a turret of sorts on the north side, complete with a spire. The roof is tiled in dark slate.

For her father's sake at least, Elizabeth tries not to be impressed, but it is difficult. This is a house *designed* to impress. As with the city's university and other public buildings, there is something unmistakably colonial about Woodbridge. This is not what enormous wealth would have provided elsewhere. Woodbridge is made of weatherboard, not stone or brick; its bones are of the finest native timbers. The slates on the roof were quarried nearby and local craftsmen created the leadlight windows using techniques and flourishes not seen on other shores. Likewise with the intricate wooden fretwork curling around the top of the verandah.

The tyres crunch on the deep shingle as Martin Templeton brings the car to a stop in front of the steps, which sweep up to the verandah. He almost leaps from his seat and has Elizabeth's door open before she can do it herself.

'Well, here we are then,' he says, then lowers his voice. 'We're a bit late. You'd better go in, pronto. Mrs Blackwell likes everything just so, if you know what I mean.'

'Thank you.'

Before Elizabeth reaches the top of the steps the front door is opened by a maid. She is a skinny red-headed girl of no more than fifteen.

'Hello, Mrs Whitman. Welcome to Woodbridge.' The girl's voice is high with nerves, the words obviously rehearsed. It is, Elizabeth thinks, as though the poor thing has been primed to greet royalty.

'Hello, and thank you.'

'This way, please.'

She follows the maid into a large vestibule, panelled in dark wood. An empty coat rack stands guard over an elephant's foot full of umbrellas and walking sticks. Family portraits cover the walls. All the Blackwells for three generations have assembled to inspect each visitor, to give them their oily nod.

Elizabeth is suddenly irritated: by the uniformed chauffeur and the maid, by the huge house with a name, by the inspection of these stony-faced ancestors. She is not annoyed by the people themselves, but by the roles they are playing. During her time nursing in England, Elizabeth witnessed more than enough of the casual subjugation of people that is class in action.

'What's your name?' she asks the girl.

'Merry,' she says hesitantly.

'Hello, Merry. I'm Elizabeth. But my friends call me Lizzy.' A wink.

The girl gives a start and then releases a broad smile, showing wildly uneven teeth. 'Nice to meet you . . .' She pauses, and finally opts not to tag on any name at all.

'Have you worked here long?'

'No, only a couple of months.' She adds in a hushed voice, 'I have a wee room upstairs at the back.'

'Don't you get lonely?'

'A little. I catch the tram home to see my mother and sisters on Sundays.' She frowns. 'Oh, Mrs Blackwell is waiting for you in the library. She told me to take you through right away.'

'Thank you, Merry. That would be very kind of you.'

'It's this way.'

The girl leads Elizabeth along a long hall where electric lights glow even in the daytime. Landscape paintings line the walls and the carefully dusted leaves of an agapanthus brush against Elizabeth's woollen skirt as she passes. The maid gives a quiet knock on a door.

A woman's voice answers. 'Yes. Come in.'

The room where Elizabeth finds herself is panelled in the same dark wood as the other parts of the house that she has seen. Morning sunlight washes in through a bay window. There is a large desk and a plush leather chair. The curtains are thick and forest-green, the room cluttered with shelves of books and display cases on which are rocks of various shapes and sizes.

Mrs Blackwell stands in front of the window. Elizabeth's first impression is of a woman about her own age, but with the stretched look of an animal whose ancestors evolved to forage high. (Elizabeth cannot put her finger on an exact species; giraffe is too obvious a choice, and too extreme.) Mrs Blackwell wears a dark dress. She gives the impression that she is just on her way to an important event.

'Mrs Whitman. I am very pleased to meet you.' She advances, hand outstretched. 'I am Margaret Blackwell. It is kind of you to come.'

Behind them the young maid makes a murmuring exit.

'Thank you, Merry,' says Elizabeth just before the door closes. She is rewarded by a flash of the girl's tortured teeth.

'Please, won't you sit down?'

Mrs Blackwell's voice is devoid of any of this country's usual rounding or elongations of the vowels. It could not be described as the least colonial.

For the record; Mrs Blackwell was in fact born and raised in Mansfield. Apart from one year-long excursion to England and the Continent, in 1909, while on her honeymoon, she has not left this country. Hers is an accent that has been cultivated through the best private schools and elocution lessons, as a lily might be carefully tended among a bed of thistles. Her father was a respected ship owner and at nineteen she was married to Paul Blackwell. Everyone considered it an excellent union.

'I'm pleased to meet you,' says Elizabeth.

Her initial impression of a treetop forager is not completely dispelled by observing Mrs Blackwell more closely. The woman's face is long and obviously inclined to the sombre, with large eyes that are slightly hooded.

'Are you interested in science, Mrs Whitman?'

Elizabeth is taken aback by this question. 'I'm a nurse, so of course I'm interested in medical science, at least.'

Mrs Blackwell nods as though this answer has provided her with more information than Elizabeth intended to part with. She gestures at the shelves lining the walls. Elizabeth realises that what she first thought were rocks and stones are in fact fossils.

'You may be aware that our family has one of the two largest private fossil collections in the empire.'

'No, I didn't know that.'

'Of course this is only a very small part of the collection. A good portion of it is on loan to the Mansfield Museum.'

'I see.'

'My husband's grandfather was Randolph Blackwell. Are you familiar with the name? No? He began the collection some years ago, and he also built this house. He was a merchant and one of the first to send frozen meat Home. In his retirement, he devoted himself entirely to expanding his collection.'

'I see,' Elizabeth repeats.

Mrs Blackwell crosses to a small case containing a semi-circular fossil. 'This is the egg of a type of marine dinosaur. I am told that it is millions of years old. Can you imagine?'

Elizabeth is pleased that she is not reduced to saying 'I see' for a third time when Merry slips back into the room carrying a tray.

'Ah yes, good. Thank you, Merry,' says Mrs Blackwell. 'Tea, Mrs Whitman?'

Elizabeth nods. 'Thank you.'

The two women sit and wait while Merry pours. Elizabeth thinks the poor girl looks nervous. The stream of tea coming from the spout of the china pot wavers from side to side across the mouth of Elizabeth's cup like a waterfall in an earthquake. There is a sudden muffled shout, seemingly from one of the rooms above them, and the stream of tea veers dangerously off course. Some of it splashes into Elizabeth's saucer.

'Merry,' chides Mrs Blackwell gently.

'Oh, I'm very sorry.' The girl looks as though she might cry.

Elizabeth smiles. 'Don't worry, no harm done.'

If it were not for its male timbre, Elizabeth would have guessed that the shout came from an angry child. Her hostess, however, has ignored the interruption.

'That will be all, thank you, Merry.' Mrs Blackwell waits until the girl has again left the room. 'I was very sorry to hear about your husband, Mrs Whitman. It is terrible. The war . . .' A solemn shake of her head removes the need for further words.

'Thank you. That's very kind.'

'Do you take milk or lemon in your tea?'

'Milk, please.'

'Sugar?'

'No.' Both women take a sip.

'I don't mean to be impolite,' says Elizabeth, 'but I imagine you haven't invited me here today simply to have tea.'

'No, of course you are right. You are a busy woman, as am I. Let me begin by saying that I know several people on the hospital board through my charitable work. I am assured by each and every one of them that you are the best nurse when it comes to caring for returned servicemen with profound injuries.'

'That's very generous.'

Mrs Blackwell takes another sip of her tea. The cup, which she holds so delicately, is bone china with pale blue flowers. 'I understand that you nursed overseas?'

'At the beginning of the war I was already in England visiting relatives, my father's sister. I immediately went to work at the Royal Herbert in London and later at Longhurst.'

'That is all commendable. You are to be congratulated.'

Elizabeth can hear in the undercurrents of Mrs Blackwell's voice the doubts that women who remained at home often have about those who went to war. There is the implication that boundaries of gender and propriety have been overstepped.

'I understand that you met your husband while overseas.'

'Yes. Jonathan was a patient. He was wounded at Mons. We fell in love and were married.'

'I thought that married women were not permitted to serve as nurses.'

'We were married secretly.'

Mrs Blackwell's eyes light up and for a moment she seems almost girlish. 'Really? A secret marriage sounds awfully exciting.'

'I suppose it was. At the time we were just doing what we felt we had to do to get through. War makes everything very intense. You live for today because you're not sure if there will be a tomorrow.'

Mrs Blackwell is leaning forward. 'And then after you were married your husband returned to the fighting?'

'Yes, he was eventually posted back to France and I went back to Longhurst. But when it was discovered that I was pregnant, I was forced to resign and came home to Mansfield.'

'The nation owes you a great debt, both of you.'

Elizabeth puts down her cup. 'Mrs Blackwell, I take it that you have someone who you think might benefit from my care.' She pointedly looks towards the ceiling.

A nod and a small sigh. 'Yes, my own husband, Paul Blackwell.'

On a table beside her chair is a small photograph in an intricate silver frame. Mrs Blackwell picks it up and hands it to Elizabeth. 'This is Paul.'

The picture shows a handsome man of about thirty. Paul Blackwell is standing next to a heavily laden bicycle, full panniers front and back. He is dressed formally in a suit and tie and looks very serious, almost scornful. Elizabeth is aware of an air of privilege in the scene: there, in the cut of the man's trousers, and again in the style of his leather shoes, in the newness of the bicycle, the jut of his chin. Everything about the man shouts money and breeding.

'Do you have any children?' asks Elizabeth.

'No. We have not been blessed, as yet.'

The way her eyes flick down to her lap tells Elizabeth that Mrs Blackwell doubts she will ever have children. As if on cue there is another angry shout and something heavy hits the floor of the room above. The noise is accompanied by a torrent of foul language. It pours down through the ceiling of the library, so rich in its invective that Elizabeth can seldom recall hearing its like before, even after years of working with wounded and feverish soldiers.

There is a long pause in their conversation. At last the gush of obscenities eases, and finally trickles into silence.

Mrs Blackwell has turned pale. 'I require someone to care for my husband. Apart from looking after his physical needs, it must be someone who can help with his rehabilitation.'

'I see. And for how long will you require this person?'

'For as long as it takes for my husband to return to his former self.'

'I'm already employed at the hospital.'

'If you were to accept the position then the hospital board is willing to grant you indefinite leave on the understanding that you could return to your present position at any time you wish. I have already spoken with Dr Hallum about the matter.'

'You've been very thorough.'

'In my husband's present state it falls to me to do what I can.'

'I'm flattered that you were referred to me, but the truth is that I'm happy at the hospital. I find my work there very rewarding. I'm not at all sure that I would find the same satisfaction in private nursing.'

Mrs Blackwell puts down her cup and saucer without the slightest sound. 'Mrs Whitman, I want the very best care for my husband. I am sure that you would want the same if our situations were reversed. From what I am told *you* are the best nurse in Mansfield. Dr Hallum tells me that you are possibly the best in the entire province.'

'That is kind of him.'

'I am willing to pay you twice what you now receive at the hospital.'

'I see.'

'Paul always said that if you want the best then you must pay for the best. If I can speak frankly, it cannot be easy raising a child on a nurse's salary.'

'We manage. Money isn't everything.'

'I agree. But too little can certainly cause problems. You must qualify for a war widow's benefit?'

'Jonathan is only missing. I'm not a widow.'

'Of course not. Forgive me.' Another sip of her tea. 'Won't you at least meet my husband, Mrs Whitman?'

Elizabeth nods. It would be churlish to leave at this point. 'Yes, now that I'm here. But I should warn you, I will almost certainly decline your offer, generous though it is.'

'Perhaps meeting Paul will change your mind.'

'Perhaps.'

Mrs Blackwell rises gracefully. 'I will take you to him. This way, please.' Elizabeth is still holding the photograph of Paul Blackwell. She takes another look at the handsome man standing so formally by the bicycle, then puts the frame carefully down on the table and follows Mrs Blackwell from the room.

eight

The house is even larger than Elizabeth imagined. She follows Mrs Blackwell to a stairway near the back, not as grand as the one at the entrance but still impressive and they ascend to the second floor and then walk down another hallway. Mrs Blackwell stops outside the last door on the right and produces a key from her pocket. She turns it in the lock with a heavy click. Elizabeth notices how the woman hesitates, her hand on the doorknob. She breathes in deeply as though steeling herself.

Elizabeth finds herself in a large bedroom. The curtains are pulled, creating a state of permanent dusk. It is insufferably hot. Although it is not a cold day, there is a large fire roaring in the grate. A basket full of split logs sits next to the fireplace. The flames crackle and leap up the chimney and the firelight flickers and prances, sending shadows over the walls. Curious, Elizabeth moves further into the room. Although the house undoubtedly has indoor toilets, there is clearly a bedpan in use here.

'He insists upon keeping his room at this temperature,' says Mrs Blackwell, almost whispering.

'He' is a figure who crouches by the fire with his back to them. Resting on his heels, knees tucked up almost beneath his chin, he has not so much as glanced in their direction. There is something bird-like in the way that he is perched by the hearth. He is wearing only striped pyjama pants tied at the waist with what looks like a piece of twine. Elizabeth moves closer. She is shocked to see how desperately underweight the man is. The firelight reveals ribs staggered up his back like the rungs of a ladder, skin tightening with every breath he takes. Although he still has not looked at them, Elizabeth is sure that he is acutely aware of their presence.

Mrs Blackwell advances a few tentative steps. 'Paul. Paul dear, it's me. Paul?' Her voice has lost all its authority. She sounds like an anxious girl trying to coax a kitten out of a tree.

The figure by the fire turns a baleful gaze on his wife and Elizabeth takes an involuntary step back. Any resemblance between the man in the photograph and this one is purely coincidental. This face is close to skeletal, his eyes dark caves. He has a heavy black beard that envelops his face and throat; tangled, knotted, all but obliterating the place where his mouth should be. The hair on his head is also long, longer than she has ever seen on a man. It hangs in clumped strands, framing his ravaged face.

'Paul, I've brought someone to see you. This is Mrs Whitman.'

Elizabeth forces herself forward. 'Hello, Mr Blackwell. My name is Elizabeth. I am a nurse. Do you mind if I talk to you for a moment?'

He does not reply. Instead he turns back towards the fire and continues to stare at the flames.

Elizabeth looks around for inspiration but apart from the bed and a single armchair the room is almost bare. On the wall next to the fireplace, however, stands a tall bookcase. 'I see that you have a lot of books.' She tilts her head and leans forward in the gloom. The titles are mostly to do with geology and palaeontology.

'Do you read a lot?'

'No,' says Mrs Blackwell, standing behind her, 'Paul doesn't touch them anymore. I try and encourage him.'

Elizabeth frowns. She keeps her attention on the man crouching by the fire. 'It's hard to see you in this light. Do you mind if I pull the curtains, just a little, so that we can meet each other properly?'

Receiving no sign either for or against the idea, she walks around the foot of the bed towards the window. She moves slowly as she might around a potentially dangerous dog but he only shuffles on his haunches. Elizabeth pulls the curtain aside and a corridor of sunlight spills across the polished wooden floor, cuts across the foot of the unmade bed.

'There, that's much better.'

Paul Blackwell turns his head away from the light. His skin is white and stretches even thinner over his bones than she had first imagined. Apart from his ribs she can now see the knobs of his vertebrae, the shoulder blades and the long curve of his clavicle. There are, however, no obvious scars or disfigurement. Elizabeth moves so that she can see him in profile. His face, as far as she can make out beneath his beard, retains the normal features; eyes, nose, lips, jaw, they are all accounted for. What, then, is his injury?

The only ornament in the room sits on the mantelpiece above the fire. It is a piece of polished stone, flat on the bottom but curved across the top. She walks over, still moving slowly, and picks it up. From the curved ridges on its surface she guesses that it is some form of fossilised shell. It is heavy in her hands and has taken for itself some of the warmth of the room. 'This is beautiful. What is it?'

She is talking to Paul but again it is his wife who answers. 'It is an ammonite, one of Paul's prize possessions from before the war. You remember that, don't you, Paul?'

At the sound of her voice the man closes his eyes and begins rocking on the balls of his feet. His wife does not appear to notice.

'You must remember the trip up the coast to Shingle Bay, Paul? You found that up in the cliff wall. You remember. I was there, and your father. It was a lovely summer's day, just before Christmas. You drove the motor up yourself and we had a picnic. You climbed up the cliff, even though I said it was too high, and took hours to dig the fossil out. My heart was in my mouth the whole time. You were so excited when you finally got it.'

Her husband's rocking has grown faster and he has begun to make a noise deep in his throat, a rumbling growl. Elizabeth holds up her hand. 'Mrs Blackwell, please.'

'If you make more of an effort I'm sure you can remember. Just look at it, Paul.'

'I think you're upsetting him.'

'If you would just take the time to look at it closely I am sure it would all come back to you. Why won't you even look at it?'

The man's head has begun to shake, moving backwards and forwards so violently that his chin comes close to touching first one shoulder and then the other. To Elizabeth he looks as though he were being slapped by an invisible hand. He raises both hands to his ears. 'Go away!'

Before Elizabeth can react, he has leapt to his feet like a skeletal jack-in-the-box. He lunges across the gap between himself and his wife. His arms are outstretched, hands grasping as though he intended to wring her long neck.

There is a clanking sound and Paul Blackwell is drawn up with a jolt.

Elizabeth is shocked to realise that the man's left leg has a metal cuff around the ankle. From this a chain snakes to a heavy ring fastened to the floor. Although his wife is out of reach, he is close enough to Elizabeth to turn and rip the heavy fossil out of her hands. For a man who looks as though he had been starved, he is surprisingly strong. He raises the ammonite above his head and Elizabeth is sure that he is going to bring it down on top of her own skull.

His eyes reflect the glowing fire. 'Go away!' he yells. 'Leave me alone!' Taking a step back, he throws the fossil at the floor between them. Mrs Blackwell screams and Elizabeth jumps back as it strikes the boards with a hollow boom. She hears wood splinter and feels the impact ripple up through the soles of her shoes. The fossil breaks into two parts, cracking along its own internal fault lines.

‘Go away!’ he roars.

Elizabeth backs slowly towards the door, her heart banging in her ears. ‘I’m sorry if we upset you, Mr Blackwell.’ At the door she turns and takes the visibly shaken Mrs Blackwell firmly by the arm so they can make their escape.

The last Elizabeth sees of Paul Blackwell is a glimpse of him before the door closes. Standing in the middle of the steaming room, his shoulders and chest heaving, he resembles nothing so much as a spent hunter from a prehistoric age, his stone tool shattered at his feet.

nine

In the moments that follow their hasty exit from the room, Elizabeth and Mrs Blackwell stand silently in the corridor. Both women are breathing hard, their faces flushed. Mrs Blackwell fumbles with the key, trying to relock the door, her hands shaking.

'I'm sorry. Paul appears to be having one of his bad days.' She struggles to control her voice. 'I should have warned you that he is easily agitated.'

'I can't believe that you keep your husband chained to the floor.'

'I realise how it must look, but without the chain he attempts to run away.'

'Surely locking the door is enough.'

'Since Paul has been here, he has twice escaped out the window.'

'Then I suggest you have it nailed shut.' Elizabeth's voice rises.

Mrs Blackwell is on the verge of tears. 'We did that after the first time. He broke the glass and climbed up onto the roof.'

Elizabeth forces herself to breathe deeply. 'Mrs Blackwell, I've nursed men whose minds have been badly affected by the war. You've heard the term "shell shock"?'

'Yes.'

'I've often seen it in the wards. I don't believe there's any shame in it. But you must understand that I'm not a psychiatric nurse.'

'Paul *is* physically injured. He has suffered a head injury. Here.' She touches her temple just in front of and slightly above her right ear. 'You cannot see the scar because of his hair, but it is there, I promise you.'

'A bullet wound?'

Mrs Blackwell hesitates, then gestures Elizabeth away from the door. They walk along the hall until they are standing at the top of the stairs. Light falling through a stained-glass window spills across the ground at Elizabeth's feet like coloured liquid, blue and red, splashing up over her shoes.

'All I have been told is in a letter from his doctor in England. Some type of fragment pierced his head in an explosion. They said that most likely it was from a shell.'

'Is there any metal still in the wound?'

'I am told that whatever was there was removed at a field hospital. I shudder to think under what circumstances.'

During her time nursing in England Elizabeth saw hundreds of wounds, raw and jagged. She knows better than anyone the very wide variation in the ways and means of inflicting damage on the human body.

'I see,' is her only comment. (She is aware that those two words are becoming something of a refrain.) 'And besides being easily agitated, what are your husband's other symptoms?'

'He cannot remember anything from before the accident.'

Elizabeth's eyes widen. Here, after all, is something new to her, not in the means but in the outcome. 'He remembers nothing at all?'

'So he claims.'

'Do you have reason to doubt him?'

'No, other than it seems so improbable.'

'How long ago was he wounded?'

'Eighteen months.'

'Of course I've heard of memory loss, but never for so long or so profound.'

'Apparently after he was wounded no one knew who he was for a long time. It was only by pure chance that someone recognised him at a special hospital for men with head injuries.'

'Eastbourne or Shand?'

'Shand. After the armistice they felt it was finally possible for him to make the voyage home. Mrs Whitman, let me be frank with you.'

'Please do.'

'Paul has been home for almost five weeks but . . .' she shakes her head, 'he is making no real progress, if I am honest, quite the opposite. He becomes wilder by the day.'

'Who's been looking after him?'

'At first I imagined that I could do it myself but, as you can see, it is clearly beyond me. Merry and the rest of the staff are terrified of him. He keeps that awful fire going in his room night and day and refuses to eat the food we give him. He insists we bring him tins of food which he hoards under the bed. If I refuse, he starves himself. It is impossible to predict what will enrage him.'

'Have you thought about sending him to a specialist hospital? Sunnyside perhaps? They have a number of the worst cases from the war.'

'I was hoping that he would not have to be institutionalised.'

'Of course, but sometimes it is for the best.'

'I am asking you, Mrs Whitman, please take over his care.'

'I do sympathise, I really do, but I'm sorry, I don't think there's anything I could do to help your husband.'

Mrs Blackwell turns her head away and her hooded eyes blink slowly. 'Well, thank you for your time, Mrs Whitman. I do appreciate it.' Without another word she leads the way down the stairs and through the house to the front door.

Outside, the autumn sun is still bright. Wisteria vines thread their way up the carved fretwork and Elizabeth can smell freshly cut grass. The car is waiting for her on the shingle driveway.

Mrs Blackwell stops on the edge of the verandah. 'I wish you could have met Paul before the war. He was a Rhodes Scholar, you know, and took his degree from Oxford. If it were not for the war and this,' she starts to raise her hand to her the side of her head but does not complete the gesture, 'he would have been the director of the Mansfield Museum by now.'

'I am sorry.'

For a moment Mrs Blackwell relaxes her stiff shoulders and her voice loses its formality. 'Won't you just consider my offer?' Elizabeth is unsettled to see that Mrs Blackwell is almost begging.

'Your husband's condition is beyond my ability to help.'

'Thank you for coming, Mrs Whitman.' She turns her face aside.

Elizabeth is tempted to lay a hand on the other woman's shoulder but is not sure how that would be received. 'Goodbye, Mrs Blackwell. I really do wish you the best of luck.'

Mrs Blackwell does not reply. She turns, walks back across the verandah and is lost in the shadows of the house.

Martin Templeton holds the car door open for Elizabeth, but this time she does not mind, as she is eager to be gone. The car throbs into life and pulls slowly away. As it swings wide on the gravel in front of the house, Elizabeth glances up and sees Paul Blackwell standing at his window, in the gap she made between the curtains. He is gazing out over the grounds. She knows that look. Despite his long, tangled hair and fierce beard, she recognises the expression common to all those who are hopelessly lost.

ten

The Mansfield Museum still has a human brain in a jar, even now in the twenty-first century. It floats in a bath of slightly milky formaldehyde. Discounting some accident — if the next curator is not a butterfingers — the brain will last almost indefinitely.

In the year of our story, this brain is not on display. It sits on a shelf in the lower artefacts room, gathering dust. It was put into storage as far back as 1893, and has been kept there ever since. It was about that time that one of the junior staff christened the brain 'Charlie'. The thought process behind this choice of name has been lost. Maybe it was named after a famous actor of the day, or perhaps after the staff member's particularly dull (brainless) uncle. Whatever the reason, the name has stuck. It was a name used only by the staff; few others even knew of the brain's existence. That was because successive museum directors judged the brain swimming in a jar too disturbing for the museum's patrons to see.

Why? Why any more so than, say, a human skeleton? There is one of those on permanent display just off to the left of the entrance to the main hall. Despite the sternly worded signage, generations of children have leant over the rail and enjoyed the macabre thrill of prodding the thin white arm, making the bones rattle together. 'Dem bones, dem bones.' If only the museum's donation box had a shilling for every time it heard that refrain.

Also, why is a human brain more likely to offend than the preserved head of one of the indigenous people of the country (which, following traditional practice, had the brains removed)? In the early days of European settlement there was a brisk trade in these heads between the local tribes and the whalers and sealers. So much so that the chins and cheeks of slaves captured in battle were sometimes tattooed like chiefs and the slaves then butchered to order. In 1919 the museum has *three* of those heads on display and they are inordinately popular with the public.

Here's a theory for you.

Perhaps the brain in a jar was kept out of sight because, more than any other part of the human anatomy, we identify the brain with our Self.

> *'I think therefore I am.'*
>
> – DÉSCARTES (*DISCOURSE ON THE METHOD*, PART IV, 1637)

See how inextricably linked the organ of thought and Self are? To lose an arm or a leg, while certainly regrettable, is not to lose a significant part of your *true* self.

If asked, that man (or the woman in Laos missing both her legs, or the Samoan boy in the newspaper article I was reading just last week who was deprived by meningitis of both legs *and* arms) would probably reply that, 'No, actually, I don't feel as if my fundamental self has been diminished. *I* am still here.' Or words to that effect.

Most people believe that their body exists as a handy device for carrying the Self around. The legs, the arms, the torso are designed to lift you up out of the dirt and transport you through life. They, in addition to a heart, lungs, the surging red blood full of oxygen and all the rest, are simply parts of a mobile life-support machine. The dark flashing eyes, the wavy hair, youth's muscular torso and strong thighs are all very well, but when we get down to the nitty-gritty, they are essentially window dressing for the brain. That is the impression most of us have, is it not?

Why else the radio report at noon today where it was announced that the police have found *the body* of Mr Jones, the missing fisherman? Note that the PR woman for the police is by implication stating that they have not found Mr Jones himself, only his body. This puts his flesh on a par with a missing wallet or a pilfered car stereo. When Mr Jones himself is eventually located, what is rightfully his will be returned to him.

For those of us who believe in the existence of a non-material something, which inhabits the body — often referred to in the western world as the soul — the part of the body where this ghostly presence chooses to dwell is behind the eyes. No one loses half a hand in an accident with a mortar shell and claims to have lost their soul. Our true Self — I, me (insert your own name at this point) — inhabits the space just here, in behind the eyes. *I* am here. Tap tap tap on the front of the head.

And what is behind the eyes? Hey presto, the brain!

Think of those science-fiction movies from the 1940s and 1950s where some boffin has managed to keep a brain alive in a jar. Say, for argument's sake, the brain of a man named Charlie.

It's not hard to imagine that inside that glass tank and all the bubbling liquid Charlie still exists. Admittedly, it's not an ideal position for him to be in. But it is undoubtedly better than if Charlie were still inside his body when it died (when it 'gave up the ghost').

Now, to postulate even further — stick with me here — what if a healthy body could be provided for the brain that is Charlie? Say, if the progress of science meant that a body could be grown in a vat, and this brain successfully implanted into that fresh unblemished vessel? Wouldn't it be true that Charlie lived on?

Charlie's wife may well be surprised when a man bearing no physical resemblance to her husband turns up at the door one Tuesday morning claiming to be Charlie. But after a relatively brief conversation and the exchange of some personal information that only Charlie could have known, surely his wife would be convinced that, yes, despite everything, this *is* Charlie.

This chain of thought leads us down a winding but ultimately circular road back to Paul Blackwell. If Self is inextricably linked to the brain and the memories it holds, then what can be said of a man who has been left with his body intact but a brain as blank as a fresh fall of snow?

eleven

Elizabeth's mother bustles around her small kitchen. She is a woman who likes things just so. Jack sits at his grandfather's feet in the living room by the coal fire and busies himself with a piece of paper and crayons, of which he owns four — red, blue, yellow and black. Jack is a quiet boy, with sandy blond hair and his father's wide, easy smile.

Her mother pointedly rattles the pots on the stove. 'Three pounds a week, Lizzy. Imagine that. And you'd only have the one to look after.'

Elizabeth sighs. 'Head injuries are difficult. I doubt that he'll improve much, if at all. I'd be more of a nanny than a proper nurse.'

'But it's still three pounds a week.' As she speaks, Elizabeth's mother strains the hot water from the peas into the sink. Steam rises up and fogs the kitchen window.

'There'd be no variety. At the hospital I have all sorts.'

'It sounds to me like less work and more money.'

'Maybe.'

'I don't see the *maybe* in it. You're looking a gift horse in the mouth, Lizzy.'

Jack appears at the kitchen door. He has heard a tone in his grandmother's voice. 'What's a gift horse?'

'It's all right, Jack,' says Elizabeth. 'Nana and I are just having a chat. You go and tell Granddad that his dinner will be ready in a few minutes.'

'All right, Mum.' Jack retreats to the living room.

Elizabeth gets out four plates and lays them on the plain wooden table. 'His wife claims that he has no memory of his life before he was wounded.'

'Claims?'

'It's far more likely that he's just another of those poor men who've cracked under the strain.'

Her mother sniffs pointedly, making it clear what she thinks about men lacking in mental fortitude. Elizabeth lets it pass. They have been bickering too much lately.

'I'm not trained to deal with that type of thing. It's not a wound that I can see and treat.'

'How do you know he won't come right?'

'It's been a long time since he was wounded.'

'Maybe all he needs is some proper care.'

'I've seen head injuries before.'

Elizabeth won't tell her mother the details, but she is thinking of a soldier she nursed in Longhurst. He was a captain. Several shell fragments nestled inside his head like a clutch of warm eggs in a nest. The doctors had deemed them too dangerous to remove. Written on his chart was: 'Keep comfortable and observe.'

At first he could shuffle around the ward and talk a little. But as the weeks went by he gradually became less coherent. Sentences slipped backwards into broken phrases, often repeated. Over a stinking hot August when no breeze came in through the open windows in the wards, the phrases became single words. By then he was bedridden. His thoughts were water draining out the bottom of a cracked bowl onto the polished wooden floor.

Three months after she met him the captain stopped speaking altogether. He stayed curled in his bed, knees to his chest, oblivious. Sometimes she found him sucking his thumb. She wonders what became of him.

Elizabeth's mother serves up the food. The meal is boiled potatoes, cabbage, peas and sheep's kidneys. The kidneys are a special treat, hand-delivered by a cousin of Elizabeth's who works in a butcher's shop.

Her mother will not let the subject of Paul Blackwell drop. 'And so what if in a year or so he does end up in Sunnyside with the rest of the loonies? By then you'll have saved a nice little nest egg. Perhaps it will be enough to get you and Jack a place of your own.'

'Perhaps.'

Elizabeth has been living with her parents since the day she came back from England, married to a man they had never met and six months pregnant. It is fair to say that there are lingering tensions. Although the hastiness of their daughter's nuptials has *almost* been forgiven — 'not even a telegram!' — the working man's cottage is undeniably too small for three adults and an active boy. On her return from Woodbridge that afternoon, Elizabeth could not help but note that their living room is only half the size of the library where she had drunk tea with Mrs Blackwell.

Elizabeth and Jack have shared the smaller of the bedrooms since the day she brought him home from the maternity hospital. At first he lay next to her at night in the double bed, snuffling like a hedgehog. Now that he is older there are two single beds in the room. Her father cut the double in half so expertly that you would swear they had been made that way.

'Ilam's a long way to travel each day,' counters Elizabeth, setting down the glass salt and pepper shakers.

'It's not the moon, Lizzy. There's always the tram. And for three pounds a week, I'd think you'd want to consider working on the moon.' She forks the boiled cabbage onto the plates and the smell thickens the air. 'Your father and I like having you around the place and Jack's a good boy, but this arrangement was never meant to last forever. I'm not sure it's the best thing, are you?'

Elizabeth pokes with her fork at the colourless, slimy cabbage on her plate. It is true that everyone in the house is headstrong. Inevitably there are frequent clashes. 'Maybe not.'

'This job is an opportunity, Lizzy. I don't see why you shouldn't grab it with both hands.'

'I'll think about it.'

'You do that. Now go tell those two boys that dinner's on the table. Let your father know it's kidneys tonight — that should hurry him along.'

twelve

Elizabeth has seven photographs of Jack's father. As with the days of the week, they are endlessly recycled. While other children have *Peter Rabbit* or the fables of Aesop before bedtime, Jack has these photographs. Through almost daily repetition, the story behind each one has assumed the familiarity of litany. Elizabeth hardly has to speak now; Jack can tell *her* the stories.

The boy always shuffles the photographs before he begins. He prides himself on being able to interpret each one, no matter what order it appears in.

The beach picture is slightly larger than the others and sits unevenly in his hands, corners out of alignment. Jack is orderly by temperament and training. He taps and jiggles the photograph into place before he begins.

'In this one, Daddy is young, but older than I am now. That other person is Uncle Roger. They're wearing their best clothes.'

'That's right,' says Elizabeth. 'They look very smart.'

'In this one you and Daddy have just got married. You're both wearing uniforms. You didn't have a proper wedding dress because of the war but you still look pretty and Daddy looks handsome.

'In this one you're smiling because you're married now. The man with the broken leg was your marriage witness.

'Daddy and you are in a big city called London. You were both on leaving.'

'On leave,' says Elizabeth. 'That's like a short holiday away from the army.'

'On leave. That tall statue is of another soldier, a ship soldier—'

'Lord Nelson. He was an admiral in the English navy.'

Jack scowls. He doesn't like being interrupted when he is telling the photographs' stories. 'The statue is up high. It always has lots of pigeons around it like that. It's only Dad in this one because you took the picture.

'In this one these are some of his friends in the war. They're wearing war uniforms and that is his artillery gun for shooting shells a long way.

'This last one isn't a very good picture of you and Daddy. It was taken at the train station when he was about to go back to the war after you were married. He looks sad and you aren't even looking at the camera.'

The seven photographs are a mixture of studio portraits and pictures taken on the Pocket Camera that travelled with Jack's father to the war — 'the soldier's camera', as the advertising of the day called it. The photographs allow the boy only imperfect glimpses into the past. Elizabeth is aware that her son will soon want to know more.

She has told Jack the facts.

His father was sent on patrol with three other men. They were ordered to scout for enemy soldiers in a forest in France. It was very near the end of the war and the Germans had been in retreat but were holding the nearby town, which had high stone walls around it, like a castle. His father's patrol left after midnight and was expected back the next morning.

'And then what happened?' Jack had asked.

Elizabeth doesn't know.

She has been left with an absence of story. She feels as if she were at a performance of a Greek drama. Offstage, armies clash, heroic duels are fought, storms blow and the gods' capricious whims are enacted. She has waited and waited. But the sounds from the wings have long ago faded. The other people in the audience have shuffled away with apologetic glances in her direction.

She still sits in the darkened auditorium waiting for the play to conclude. There is, however, no sign of a messenger; no last surviving member of the three hundred has turned up mortally wounded, to gasp out his tale.

But how do you explain *that* to a four-year-old?

Undoubtedly there are some mothers who would have spelt out the hard facts, laid out the slim odds and the dire possibilities under a harsh light, one by one.

There's a good chance that your father is dead. You'll almost certainly never see him again.

Elizabeth has considered that approach but she is loath to leave Jack to the mercy of the facts, which are limited, and doubt. She doesn't believe that facts and doubt are a suitable foundation on which her son should be expected to build a decent life.

That is why she has, slowly, hesitantly at first, unsure if she is doing the right thing, but then with growing confidence, begun filling the emptiness with a story.

It began on Jack's fourth birthday.

She tucked him into bed, turned out the lights, and at the point when she would usually kiss him on the forehead and slip from the room, she sat on the edge of the bed in the darkness. Jack turned his face to her expectantly.

She spoke slowly but with certainty, as though she had heard this story before, as if she knew how it proceeded and how it would end.

Once there was a man who went away in a hot air balloon. He waved goodbye to his family as he lifted off. He promised them that he would be back in exactly one year. The balloon drifted up and up and up and soon they were so far away that they looked like black ants way down, far below him.

That's how the story started. That was the very first telling.

As is true with many stories, it began with something familiar. Jack had recently seen a weather balloon being launched from a park close to where he lived. He had been on an outing with his grandmother and Elizabeth had heard all about it when she came home. Also, like most boys of that age, he was fascinated by the insects in the garden, particularly by ants.

Don't imagine that the story was as polished on that first day as it appears when written down. Of course I'm surmising: there is no transcript of that first rough draft. But undoubtedly the story would have been a clumsy soup of half-cooked words and ideas. That's just how first drafts are, even more so if they're spoken.

But Jack seemed satisfied when, after just a few minutes, Elizabeth said, 'It's late and you're tired.' She would tell him some more of the story another night if he wanted.

'All right.'

For the next two nights, Jack did not mention the story. Elizabeth was relieved. She had come to question the wisdom of her approach. She was uncertain about her ability to string together a coherent story, let alone one that would give her son something to cling to in an ocean of doubt.

And then three nights later, as Jack was pulling on his pyjamas, he said, 'I liked that story.'

'Which one?' she asked, although she knew.

'The one about the man and the balloon. Tell me some more.'

'Tell me some more, *please*.'

'Please.'

Elizabeth found it necessary to go back, repeating the start as best she could recall. She found herself refining and polishing the words so that they flowed, and better expressed what she hoped to say.

Once there was a man who left his family so that he could go and explore the world in a hot air balloon. He wore a special balloonist's uniform of blue and red and looked very smart and handsome as he waved goodbye to his wife and his young son. As the balloon lifted off from the ground, the man called out to them, repeating his promise that he would be back in exactly one year. The ground fell away beneath him as the balloon carried him up into the sky. Soon his little house, his wife and his boy were all so distant that they looked like black ants far, far below. And then they were lost from his view.

Over the weeks since his birthday the telling of this story has become a comforting routine. Elizabeth always sits on the edge of the bed, the light turned off, the door open a crack so there is just enough light for her to see Jack's face. He is generally still and silent, an audience only known by its breathing, or through small murmurs of wonder or sympathy. Sometimes Jack will ask her to stop. He rolls over onto his tummy and reaches for the glass of water on the chair next to his bed.

'Not too much or you'll need to go in the dark.'

'Oh, Mum,' he protests.

Jack doesn't request the story every night. Sometimes it will be a full week before he asks for it again. Occasionally, there will be a flurry of story nights, three or four in a row.

Elizabeth often starts by repeating what she has told him in the last instalment. Sometimes she will even go right back to the start of the story and in a few succinct sentences sum up the entire tale to date. Jack does not seem to mind the repetition. He is content just to listen.

There are other bedtime stories as well. She reads to Jack books borrowed from the Mansfield Children's Library, a brick building near the centre of the city. Jack finds some of these stories original and enthralling. Many, however, are less so. *The Balloonist*, as she comes to call her story, is the only one Elizabeth has the energy or motivation to make up.

The Balloonist is requested regularly enough that it becomes a fixture in their lives. Every time the story is told, a little more is added until it is populated with a number of different characters. There is an African named Mboli, whom the Balloonist first met when the tribesman was falling off a waterfall, over which he had been chased by an enraged white rhinoceros. The Balloonist had plucked him to safety. Mboli was a clumsy chap and often needed rescuing. (This was 1919. People whose skin was anything less than white often found themselves taking secondary roles in fiction — just as they did in colonial societies.)

Jack also likes the character of Dougal MacTavish, who chanced his way into the Balloonist's company while fleeing from the clutches of pirates whom he owed money. What a whisky-drinking, bumbling laugh the red-nosed Scotsman turned out to be.

As she walks to and from the hospital, Elizabeth finds herself thinking about directions the story could take. Her mind sifts through the possibilities, even as she performs the tasks that are part of her daily routine.

On the evening of the day when Elizabeth first meets Paul Blackwell, this is what she adds to *The Balloonist*.

thirteen

After many adventures, the Balloonist found himself flying high over a land of jungles. Or perhaps it was just one jungle; it was impossible to tell. The trees stretched in every direction as far as he could see. It was early morning and the sun had just risen above the green horizon to the east. Both Mboli and Dougal MacTavish were asleep in their hammocks in the section of the large basket separated by a blanket strung on a rope and under cover of a roof of banana-tree leaves that Mboli had fashioned. MacTavish was snoring loudly.

Peering over the edge of the basket, the Balloonist could occasionally see clearings among the trees. In some there were villages with huts of mud and roofs made of leaves. In one village he observed a naked child jump back in alarm as the balloon's shadow passed close to her feet. The child looked up and began to shout. Soon people were hurrying out from the huts. They pointed excitedly to where the balloon drifted in the sky. Some of the men threw spears and the Balloonist was glad when the breeze carried the balloon over the treetops and out of sight.

Later that day, he saw thousands of brightly coloured birds roosting in the tops of the giant trees. Startled by the balloon, the birds all took off at the same time and flew just below the basket. The flock was so thick that the Balloonist imagined he could step right out of the basket and walk across their backs just as you or I might walk over a brightly coloured rug. Of course he did not do that. As you will know, the carpet of birds would not have supported his weight and he could have fallen right through them to his death in the jungle below.

A flash of lightning arced across the sky. The boom of thunder was so close that it shook the basket. The man looked up from the birds and was surprised to see that a storm had suddenly sprung up in front of him. Storms near the equator — for that is where he now was — are not at all like the storms we have here in Mansfield. They do not gather slowly, allowing children time to come in from their games or giving mothers a chance to bring in their washing from the clothesline. In the tropics, storms leap out like a big black dog appearing from behind a bush. You always have to be on your guard.

Churning clouds stretched from the top of the trees to the tip of the sky. Within minutes the storm had overtaken the balloon, sucked it in, swallowed it whole; basket, men, supplies and all. Inside the clouds it was as dark as night. The howling wind blew rain into the Balloonist's face and shook the basket so hard that it was as if the storm were intent on tossing him out. The thunder was close enough to rattle his teeth. Somewhere behind him he heard Dougal MacTavish fall out of his hammock and curse loudly. There was the sound of breaking glass. MacTavish cursed louder still at the loss of his last bottle of whisky.

The man peered over the edge of the basket. He could not see more than a few feet so did not know if the howling wind had pushed them high or low.

As it turned out, the storm had chosen to drive the balloon downwards. The man discovered this when a branch flicked by in the darkness. And then another and another. They were flying through the treetops. Desperately he began to throw out the heavy sandbags from the bottom of the basket. Normally this would make the basket rise, but it was already too late. The storm had them in an iron grip. The basket hit a wall of branches and somehow drove through. The Balloonist had a fleeting glimpse of a startled family of orang-utans as he shot past, close enough that he could have reached out a hand and stroked their long auburn hair.

And then came the sound that he had been dreading.

Riiiiiiip.

He looked up and saw a gaping, flapping tear in the silk of the balloon. The only thing that he could do as the basket began to crash down through the trees was throw himself onto the wicker floor where he was flung around like a ball, his stomach in his mouth.

The basket plummeted through the jungle canopy. Sometimes it held up for a moment. But mostly it bounced and crashed and shuddered from one branch to another. At long last it seemed to be over when the tattered silk and the ropes snagged and the basket hung in the air. Looking up, the man saw that they were caught on a thick branch and breathed a sigh of relief. But before he could even stagger to his feet a rope snapped, the whole basket tilted and slid and began to fall again.

Finally, with a terrible thump, it hit the floor of the jungle.

The Balloonist felt something hard strike his head. Or possibly his head struck something hard: it was difficult to tell, given all the noise and the confusion. Either way, that was the last thing he knew for a long time.

fourteen

In the week after her first encounter with Paul Blackwell, Elizabeth isn't herself. In the typically imprecise way of idiom, that's not to say that she has become another person, but simply that she's distracted.

Everyone notices.

Her mother tut-tuts when Elizabeth burns the toast. Her father mumbles affectionate platitudes when he discovers her standing on the back lawn staring vacantly into the distance, her brow creased, only half the wrung washing on the clothesline. He pats her reassuringly on the shoulder with a hand caked in manured earth from the vegetable patch.

The men in Ward Six also notice but they have other things to think about. One of their number, Ian Webster — Webby, Webs — for so long a patient that he finds clothes other than his hospital pyjamas completely alien, is finally being discharged.

He is being released into the care of his mother. Anyone who has seen them together couldn't help doubting whether their relationship is going to be harmonious. Mrs Webster is a sagging woman with a flat nose and eyes like two dark raisins firmly pushed into the doughy flesh of her face. During her frequent visits to the ward she habitually leans over her son's bed, keeping up a steady stream of endearments and encouragement more suited to a five year old learning to swim than a man who has spent a considerable portion of his young life manning a Vickers machine gun. (It is worth noting that *mothering* is only a single sibilant slip away from *smothering*.)

In May 1919 the world is looking for any excuse to push the recent war to the back of its collective consciousness and kick up its heels. To celebrate Ian Webster's discharge the men of Ward Six are throwing a party. They spend that whole week preparing, gathering together the ingredients for cake and biscuits, which the kitchen staff have agreed to bake. There will be beer and gin; not sanctioned by the nurses but not explicitly forbidden either. Other small luxuries appear via friends and family. The men make paper hats out of newspaper and paint them blue and red. On Friday they decorate the ward for that evening's festivities. A line of red and blue bunting is hung over the doorway. A banner is placed along the wall above the windows on the north side of the room — GOOD LUCK WEBBY. Real balloons are in short supply so cardboard imitations have been cut out and painted festive colours. They are tied in two-dimensional bunches to the bed-heads.

When everything is ready the men help each other with buttons and belts where a missing hand or chronic trembling means that someone is unable. They joke as they wrestle with Windsor knots and the awkward bows in shoe laces.

Elizabeth stays after her shift so that she can attend.

At 4.30 the gramophone is cranked up and Al Jolson sings. He is followed by the Original Dixieland Jazz Band and by six o'clock the party is in full swing. Someone has spiked the punch with gin. Nobody minds. Half a dozen of the other nurses from the hospital have come. They laugh and talk with the men, who show off and make jokes that sometimes sail close to the wind.

Ian Webster rolls his wheelchair up and down the aisle between the beds, 'working the room', as they would say these days. A large black patch over his right eye hides the worst of the scarring. The lower halves of his trouser legs are neatly folded up and held in place by safety pins. His newspaper hat sits at a jaunty angle on his head. As the evening progresses, however, Ian becomes more and more morose. Maybe it is the gin. More likely, the cause of his dark mood is the haunting thought that, come morning, his mother will appear. She will fuss and coo over him. After they leave the hospital she will push him along the footpath, just as she used to do when he was a baby in a perambulator.

Will his wheelchair fit through the door of the tram? Or will there be a humiliating moment when they both realise that he is jammed? He imagines his mother pushing and grunting like a furrowing sow, her face turning red. People will stare. No matter what happens on the way home, soon enough he will find himself back at the house where he grew up, dossing down in the same small bedroom where he slept as a boy. He grimaces and takes another drink.

Back in the bitter winter of '17, during a raid, Private Webster's platoon overran an enemy trench. He had bayoneted a Hun through the chest, slipped the metal between his ribs. The young German had been so close, only the length of the rifle between them. Ian could see each hair on his unshaved chin and smell the wet wool of his scarf. The German's eyes were grey and scared as all hell. He was so close that Ian could have leant forward and placed a goodbye kiss on his blue lips.

Ian's hand trembles as he takes another drink and he wonders how much of his mother's care he can stand before he snaps. It was no wonder that his old man buggered off when Ian was just a kid. How long can he stomach being alone with her in the house? He fears what could happen. After all, Ian Webster knows exactly what he is capable of.

Eventually, he picks a drunken fight with the man two beds down, more to take his mind off things than out of any real animosity.

(For those who might be tempted to put a wager on such a fight, deciding on the odds would be difficult. In a brawl between a man with no legs and one eye, and another who is missing his favoured arm, his left, along with most of his shoulder and a good percentage of the capacity of his lungs, neither stands out as having an obvious advantage. What one pugilist gives away in height the other forfeits through lack of a left hook. Or jab or uppercut. Lungs damaged by gas or not, after their long convalescence both lack stamina.)

Elizabeth watches while an orderly attempts to drag the two men apart. She has been thinking about Paul Blackwell all week. Now, the sight of the two invalids rolling together on the floor spurs her to make a decision. There is a telephone in the nurses' office on the second floor. Elizabeth asks the operator for an outside line and then requests a connection to the Blackwells' house. The maid, Merry, answers and eventually Mrs Blackwell is found.

'I have decided to accept your offer, but only on a trial basis. If after a month I feel that your husband has made no progress, then I will return to my work here at the hospital.'

Mrs Blackwell sounds deeply relieved. 'Thank you, Mrs Whitman. I was beginning to despair that we would be able to keep Paul with us here much longer.'

'Has his behaviour become worse?'

A hesitation. *Yes then*, thinks Elizabeth.

'It has certainly not improved.'

'You understand that I can't promise anything.'

'Of course. I am really not expecting miracles.'

'Good. I'll start on Monday at nine.'

'How will you travel here?'

'I'll take the tram. It's only a fifteen-minute walk from the last stop.'

'I will ask Martin to pick you up from the tram.'

'No, thank you, I prefer to walk. Having spent a great deal of time caring for patients who are bedridden, I've come to believe that walking is one of the best things for a person's health.'

'Are you sure?'

'Definitely. I'll see you first thing on Monday. Good evening, Mrs Blackwell.'

When Elizabeth returns to the ward the fight is forgotten. Everyone is singing. The men roar out the lyrics at the top of their voices.

'For he's a jolly good fellow,
For he's a jolly good fellow,
For he's a jolly good fe-ellow,
And so say all of us!'

Elizabeth is just in time to join in with the cheers.

Ian Webster sits on his bed where the orderly has deposited him and grins as the tears from his remaining eye run freely down his cheek.

fifteen

It takes Elizabeth slightly longer than she had anticipated to walk from the tram stop to the stone gateposts at the entrance to Woodbridge. She doesn't mind in the least. It is another sunny autumn day. Here on the edge of the city the distinction between rural and urban blurs among sprawling gardens, long driveways and open paddocks. It is all most pleasant.

If anything, the grounds of Woodbridge are even more impressive when seen on foot; so many senses are excluded by the sealed interior of a motor car. Elizabeth smells cut grass, and the smoke from a bonfire burning somewhere out of sight. She hears the wind in the lime trees that run the length of the drive (her point exactly; from inside the car they were merely trees). A slow stream follows the driveway before curving away and disappearing into the greenery. Seen from the shadows, the lawns are patches of emerald where the morning sunshine lies upon the grass. Further along she spies a small brick chapel set back among the trees.

Today, Mrs Blackwell is waiting to greet her at the door. She is smiling, eager to begin. 'Good morning, Mrs Whitman.'

'Good morning.'

'Thank you for coming.'

'As I said, it's only a trial.'

'I understand. Still, I am pleased. I see that you wore your uniform.'

'I thought it appropriate.'

'Of course. I will take you up to Paul. I have a few new ideas as to how we might encourage him to remember who he is.'

'Actually, Mrs Blackwell, I'd like to work with your husband alone for a while, if you don't mind. At least to begin with.'

Mrs Blackwell purses her lips. 'I see. Of course.' She hesitates. 'I do not like to say this about my own husband, but I am not sure that you will be entirely *safe* if you are alone with him.'

'I've thought of that and I agree. I'd like to have someone waiting outside the room, just in case — perhaps Mr Templeton?'

Mrs Blackwell seems relieved. 'Yes, I think that would be best.' She pulls a bell rope that is hanging near the door. Merry appears, looking flustered, and is dispatched to fetch the chauffeur. 'Tell him to meet us outside Mr Blackwell's room.'

'Okay.'

'Merry,' she chastises.

'Sorry. I mean, yes, Mrs Blackwell. Right away, ma'am.'

The two women take the main staircase up to the second floor, Mrs Blackwell leading the way, and wait outside the last door at the end of the hallway. When Martin Templeton arrives he is still awkwardly buttoning the jacket of his uniform. His remaining finger and thumb pinch at the silver buttons. Elizabeth notices the involuntary expression of disgust on Mrs Blackwell's face and sees her look away from the mutilated hand.

'Morning, Mrs Blackwell. Do you want me to bring the car round to the front?'

'No, thank you, Martin. Mrs Whitman is going to spend some

time with my husband and we would both feel more comfortable if you could wait outside the door.'

'Oh, right. Good as gold. I'll grab a chair and park myself just here.'

'Thank you,' says Elizabeth.

'Happy to help.' He flashes her a grin that makes Mrs Blackwell frown. Although not a harsh person by nature, she has certain expectations of her staff inherited from her husband. Before the war Paul would not have tolerated such informality.

'I think there's a chair in Paul's mother's old room.'

'Right,' says Martin. 'I'll fetch it.'

Martin hurries off down the hall and Mrs Blackwell turns back to Elizabeth. 'Are you sure that you don't want me to go in there with you? After all, I know Paul better than anyone.'

'No, thank you. It's important that I build a rapport with him.'

'It's just that I know so much about his history, you see.'

Elizabeth is adamant. 'Perhaps later. I do think it's best that I'm left to talk to him alone.'

Martin returns holding a bentwood chair. Elizabeth waits until Mrs Blackwell goes back to whatever she does downstairs, although she cannot really imagine how the very wealthy occupy themselves.

'I'll be right here if you need me,' says Martin.

'Thank you.'

'Be careful.'

'I'm sure I'll be fine.' She speaks with more certainty than she feels.

The bedroom is even hotter than it was on Elizabeth's first visit. She closes the door behind her but does not lock it. She is glad to see that her patient is no longer chained. Instead, five iron bars have been fitted across the window on the inside of the glass. Paul Blackwell is standing by the window staring out between those very bars. It is as if he had not moved an inch since she saw him from the car. That is not quite true: there is one difference. He is still wearing the pyjama pants but now a matching top is draped off his coat-hanger shoulders. Obviously the pyjamas were once owned by a much larger man.

No, she corrects herself, *it's more likely that they were owned by the same man, once larger*.

Paul Blackwell studiously ignores her.

Two can play at that game.

There is a comfortable-looking armchair against the wall near the door. She moves cautiously over to it and sits. This is what she has resolved to do: sit and wait. She has already seen how a flurry of attention upsets her patient. Now she will determine how he responds to her silent presence.

He remains standing, staring out the window. When it becomes obvious that she is not going away, he flicks her an irritated look as though she were a mosquito that had invaded the room and was sawing the air. She smiles but he has already turned his head back to the view.

An hour later, he adds two sizable pieces of wood to the fire before returning to his gazing. Elizabeth watches as the dry wood catches and the flames jump and stretch. A fresh wave of heat rolls into the room. She is overdressed for the conditions and wonders how long she can stand it.

Around mid-morning her patient grows hungry. He continues to ignore her as he crouches and slides out a tray from beneath the bed. On it are several tins. She identifies a half-finished tin of bully beef. He opens what may be a tin of beans, sawing at the lid with an opener until it peels away. He eats everything cold with a spoon, sitting on the edge of his bed, his back to her.

Elizabeth is sorely tempted to tell him that he need not fear her trying to steal his lunch. A brief glimpse of the pale and fatty corned beef, in combination with the oppressive heat, has been enough to make her nauseous.

When he finishes the contents of both tins, Paul Blackwell drinks deeply from a canteen. Elizabeth imagines the water must be tepid. He returns everything, including the empty tins, to the tray, slips it back under the bed and resumes his post at the window. It is all Elizabeth can do to restrain herself from clearing away the mess, refreshing the water, emptying the bedpan, pulling back the curtain to let in the light.

At midday she stands quietly and leaves the room. Martin jumps to his feet, folding a newspaper as she closes the door behind her.

'That seems like it's going pretty well.'

'I'm not sure. He hasn't said a word.'

'There's been no fireworks anyway. Mrs Blackwell only lasts five minutes before he's shouting and throwing things around.'

'Do you know what makes him so mad?'

'Nothing really. Mostly she just shows him old photos or tries to talk about things that he was fond of doing before the war.'

'I see.' She sighs. 'Well, it's early days yet. I'm feeling hungry. Mrs Blackwell said that she'd organise some lunch for me.'

'I'll take you down to see Mrs Booker — she's the cook. Booker the Cooker we call her round here, though not to her face. She'll rustle you up something nice. How long do you think you'll be?'

'I'll take half an hour.'

'Right-o. I'll come back then as well.' He stretches and rolls his shoulders. 'This sitting around is pretty tough work.'

'I'm sorry, it must be boring for you.'

'Oh, not really. I've had my fair share of excitement. This beats getting shot at by the Kaiser's lot.'

He smiles. There is something about the way that Martin Templeton looks at her in that moment that tells Elizabeth that he finds her attractive, that he is considering the possibilities. His gaze has a certain *weight*. It is a look that has crept back into her life over the last few months, always from men who are aware of her circumstances. It was there the other day in the eyes of the red-headed apprentice at her cousin's butcher's shop, although he can be no more than seventeen. She's seen it in the heavy gaze of the returned soldier living down the road. Her wedding ring seems to have become mere costume jewellery.

The kitchen at Woodbridge is at the back of the house. It is an enormous room that smells of baking and soap and wood smoke. Mrs Booker is a slim woman of about sixty whose hair is grey, her cheeks and nose red with broken capillaries. She greets Elizabeth and then fusses around the kitchen, talking all the time.

Elizabeth sits at the wooden table in the middle of the room and is soon served chicken and vegetable soup. She eats it with crusty bread fresh from the oven and butter that Mrs Booker has smeared on thick as mortar. It takes little encouragement from Elizabeth to gather from the cook information about Woodbridge, the Blackwell family and Paul himself.

'At first the poor man used to eat everything I gave him: soup, meat, vegetables, even scones and cakes — he wolfed down the lot. It did my heart good to see it, what with him being so skinny. I don't know what they fed him in that hospital where they had him in England but it looked like they'd given him nothing but bread and water.'

'It's possible he lost weight because of his wound.'

Mrs Booker huffs sceptically. 'But then one day he just stopped eating anything I fixed him. Now he only eats that terrible tinned rot. Even then the tin can't have been opened, otherwise he won't touch it.'

'Why do you think that is?'

'I've no idea, love.'

Elizabeth takes another spoonful of the soup. It is excellent. Given a choice between tinned food and Mrs Booker's cooking she knows which one she would opt for. 'How long have you worked here?'

'Oh, I've worked for the Blackwells for almost thirty years now. I started out as a maid, like little Merry. I remember Paul from when he was just a boy.'

'What was he like?'

'To tell the truth he was a strange wee chap, very serious and polite. I used to say to my Ben, that's my husband, that the boy was afraid of his own shadow. His mother used to dress him up so that he looked like he was in his Sunday best every day of the week. The worst of it was he never got sent to school when he was little. His father paid for tutors to come to the house. I think a boy needs to mix with children his own age, laugh a bit, have some rough and tumble, learn about life, you know.'

'Didn't he have any friends?'

'Not to speak of. I think he was quite lonely here in this big old place.'

'He had no one at all?'

'His cousins would visit once in a while but he didn't seem to know what to make of them. I don't think he really knew how to talk to them or play their little games. What he liked best was collecting things. Paul was always off by himself finding birds' nests and interesting stones and whatnot. He had dozens of different types of eggs at one point, all in boxes in his room. I was the one who taught him how to make a wee hole in each end with a needle and blow them so they wouldn't go off.'

'How old was he when he got interested in fossils?'

She pauses to think. 'Older, after he went off to boarding school up north. He must've been about eleven or twelve by then. He only came home for the holidays.'

'Couldn't he have gone to school in Mansfield?'

'I think mainly they sent him off because he,' she looks around the kitchen and lowers her voice, 'he didn't get on with his father that well. I shouldn't really say, because every boy loves his father, don't they? But the truth is that Mr Blackwell was a very stern man. I think Paul was scared of him. God knows, I was more than a bit scared of him myself.' She looks around the kitchen again and her ruddy face twitches slightly, making the broken capillaries squirm. 'Not that his father was at home that much. Most of the time he lived at his club. But I'll tell you one thing for free, that man knew which end of a pound note was which.'

After half an hour Elizabeth thanks Mrs Booker. 'That soup was delicious.'

'I'm pleased you enjoyed it, dear. Will you be eating here from now on?'

'Yes, if that's all right? For the next month a least. I hope it's not too much trouble for you.'

'The more the merrier, love. Nothing I hate more than having too much time on my hands.'

~

For the rest of the day Elizabeth sits in Paul Blackwell's room and simply observes him. For a while he lies on his back on the floor next to his bed and shuts his eyes, although she dares not move from her chair to see if he is actually asleep or just resting. If he is sleeping she is not surprised. It must be extremely difficult for a man so frail to keep up his energy on a diet of tinned food, no matter how curtailed his range of activities. He spends most of the afternoon staring at the fire, occasionally scratching at his beard.

Come five o'clock, Elizabeth leaves the room as silently as she entered it, locking the door behind her. Not a single word has been said all day. As to what she has seen . . . well, it is hardly a revelation that her patient eats from tins, dozes, stokes the fire and stares out the window.

'So, any luck?' asks Martin Templeton, who has swapped his newspaper for a greasy square of tarpaulin on the floor, on which is lying what appear to be parts of an engine. His hands are black with grease.

'He spends a lot of time just looking out the window.'

'Probably thanking his lucky stars he's home again.'

'Maybe.'

'Anyway, you're doing a great job.'

But Elizabeth is not at all sure. As she rides the tram home that evening, she looks out at the weatherboard suburbs. The closer the tram gets to the centre of Mansfield the more crowded it becomes. Soon all the seats are taken. People are swaying and jolting, shoulder to shoulder in the aisle, and Elizabeth is hemmed in. Looking around at the blank faces and tired eyes, she ponders the fact that, as she has heard said many times, it is indeed possible to be alone in a crowd. It can, however, be equally lonely in a room with just one other person.

sixteen

Mrs Blackwell was wrong.

It was not a piece of metal that pierced her husband's skull; neither a bullet nor a fragment of shell. Fractured steel did not wipe away Paul Blackwell's memory of his life as efficiently as a schoolteacher erasing the day's lessons from a blackboard. The doctors in England had filled in the details of what happened by relying on what was probable, but without regard for the almost infinite variations and random cruel jests that reality is always throwing up, especially in wartime.

It was a bone.

The bone was similar in appearance to the fossilised remains that Paul Blackwell once collected so avidly. Except, this was no splinter of ammonite left high and dry halfway up a limestone cliff, no shard of *Tyrannosaurus rex* rib or tooth of a marine reptile. The truth was that the bone that pierced Paul Blackwell's skull was the splintered femur from the right leg of another soldier.

The incident happened in a trench in France (exact geography is irrelevant; one trench looked pretty much the same as another all the way from the Swiss border to the North Sea coast of Belgium). Paul was standing a short way off from his platoon, a map in his hand. They had orders to relieve another platoon in the forward trenches but were lost among the labyrinth. The day was so cold that the mud was frozen in clumps and the tread on his boots failed to make any impression. He was wearing a heavy coat and good leather gloves with wool linings that his wife had sent him. Even so, he was freezing. He was arguing with his sergeant about their exact location, aware that he was probably wrong but unwilling to back down.

The calico-tearing sound of a shell from German artillery.

Paul had time to think, *God, that one's close.*

Light-flame-heat-pain.

A volcano erupted from the floor of the trench. There was a searing white flash, and a sulphuric blast from the hell's mouth that had opened up where his men had until a second ago been huddled.

The femur is the largest and strongest bone in the human body. The fragment that struck Paul Blackwell was 8 inches long and travelled at an average velocity of 150 feet per second, across 12 feet (do you remember the formula?) to where he was standing. The bone did not spin end over end but flew like a gory arrow. The sharpest, most tapered end entered through the right side of Paul's head, just in front of his ear. It lodged there, projecting some 5 inches.

The impact felt like a heavy slap to the side of the head. The type of slap his father used to administer for minor misdemeanours. *Don't snivel, little man. Act your age. Admit you've done something wrong and take the consequences.*

He tried to open his mouth to scream and may have made a sound but it was lost in the detonation of another shell that fell close to the first. He seemed to be flying through the air, his body flung backwards. It was strange having no control. He glimpsed the grey clouds above him before he came to a jarring halt, crumpling into the sodden wall of the trench, somehow 20 feet from where he'd been standing, and slid down onto the boards. He lay there for a moment unable to breathe, limp, sharp pain in his chest and in his leg. The earth above him shuddered and groaned and collapsed on top of him. Everything went black.

seventeen

At this point the story will be frustrating certain readers.

'Impossible!' or 'Isn't this supposed to be based on a *true* story?'

Perhaps you have already drawn back the book, set to lob it towards the far wall. No doubt there are other much more credible narratives stacked upon your bedside table. Or perhaps you prefer your books to be more explicitly *incredible* — strange planets, or goblins and dragons.

I understand. It is an entirely valid position to take. How can a man have an object — be it bone, shell fragment or bullet — enter his brain at such speed, to such a depth, in such circumstances, and yet survive? The chances are too small to be remotely probable. And if he did live for a short while, the infection that would inevitably follow such a wound when antiseptic treatments were still in their infancy — penicillin would not even be discovered for another decade — would have finished him off. During the Great War, tens of thousands of men died from blood poisoning.

Perhaps some earnest book reviewer is scribbling in the margin of his or her uncorrected proof copy, 'Too much suspension of disbelief required.'

Wait. Please. Just a moment.

Consider the case of one Phineas P. Gage. He was born in 1823 in New Hampshire, USA. At the age of twenty-five, while foreman of a work gang blasting rock for a railway company in Vermont, Mr Gage was tamping down blasting powder with an iron bar 3 feet 7 inches in length into a hole bored into rock. The powder exploded prematurely. It was a known risk if not enough sand was mixed with the gunpowder.

The resulting explosion fired the tamping iron some 80 feet through the air, but not before it had passed directly and completely through the skull of Mr Gage. The bar entered through his left cheek just below the eye socket and passed out the top of his skull. Worn smooth through use, the iron bar was an inch and a quarter in diameter and had been custom-made by a blacksmith to taper at one end to a quarter-inch leading point, almost exactly like a spear.

It is a historical fact that Phineas Gage was walking and talking within minutes of the accident. He chatted about the event with the small-town doctor who first examined him. This doctor was to be the first of many marvelling medics. After a surprisingly brief illness of only three months, Mr Gage returned to paid employment. Years later he was a stage coach driver in Chile on the Valparaiso to Santiago route.

There are two known portraits of Mr Gage taken in later life. In both he is wearing his finest jacket and waistcoat, thick dark hair combed to one side, proudly holding a tamping iron — *the* tamping iron.

The Vermont doctor's name was Williams. He must have wondered what he would find when, less than half an hour after the explosion, he carefully cleaned away the blood and matted hair, the fragments of bone, and gently probed beneath his patient's cranium with his fingers. The Mansfield Museum has the words 'Lo, these are parts of His ways, but how little a portion is heard of Him' carved in stone above the main entrance. To Dr Williams these words from the Book of Job could equally have been stamped upon the exposed grey matter he saw that summer day in 1848, pulsing in the shaft of sunlight coming through his surgery window.

~

These days the brain is mapped and its regions charted and plumbed. As with nearly everything else in the natural world, science is well on the way to removing the mystery and wonder of the unknown through continuing research on the organ of thought. This isn't a complaint, just an observation.

Scientists can ask a patient a question and watch in real time on a colour monitor those regions of her brain that light up in response. They can see what cogs and wheels inside us turn when we cry and laugh. They know which springs go slack when we despair and take to our beds.

Those same scientists could explain that the bone that hit Paul Blackwell undoubtedly pierced his temporal lobe: the seat of memory. Seen in a diagram, the temporal lobe resembles nothing so much as one of those hats favoured by Canadian males whose work or lifestyle choices take them into the great outdoors: the hat with the flaps that hang down over the wearer's ears, turning him into some type of hound. The temporal lobes are similar in design to those flaps, but angled slightly forward.

The brain is almost infinitely complex. Having had his temporal lobe damaged by the splintered bone, the outcome for Paul Blackwell was far from determined. Charles S. Sherrington, an early explorer of the brain's wonders, described it as 'an enchanted loom where millions of flashing shuttles weave a dissolving pattern'. At the time, a spinning loom was the height of mechanical sophistication. Born into this age, Sherrington might have described the brain as being similar to the world's most powerful computer. Stab a computer randomly with a screwdriver and the exact results would be far from certain.

If the bone had been blunt, Paul's temporal lobe could have been almost entirely crushed. If the damage had been a fraction to the right or the left . . . who knows? He could have ended up in a similar state to the man from the medical case studies who lost the ability to store information in long-term memory. Like Paul Blackwell, he remembered nothing of his past. But, what's more, that man could remember nothing *at all* for longer than fifteen minutes.

Another man from the medical literature — look it up yourself, it's all true — let's call him Patient B, remembered everything up until the day when he was twenty-three and fell from a ladder, hitting his head against one of the cobbled streets of Edinburgh. From that day on every time Patient B fell asleep the events of the preceding day were lost. Sleep bleached the accumulated words from each day's mental diary so they grew fainter and fainter until sometime before dawn they vanished. With no fresh pages added to the story of his life, Patient B was in his own mind forever twenty-three. Every day was the day after he fell and hit his head.

How alarming it must have been to look in the mirror and see a man of sixty looking back, when you expected to see the face of someone who was little more than a teenager. Instead Patient B discovered a stranger, lined and stained, greyed by experience he did not recall.

'Where's Lucy?' he asked on his sixtieth birthday, as he did almost every day. 'Where's my little girl?'

By this time, Lucy was aged thirty-seven and had children of her own. She was not there on her father's birthday. He did not recognise her anyway. Even when Lucy explained the situation to him (yet again), he refused to believe that she was his daughter. He would not listen to what he called 'some strange woman's loony story'.

In a way, Paul Blackwell's injury produced a result diagonally opposite to Patient B's, although both sustained damage to their temporal lobes. While Patient B remembered nothing from after his accident, not for more than a day anyway, Paul remembers nothing of his old life. However he recalls very well everything from the moment he awoke buried in earth, surrounded by the scattered remains of his men.

Who was the more cursed is hard to argue.

eighteen

On the second day working for her new employer, Elizabeth returns to Woodbridge by means of the tram and her own two feet. Once again, Martin Templeton sits outside the bedroom door with his newspaper while Elizabeth sits inside the room with Paul Blackwell. She has resolved not to speak, not so much as a greeting until he acknowledges her.

It is as it was the day before. He gazes at the flames and stares out the window, feeds the fire, eats from a tin. The first thing Elizabeth does is empty his bedpan. Apart from that the only other time she leaves the room is to eat lunch. Today Mrs Booker serves mutton hash.

By early afternoon, when her patient sleeps, or gives the appearance of doing so, Elizabeth finds her chin beginning to sag and her eyes to close of their own accord. Of course it is the heat.

She is sorely tempted to open a window but does not want to make such a proprietary claim on her patient's space. In an effort to rouse herself she stands and goes to the bookcase. Head tilted to the side in the manner of one of the birds in the trees outside the bedroom window, she scans the shelves. Elizabeth is disappointed. She had been hoping for a romance novel.

Although she is not a fanciful woman by nature, fiction featuring a headstrong female protagonist and a complicated romance has always appealed to her. *Pride and Prejudice* has long been her favourite book, and although she finds modern variations are not nearly as well written, they follow a similar pattern. There is something very satisfying about a woman meeting a seemingly unlikeable but undeniably charismatic, mysterious and often wealthy man. Misunderstanding and unforeseen complications ensue until they are both free to declare their love and to be married.

Unfortunately there seems to be nothing of that nature on Paul Blackwell's shelves. This is a man's collection. As far as she can see, there is no fiction at all. The books seem to be mostly about geology, archaeology and anthropology. *The Rituals and Rites of the North American Indians* nestles up to *The Stone-Age World of the Maori*, which in turn keeps company with *The British Museum's Compendium of the Jurassic Epoch*.

Elizabeth's eyes stumble over a name written vertically up the spine of one of the books — P. Blackwell. She slips it free. The title is embossed on the cover in gold lettering: *Recent Developments in Dating the Fossil Record*. Still standing, she begins to read.

The rest of the afternoon is spent wading through Paul Blackwell's book. It is heavy going but she perseveres because she feels as though the text were a clue to the personality of the man in front of her. His argument is very technical and the sentences sometimes stretch so far as to be positively labyrinthine.

When she finally closes the book, all Elizabeth has is a list of adjectives to describe its author: *orderly*, *thorough*, undoubtedly *intelligent*, *educated* and *serious* (there is not the smallest sprinkling of levity in the whole thing). She sighs and replaces the book on the shelf. It is almost five o'clock so she slips from the room. Paul

Blackwell does not stir. Martin Templeton is still on duty in the hallway.

'Another good day then.'

'I suppose so.'

'Same time tomorrow?'

'Yes. I'll see you then.'

Before Elizabeth leaves the house for the day, she wanders about the ground floor. Mrs Blackwell seems to spend most of her waking hours in the library and Elizabeth has no fear of being interrupted, unless it is by Merry or Mrs Booker or one of the two permanent gardeners who work at Woodbridge, although she has never seen either of those men inside the house. She fancies that she is playing detective, searching for further clues to her patient's past, but also acknowledges that perhaps she is just being what her mother would call a *nosey parker*.

The first room she enters is a very large formal dining room with a table that can seat — she counts the chairs — twenty. At the end of the room is a fireplace, tiled in green and black, the grate neatly stacked with kindling. Woodbridge has no fewer than six chimneys poking above its snaggletooth roofline. As well as the dining room and the kitchen, with the pantry and the scullery beyond, the ground floor comprises the library where she first met Mrs Blackwell, a drawing room and a ballroom with a lustrous wooden floor.

Next to the ballroom she discovers a music room with a piano. Elizabeth runs her hand over the rows of black and white keys. They are slightly dusty. She imagines the younger Paul Blackwell studiously and seriously practising at this instrument. It is probably just because of what Mrs Booker told her yesterday, but in her imagination Paul is a lonely figure. She feels sorry for him, with only tutors and servants for company in this big house. Or is she just being fanciful? What would the daughter of a stevedore know about what goes on in a house like this? She gently closes the piano lid. The whole day has turned out to be very unsatisfactory and she is beginning to doubt the wisdom of accepting Mrs Blackwell's offer.

Even though she will have to hurry to catch the last tram back into town, she stops for a moment at the main entrance to inspect the family portraits. They run in chronological order from left to right, starting with the grandfather. He appears to have been about sixty when his portrait was painted. The man's furrowed brow, his jutting jaw and slightly narrowed eyes staring into the middle distance are the definition of stoic. Attached to the inner edge of the heavy frame is a small brass plate on which is engraved the name *Randolph J. Blackwell.*

She wonders if there was ever a portrait of old Randolph's wife, Paul's grandmother? Its absence is interesting. If the woman had died young it would be all the more likely that there would be a painting of her. The lack of one suggests a scandal or at least a falling out. She will ask Mrs Booker tomorrow. The ruddy-faced cook is sure to have the story.

Next in line are Paul's parents, first the father and then the mother, each in their own frame; Charles and Victoria Blackwell, according to the name plates. Charles inherited his own father's craggy and brooding brow. His hair is dark and thick. In contrast his wife is pale and thin. She seems somehow distant. Her expression suggests that the whole business of having her portrait painted bored her profoundly.

Paul and Mrs Blackwell share a frame. As with the photograph she saw on her first visit to the house, there is almost no resemblance to the man upstairs. In the portrait he is slightly plump, but still undeniably handsome, with brown eyes and dark wavy hair. His cheeks and his lips are full. Paul sits in chair that has an ornately carved back and legs, while his wife stands behind his right shoulder. Mrs Blackwell looks, perhaps ten years younger. Her hand is on Paul's shoulder and the hint of a satisfied smile lingers in the corners of her lips. In an act that seems to Elizabeth more one of ownership than affection, Paul's right arm is folded across his chest so that his hand is resting on his wife's. The brass plate is engraved *Paul Edward Blackwell and Margaret Blackwell.*

Staring at the portrait, she wonders how she can possibly bring this man back. What tools does she have at her disposal to rekindle him? Put simply, how on earth can she get him to remember who he was?

nineteen

Elizabeth is late for the tram. As she hurries down the driveway, striding through the shadows of the lime trees, the sun dips behind the mountain range to the west. The shadows fade and blur and the air becomes chill. The tram is just rattling up as she arrives at the stop, slightly out of breath.

She waits her turn in the queue of half a dozen people and eventually finds herself standing in front of the driver just as an idea rolls over inside her. She tries to grasp it but somehow misses. Something to do with the engraved brass plates beneath the portraits at Woodbridge.

Paul Blackwell.

The same name as the one that ran up the spine of the book she had been reading earlier.

As Elizabeth stands like a statue in front of the tram driver, one idea jostles another idea and then, in a small cascade of thoughts and connections, something known and assumed to be true teeters and wobbles and eventually falls.

'You going to buy a ticket?' asks the driver.

'Sorry?'

'A ticket, love?'

'No. Sorry. I've changed my mind.'

Elizabeth turns and apologises her way past a man who has joined the queue behind her. Almost running, she rushes back down the road. She is breathing hard when she eventually pushes open the front door of the house. Merry, standing in the foyer holding a small tower of ironed and folded sheets, jumps back in surprise. The sheets sway and several of them fall to the floor.

'Bugger,' says Merry and then her eyes go wide. 'Sorry. I didn't mean to say that.'

'That's all right. I've heard worse.'

'Is everything all right, ma'am?'

'Everything's fine, Merry. And I've told you before, call me Elizabeth. Or Lizzy if you like.'

'Yes, ma'am.'

Elizabeth leaves the girl picking up her lost sheets and rushes up to Paul Blackwell's room. The key is still in the lock. She gives no consideration to the danger of entering the room without Martin Templeton as her bodyguard. Taking a moment to compose herself, Elizabeth slowly opens the door and enters.

He is lying on the bed. His eyes are open, staring at the stippled ceiling. He turns his head to look at her.

'Excuse me,' she says, 'but I have a question.' His eyes are large in his gaunt face, his mouth lost in his wildman's beard. 'Would you mind telling me your name?'

There is a long pause while he considers. He sits up, swings his feet to the floor and standing slowly walks to within a few feet of her. When he speaks his voice is a rusty tool that creaks from lack of use.

'Lucky. My name is Lucky.'

'Lucky,' she repeats.

He stares into her eyes. 'Thank you.'

'For what?'

'You're the first person here who's asked. The others think I'm someone else.'

'Someone else?' says Elizabeth.

'Yes. But they're wrong.'

twenty

Lucky.

It's the laconic punch line of a joke: 'A man with a bone through the side of his head walks into a bar . . .'

What else, though, would you call a soldier whose companions were, without exception, blown to pieces by a shell?

Lucky.

It's just right for a man who survived the rest of that day and the night which followed with everything except his head and one shoulder buried under the collapsed earth wall, half smothered among the dead and the pieces of the dead. He lay there the next day as well, lapsing in and out of consciousness. The trench was briefly overrun by the Germans but none of them looked at him closely. Dead bodies were a dime a dozen. They were so common that they were sometimes buried strategically so they formed temporary steps or became infill when repairing a trench wall.

He lay listening to the constant pound of artillery fire that went on day and night, the devil's orchestra, until the tide of the battle turned and a platoon of Australians recaptured his position.

'Jesus wept, this bloke's still alive.'

He opened his eyes and there was a face peering down at him.

'G'day, mate, you're lucky.'

Lucky.

Of course that's what you call a man carried back by the stretcher bearers, lurching and stumbling over a mile of broken earth. At the clearing station he was put to one side, among those deemed too close to death to bother with. The young doctor who re-examined him four hours later was just on his way to get some sleep.

Lucky.

A good name for the man who didn't die after all. They took him to an old hall in a French town once famous for its soft cheeses but now deserted by everyone except those who had absolutely nowhere else to go. The town hall had become a makeshift surgery and hospital. It was there that a surgeon carefully removed the bone from the side of his head. It came out with the same sound a boot makes when pulled from thick mud. In the days that followed, he burned with fever. On the wall above him was a plaque, a list of French names — those who had represented the town in cycling.

The surgeon had placed a steel plate the size of a shilling over the hole in Lucky's skull before drawing the skin back and sewing it together the best he could. He had no doubt the man would die. Everybody from the stretcher bearers to the nurses to the doctors thought he would die. Even the wizened Frenchman who mopped the floor was sure of it.

Lucky. The name is perfect.

twenty-one

Only a second has passed since Elizabeth asked the man standing in front of her for his name. The implications are still hanging in the air between them.

'What is *your* name?' he asks.

'Elizabeth Whitman. Some people call me Lizzy.'

He stares at her openly, some might say brazenly, although not like the young Arabs with switchblade eyes who trailed her during her ship's stopover in Alexandria on her way to England. This man, Lucky, seems merely curious. It is as though he has found something — a fossil, or mottled goose egg, a frost-frozen thrush — that he has not seen before.

Even so, Elizabeth has to force herself not to step back as he moves close to her; close enough that the heavy musk of his unwashed body threatens to overwhelm her. Standing this close to him, she can see how thick and dark his eyelashes are and the thought occurs to her that such beautiful lashes are wasted on a man. His matted beard is dense as a hearth-brush and his long hair provides an unruly frame for his face. All this she now sees in detail. It is to her credit that Elizabeth does not flinch when he reaches out and gently touches the shoulder of her uniform. She can feel the heat of his skin through the fabric.

'You are a nurse.'

'Yes. That's right.'

'There are always nurses.'

'You mean the nurses at the hospitals where you've been treated?'

He nods. 'And on the ship coming to this place. The nurses always think that I am broken.'

'What do you mean?'

He holds her gaze in a way that she finds disconcerting. His eyes are dark brown with flecks of gold.

'I did not understand most of the things they tried to talk to me about. I couldn't answer their questions. I heard one of the nurses say that this,' he touches the side of his head, 'had made me *simple*. That means broken, doesn't it?'

'Yes, it does.'

'Do you think that I'm simple?'

'Actually, Lucky, I'm starting to think that you're not at all simple. Quite the opposite, in fact.'

twenty-two

Mrs Blackwell is appalled. 'I am sorry, Mrs Whitman, no. My husband's name is Paul Edward Blackwell.'

They are in the library and Elizabeth's revelation has transformed Mrs Blackwell into an animal pacing in a small cage. When she reaches the shelves full of fossil crabs she is forced to turn for another agitated length of the room.

'How can he possibly not know his own name?'

'He believes that his name is Lucky.'

'Lucky,' she repeats. 'It is not even a proper name, it is an adjective.'

'Soldiers often give each other nicknames. They probably called him Lucky because in many ways he was. Apparently there was some confusion because his identity tags were lost. It's not uncommon. For a long time nobody knew what his name was. He told them that it was Lucky.'

'He said all this?'

'Some of the details I've had to surmise, but yes, we talked for quite some time.'

Mrs Blackwell shakes her head in amazement. 'Well, at least he's talking. That is certainly progress, and more than I would have expected. He has not said more than a dozen words to me in all the time he has been home. Now I can concentrate on retrieving his memories.'

'I'm not sure about that.'

'What do you mean?'

'Having questioned him in some depth, I think we may have to consider the possibility that he has no memory left to retrieve.'

A more vigorous shake of the head perched upon that long neck shows Elizabeth how Mrs Blackwell feels about that idea. 'No. Paul's memories are not lost, I am certain of it. They can be found.'

'You should at least consider the possibility.'

'I will not, not yet. It is too soon.'

'It's been eighteen months since your husband was wounded. He told me that he has never, in that time, remembered *anything at all* from his previous life.'

'But now that he is home there is so much more to stimulate his memories.'

'Granted, that is true.'

'I cannot give up hope, Mrs Whitman. We must persevere.'

'Any solution is going to take time. Your husband will have to be handled very carefully. Try and put yourself in his shoes. All this must be very foreign.'

'Foreign?' Mrs Blackwell looks around at the panelled walls, the bookshelves, the rows of fossils. 'But this is Paul's home. He grew up here.'

'The man who believes that his name is Lucky insists that he has never seen this place before in his life,' says Elizabeth patiently. 'I'm sorry, this must be very difficult for you.'

'His memory *will* return.' Mrs Blackwell's voice is firm.

'I hope so. I'd like your permission to take him out into the grounds tomorrow.'

'Is that safe?'

'I think a brief expedition would be good for him. I suspect that he becomes agitated only when pressured to remember. When I talked to him this evening he was quite calm.'

'If you take him out then it must only be inside the grounds and I must insist that Mr Templeton accompany you at all times.'

'All right, but Martin can keep a discreet distance.'

'Agreed.'

'There's one more matter I'd like to discuss.'

'Yes?'

'I asked your husband why he won't eat anything except food from a can. He said that when he first came here he ate the food Mrs Booker prepared for him. Is that true?'

'Yes.'

'He told me that you began poisoning his food.'

Mrs Blackwell looks indignant. 'That is, of course, a complete delusion. As if I would poison my own husband.'

'I didn't think so, of course. However, I must ask if *anything* was added to his food?'

The hooded eyes flicker for a moment. 'Certainly not poison.'

'Something else, though?' Elizabeth insists.

Mrs Blackwell sighs. 'Dr Frengley has been our family physician for many years. He recommended that we add some medication to Paul's food. You have to understand, my husband was very agitated.'

'What type of medication?'

'Something to make him calmer. That's all it was.'

'Perhaps an opiate of some sort? Or lithium bromide?'

'The doctor may have mentioned lithium,' Mrs Blackwell concedes. 'It certainly did make him calmer.'

'Yes, it would. It's a powerful sedative.'

'It was done on medical advice.'

'I understand. But when your husband realised that his food was being drugged it was no wonder that he began to eat only from sealed tins.'

'At the time I believed that it was the right thing to do. Do you think I was wrong?'

‘I’m sure you did what you thought was best. However, drugging his food has left your husband with a profound lack of trust. It has reinforced the impression that he’s a prisoner here.’

‘He is not a prisoner. This is Paul’s home.’

‘On the day I first saw him, he was chained to the floor.’

‘I explained all that. Mrs Whitman, I am not on trial here. Everything, absolutely everything, that I have done has been for Paul’s own good. ‘

Elizabeth can see that she is getting nowhere. ‘Of course. It’s a very complex situation.’

Mrs Blackwell makes an effort to regain her composure. ‘All these arrangements are just temporary. This is simply what must be done until Paul has recovered. Afterwards he will thank me.’

There are certain people whose opinions are like reeds. Elizabeth has met them before. No matter how hard the wind of reasoned argument blows they always return to the same position.

‘I’ll try to persuade your husband to eat Mrs Booker’s food again. We can’t expect him to return to physical health on a diet of tinned meat. I’ll need your word that nothing else will find its way into his food.’

A curt nod.

Elizabeth waits but Mrs Blackwell has turned back to the window. Behind the glass the grounds are dark and the other woman’s face is a pale reflection. Elizabeth herself hovers over the poor woman’s shoulder, as if she were about to whisper in her ear. Whether she is an angel or a devil is uncertain, even to her.

twenty-three

Whether you think of the man living upstairs at Woodbridge as Lucky or Paul Blackwell during the rest of this story is, at the end of the day, a philosophical choice.

Elizabeth calls him Lucky to his face. In Mrs Blackwell's presence she fudges the question out of consideration for the other woman's feelings. She refers to 'your husband' or simply 'he'. For the purpose of our story I will side with Elizabeth and also call him Lucky.

Shortly after ten o'clock the next morning Elizabeth escorts Lucky into the grounds. She has already spent an hour cleaning and tidying his room, something that he only reluctantly agrees to. It is a cool morning but as they leave the house the windless day warms. Lucky moves tentatively down the gravel paths, in and out of patches of sunlight, seemingly unsure of what to make of such boundless space. He seems to prefer to walk slightly ahead of Elizabeth and stops often to examine things that catch his eye: a serrated leaf here, a caterpillar mountaineering on a stone sundial there. Elizabeth, not wanting to crowd or hurry him, mirrors his stuttering progress.

As instructed by Mrs Blackwell, Martin Templeton follows. He ambles among the trees, holding a thin switch picked up from the ground and occasionally slicing listlessly at the air or punishing a tree trunk for some misdemeanour. On the whole, he keeps far enough away not to bother them.

Elizabeth has persuaded Lucky to relinquish his pyjamas in favour of a pair of corduroy trousers that billow out from his legs. The belt that Merry found required a new hole punched into the leather before it would function properly. He wears a white shirt open at the collar and a faded jacket. Elizabeth suspects that the clothes may have been his when he was an adolescent but says nothing of this to Lucky. For some reason that he cannot explain, he categorically refuses to wear shoes. Elizabeth does not press the matter. She sees no harm in it, despite her mother's dire warning every time Elizabeth allows Jack to go barefoot.

The grounds of Woodbridge are even more extensive than Elizabeth had imagined — acre after acre. Oak and plane, maple and eucalyptus, pine and lime are only some of the trees that she can identify. They are dotted around, singly and in small stands. She eventually gives up trying to keep track of where they are and allows the magnetism of the shingle paths to draw Lucky where they will.

Shortly after they leave the house he points up into the branches of an oak. 'Look.'

'It's a bird's nest,' she said.

He nods thoughtfully. Since then he has been silent.

Elizabeth is aware of the soft crunch of their footsteps, the sound of a blackbird flicking aside autumn leaves, unseen water bubbling among shaded ferns. By sheer chance, they come across a rhododendron walk. They eventually reach a meadow where the grass brushes her knees. On the far side, they enter the shadows beneath a stand of eucalyptus trees. There seem to be many different varieties of tree and Elizabeth finds herself wishing that she knew their names. Some are moulting, the bark peeling away in strips. Others have trunks that twist like giant plaited ropes or contain pregnant bulges. There is no undergrowth but Elizabeth and Lucky have to contend with fallen branches and flayed bark.

'Yes,' says Lucky when Elizabeth suggests they turn back. He is beginning to look tired. They retrace their footsteps and when they come across a narrow stream that cuts across their path they follow its course until they reach a large pond not far from the house.

'Let's rest for a while,' says Elizabeth.

She sits on a stone bench and Lucky squats by the water. He watches half a dozen large goldfish circle the stems of lily pads close to the bank. Elizabeth observes that his hands are shaking. He holds them, fluttering lightly, in his lap. She cannot say whether this is a new symptom or something familiar that ceased for a time but has now returned. It is also impossible for her to separate the physical symptoms resulting from his head wound from the results of the stress caused by what has happened to him, what *is* happening. Since he does not seem to be paying any attention to her she examines him as unobtrusively as possible. The sunlight reflecting off the water flickers over his pale skin. There is a patch near his right ear where the hair does not grow although it is not obvious among the dark tangle of his heavy mane.

'Can I ask you something?' she says. Lucky does not turn his head but makes a small sound that may be acquiescence.

'What is your first memory?'

'Smells.'

'The smell of what?'

He does not take his eyes of the slowly circling goldfish. 'It was night so I couldn't see but I could smell. The earth that covered me stank of manure and of mud that has been wet for a long time. There was also the smell of blood from the dead men. Shit and piss from the ones who'd had the time before they died. There was one body lying very close to me. He smelled of . . .' Lucky pauses while his mind fumbles for the right word, 'something strong that soldiers drink.'

'Gin? Whisky?'

'Maybe whisky. He had a flask in his jacket. It had leaked.'

Elizabeth shuffles uncomfortably. 'And then what happened?'

'I couldn't move, nothing except my head. All that first night the artillery hardly stopped. I could hear the shells flying overheard and later the explosions. It was like . . .'

'Thunder?'

'Maybe. Sometime in the night, a red flare lit up in the air right above me. It drifted slowly and I thought it was very beautiful. I must have been asleep or unconscious for a time because in the red light I could see new snow over everything but I hadn't seen it fall. The snow looked pink. And then I saw a rat moving up the trench towards me.' Lucky holds up his hands, forming a gap that makes Elizabeth shudder. 'I couldn't remember how I came to be in that place but I knew the word *rat* and I knew the words *snow* and *trench*. At first the rat moved slowly. It was afraid, ready to turn and run away. It was aware that I was watching it. In the end it came very close to me. It must have decided that I wasn't dangerous because it started to feed on a nearby body.'

'How long was it before someone found you?'

'I was there that night, and most of the next day. I would have frozen to death except I was wearing a heavy coat and gloves and I was covered by a blanket of earth. The trench was overrun by men who spoke but I couldn't understand them, and later by men in a different uniform. Nobody noticed me. There was fighting. I saw a man shot through the eye. Another bled to death leaning on the wall very close to me. He tried to speak to me but I couldn't understand his words either. I was relieved when he finally died because I was able to go to sleep.'

twenty-four

What is your first memory?

Perhaps it is of a flurry of ducks squabbling, flapping and splashing over the bread your grandmother gave you to throw into the pond. It may have been scary at the time, or thrilling. Probably that is why you still remember it.

Or is your first memory of the bolder girl, a neighbour or cousin, who picked you out as her friend and sealed the deal by giving you her third-best doll to keep forever?

A birthday party. Candles and cake and music and squealing as the parcel is passed round and round with only one prize buried deep in the folded newspaper. There were tears when you lost and the humiliation of being sent from your own party to your bedroom.

The smell of eucalyptus oil and petroleum jelly being rubbed onto your chest.

Is it of your mother hurling insults and crockery at the man in the doorway?

You were running away from home that day with the family dog for company.

The big snow of 1972, the one that left behind a marshmallow world.

A grave injustice.

A triumph.

Perhaps you remember something that is seemingly trivial to you now you are an adult, but for some reason has been selected for preservation.

And how old were you when this memory was first stored in the wide shallow drawers of your mind? When was it pinned down and labelled, carefully slid back into place so that now it can be brought out and examined at will?

Perhaps you were not yet two years old (a precocious child), or three, four? There's no shame in being five: the first day at school is a common seminal memory.

Lucky has all of us beaten in the memory stakes. He remembers clearly the moment that he first opened his eyes. Not just the day, although that would still make him unique, but the very *moment* when his consciousness awoke. Consider what it must be like to be born as an adult, as the Bible tells us only Adam and Eve have been. Lucky was also drawn forth from the earth, fully formed, capable in body and mind.

twenty-five

'Listen,' says Elizabeth. 'I want to tell you a story.'

It is two days after their first walk in the grounds of Woodbridge, their third excursion. They have come across the fern house. The building is small, really just a circular room with stone walls up to waist height and cedar boards above. There are opaque windows set all the way around and the ceiling comes to a high point in the middle. A brook has been diverted so that water runs through the middle of the building, falling over a construction of rocks and bisecting the path where a flagstone acts as a bridge. The room is full of ferns, in all sizes and shapes. The tallest, planted in the middle, brush their serrated leaves across the ceiling. One of the gardeners turns on the sprinkler system every morning and when Elizabeth and Lucky find the house everything is already damp and dripping. Martin Templeton waits outside.

Lucky stands by the door and watches a spider spin between two leaves. 'Why?'

'Because I think you'll like it.'

'What's this story about?'

'Just listen. While I was travelling to England before the war, I met an Irish nurse who was on her way home. Her name was Patience Flannery. We became very good friends for a short while, as you do on a long sea voyage and Patience told me the story of her childhood. Her parents worked in a circus in England: her father was a knife thrower and her mother mended costumes and tents and sold tickets to the various acts. Unfortunately, her mother died when Patience was seven years old.

'After his wife's death, her father quit the circus and took his daughter back to County Cork, where he had been born. Cork is one of the Irish counties in the far south. Her father found himself with nothing to his name but a daughter and a set of five well-balanced knives with ivory inlays in the handles. Apparently, for a knife thrower, a pretty daughter is a good thing. She told me that a young girl's innocence stands out in stark contrast to the hard gleam of the steel knives.'

Lucky shifts his eyes from the spider to regard her thoughtfully.

'So that's how my friend came to grow up travelling around Ireland working as her father's assistant. She told me that in spring and summer the two of them worked county fairs, but in the wet and cold Irish winters they were forced into smoky pubs. Her father would set up against a wall a wooden circle the size of a cartwheel, with a red bullseye painted on it. The wheel had hinges that allowed it to be folded and transported. Before he even spoke, he always placed a dented black top-hat on the ground. He never referred to the hat directly but would nod in appreciation whenever anyone dropped in a coin. First, he would invite people from the crowd to inspect the five knives. Men would run their thumbs lightly down a razor-sharp edge or weigh one appreciatively in their hands. Women tended to touch the tips and withdraw their fingers quickly.

'Some people grinned, certain they were being conned. They

predicted that the knives would never actually leave the man's hand. Others believed that if the knives *were* thrown they wouldn't come within spitting distance of the pretty colleen. Even so, it was not unknown for women to step forward from the crowd and offer Patience's father money *not* to throw the knives.'

Elizabeth brushes a stray strand of hair from her face. 'Patience demonstrated for me how she used to stand. She stood on the ship's deck with her legs apart, arms out between waist and shoulder height, fingers splayed like a starfish. Other passengers stared at her as though she were mad. Patience said she pressed her back hard against the wooden circle but she always kept her eyes open as her father drew back his arm and threw, hard and fast.

'One above her left shoulder close to her ear.

'One above her right.

'The third between her hip and outstretched right arm.

'The fourth in the same spot but on the other side of her body.

'The fifth and final knife went between her legs. It sank into the wood at knee height.

'Patience straightened up and laughed. She told me that not one knife was ever more than a hand's distance away from her. She was her father's assistant from the time she was seven years old until he died of pneumonia. That was when she was seventeen. Patience admitted to me that sometimes the constant travelling did grow tiring. Her father taught her to read and write and to do her sums, but he was not always the best company. In all those years she never seriously contemplated leaving him, even though after she turned fourteen there were many offers of marriage, three of them serious. There was also an aunt up north in Dublin who every year wrote to Patience repeating the offer of a decent place to live and a proper school. She accepted the offer after her father died.

'I told Patience that I thought it sounded like a terrible way to grow up, but she insisted that it wasn't bad at all. Apparently, her father loved her dearly. She always had a warm bed and a full stomach. Standing near the rail of that ship, somewhere off the west coast of Africa, she said that in all those years her father had only ever missed twice.

'She said, "All things considered, I carry fewer scars from my childhood than most people."'

twenty-six

Lucky has an undeniable pungency.

Elizabeth questions Merry and discovers that since his arrival at Woodbridge her patient has occasionally and then very reluctantly agreed to exchange his pyjamas for a laundered pair. Apparently he has not bathed at all.

The morning after their visit to the fern house she leads him to the bathroom halfway down the corridor. The floor and walls are tiled in white and black.

'Why are we here?' His voice echoes off the tiles.

'I think it would be a good idea if you took a bath.'

He scowls at her. 'The nurses at the hospital were always trying to dab at me with wet cloths. I don't like it.'

'Not a bed-bath. You're more than well enough for a proper bath.'

Lucky looks sceptically at the bathtub. It is deep and narrow and rests on four cast-iron legs, each one shaped into a clawed lion's foot grasping a metal ball. The inside of the bath is enamelled a stark white.

'In this?' he says.

Although he claims to remember objects and concepts Elizabeth is sure that he doesn't recall everything. Sometimes words, nouns especially, dance on the tip of his tongue. That very morning he had been reduced to calling an egg *the child of a bird*. Now he looks at the bath as though it were an alien artefact.

'You turn on these taps, like this.'

The copper pipe shudders inside the walls and the tap splutters before a steady stream of water begins to pour into the bottom of the bath. Elizabeth fits the plug into place. Lucky puts his hand into the water and pulls it back. 'It's cold.'

'It takes a while for the hot water to travel from the boiler. There, see, it's getting warmer already.'

The sound of the falling water rolls and surges back and forth between the tiled walls like surf in a narrow strait. Soon the water is steaming hot. 'You have to turn on this tap as well to let cold water in. That way you can get the temperature just right.'

When the bath is three-quarters full Elizabeth turns the water off. 'Take off your clothes. I'll have them washed. I'll ask Merry to leave some fresh ones outside the door, but not pyjamas.'

'Why?'

'You should start wearing proper clothes and not just when we go walking.'

'Why?' he repeats.

'Because that's what people do.'

Lucky frowns but accepts this without comment. Now that he has committed himself to the idea of the bath he seems anxious to get in. His pyjama top is so baggy that he can easily pull it above his head. Elizabeth watches the muscles in his shoulders as they slide over each other, contract and expand to achieve the manoeuvre. His shoulder blades protrude alarmingly. When he turns to face her she can see the half-dozen shrapnel scars on his chest and torso. Steam rises up from the hot water, filling the air between them.

'Do any of those old wounds still give you pain?'

'No.'

'You were fortunate with this one. It's very close to your jugular.'

The scar is about half an inch long and slightly raised. It nestles near the base of his neck in against the raised collarbone. She reaches out and touches it with the tip of her index finger. Lucky shivers.

Elizabeth steps back. 'You're cold. You should get in. There's soap in the dish. Make sure you use it. Give your hair and beard a good scrub as well.'

She has barely turned away, let alone left the room, before Lucky has lowered his trousers. Elizabeth focuses on gathering together his discarded clothes but she cannot help catching a glimpse of his flanks — as thin as a greyhound's — as he steps into the hot water. He lowers himself slowly. 'Ahhh, that's good.'

She addresses the wall. 'I told you that you'd like it.'

Lucky stretches himself out. The steam rises up into the cooler air. His beard has become a clump of seaweed hanging just below the surface.

'If it cools off, you can add more hot water later.'

There is no reply so Elizabeth slips from the bathroom, followed into the hallway by a swirl of steam.

She finds Merry in the kitchen talking to Mrs Booker and hands over the washing with instructions for fresh clothes to be delivered to the bathroom. In Lucky's bedroom Elizabeth opens the window to let in fresh air and then changes the linen on the bed. Technically, this is Merry's job, but Elizabeth hates having nothing to do. Her mother has always been fond of saying that the devil takes a special interest in the idle. Although the war has destroyed the last vestiges of Elizabeth's belief in devils and angels — but not good and evil — she still prefers to keep busy. Besides, if there is one thing a nurse knows how to do properly, it is make a bed.

She has just finished smoothing out the bedspread when she hears a scream from the corridor. Running out of the room she finds Merry by the open bathroom door, both hands pressed over her eyes. Lucky is standing in front of the girl, frowning. He is stark naked and dripping wet. His penis points at the ceiling.

Lucky turns to her. 'Why is she making that awful noise?'

Elizabeth stoops to pick up the clothes that Merry has dropped and thrusts them at him.

'Here, take these. For God's sake go back in the bathroom.'

'She knocked. All I did was open the door to see what she wanted.'

'I know.'

Merry's screams have turned to wails. 'That's a very annoying noise,' says Lucky, frowning deeply at the girl, whose eyes are still clamped shut.

'Just go back inside and get dressed.'

Lucky retreats into the bathroom, shaking his head, and Elizabeth closes the door firmly. Merry is still crying as Elizabeth helps her down the back stairs and into the kitchen. She finds Mrs Booker preparing a leg of mutton. The cook has been delighted that Mr Blackwell is again eating her food. She looks up in surprise.

'Oh dear, what's the matter with her then? What happened?'

Elizabeth sits the sobbing girl at the table. 'Merry's had a bit of a shock, I'm afraid.'

'Broke some of the good china, did she?'

'No, nothing like that. She's accidentally seen Mr Blackwell without any clothes on.'

'Is that all?'

'Perhaps if you could get her a nice cup of tea, Mrs Booker.'

'Fine, but I don't see what all the fuss is about.' Muttering to herself, the cook walks over to the stove.

Merry's eyes are puffy and red. She sniffs. 'I'm sorry, ma'am.'

'I've told you to call me Elizabeth.'

'I just brought his clothes like you said to. You told me to leave them on the floor outside so I knocked, just to let him know they were there, and then suddenly the door opened and there he was all . . . big.'

Over at the stove, Mrs Booker laughs. 'Oh, is that what happened?'

'It was just an accident,' says Elizabeth. 'It was nobody's fault.'

Merry's bottom lip quivers. 'But why was it like that?'

'Sometimes if a man has been . . .' Elizabeth pauses, lost. She starts again. 'Well, in warm water for example, that can happen. Mr Blackwell was taking a bath.'

'Or if he hasn't been getting his oats regular,' chips in Mrs Booker. 'You sure he wasn't just showing off? He wouldn't be the first young fella to show his cock to the maid.'

Merry's eyes go as wide as the saucers lined up on the sideboard.

'No, Mrs Booker, it wasn't like that,' says Elizabeth quickly. 'Something about Mr Blackwell's injury has made him unself-conscious, unusually so. He doesn't think of nudity as at all unnatural. Which, if you think about it, of course it isn't.'

'If you say so, love,' says the cook sceptically.

Mrs Booker brings the kettle and pours a cup for Merry. Both women watch as the girl ladles in three heaped teaspoons of sugar.

'I think I'll have a cup as well,' says Mrs Booker. 'Do you want one, dear?'

'Yes, thank you,' says Elizabeth.

Mrs Booker peers at Merry above her cup. 'You shouldn't carry on like that. It's nothing really. When I was a girl we had a neighbour who was always pulling down his trousers and showing us his funny pete.'

Elizabeth is not sure that this story will be helpful but before she can change the subject Mrs Booker has ploughed on.

'That's what my mother used to call it, a funny pete, or a peter. There were five girls in my family, and it got to the point where the neighbour's one was more out than in. We all just used to laugh at him. In the end, though, my father threatened to chop it off with a meat cleaver if it happened again. He was a butcher and a red-headed Scot to boot so I think the fella next door believed him. Leastways, he kept it in his trousers after that.'

'I'm sure in *this* case, though, Mr Blackwell didn't mean to frighten you, Merry,' says Elizabeth. 'It just didn't occur to him that you'd be upset.'

'It wouldn't be the first time I've seen Mr Blackwell's funny pete,' says the cook thoughtfully. 'Mind you, the last time was when he was about six.'

'It's the first one I've seen apart from on little boys,' says Merry and lowers her voice. 'Are they always that big?'

Mrs Booker laughs. 'Only if you're lucky, girl.'

Elizabeth tries to keep a straight face. 'Speaking as a nurse, Merry, I think it's possible for me to say that Mr Blackwell may very well be more generously endowed than some other men.'

Merry sighs. 'Thank the Lord for that, otherwise I'm never getting married.'

There is a slight pause. First Mrs Booker starts laughing, and then Elizabeth. The cup in her hand shakes so much that tea sloshes into the saucer and she has to put it down. Confused, Merry looks from one woman to the other. Finally she begins to laugh as well. Soon all three are roaring, until tears roll down their faces. They laugh and laugh until it hurts.

twenty-seven

Over the next fortnight, it becomes Elizabeth and Lucky's routine to walk the grounds every day, setting off from the house around mid-morning. Sometimes they make for a predetermined destination, such as the pond or the fern house. They discover a disused barn with gaps in the walls and roof and small grey mice that act more boldly than is wise.

Although Martin still escorts them, Elizabeth believes that his presence is redundant. Any reservations she had about Lucky have vanished. She no longer fears him at all, quite the opposite. It is refreshing to be around someone who is so open in his manner, so willing to give her his full attention when she talks. As they walk, now side by side, Lucky pockets small treasures that catch his eye to line up later along the windowsill in his room: a chestnut, shiny as polished mahogany; the clean white skull of a hedgehog. Sometimes he holds out one of his finds for her to inspect. She soon discovers that he does not require her to comment on them at any length. A smile or a nod is often enough.

Most mornings he is content simply to observe the angle of the light through a patch of mist hanging above the lawn, the turning leaves, or the flight of a pair of magpies. For her part, Elizabeth is happy to try and see the world as he does and to bookend his silence.

Lucky still tires easily, although the trembling in his hands has subsided for the time being. By lunchtime he is normally ready to return to the house and seems relieved when he spots the tallest chimney above the tops of the pines. In the afternoons he bathes and then sleeps or simply stares at the fire. Bathing has become his favourite activity. Since the incident with Merry, Elizabeth has gone to pains to explain to him that there are certain protocols about nudity. He obviously considers these rules to be eccentric, but adheres to them nonetheless. He makes the bathwater hotter each day until Elizabeth would find it almost unbearable, yet Lucky sinks into it without pause.

'I don't know how you do it, the water is scalding.'

'I like the heat to reach my bones.'

After he has slept, never for more than an hour, Lucky often asks Elizabeth to read to him from the books in his room.

'I could find some fiction in the library, a story you might enjoy.'

He shakes his head, his hair still slightly damp. 'I don't care about the meaning.'

'I don't understand. Why not?'

He regards her, his face serious. 'I just like the sound of your voice.'

That is how she comes to read aloud from *An Encyclopaedia of Geological Discovery*, and the even less engaging *Davin's Guide to Archaeology*.

It is now a condition of her employment that every afternoon before she leaves the house and walks to the tram stop, Elizabeth reports to Mrs Blackwell in the library. Her employer is very pleased with the change in her husband's demeanour, but each day without fail she asks Elizabeth if he has fished up a memory of the time before he was wounded. Every time Elizabeth is forced to say, 'No, I'm sorry, nothing like that today.'

Without fail Mrs Blackwell looks disappointed. 'Maybe tomorrow.'

'Yes, perhaps,' Elizabeth says.

In the late afternoon she catches the tram back to Sydenham Street. Ever since Elizabeth accepted the job at Woodbridge, her mother has been in an excellent mood. There is nothing like a large and steady wage to put a spring in an old woman's step. With her first pay packet, Elizabeth buys lamb, to be roasted, and ice cream for dessert.

'It's like Christmas,' says Jack, delighted, as they all sit at the table in the kitchen.

Elizabeth's father laughs, 'Aye, it is.' He ruffles his grandson's hair with a big hand. Even his coughing seems to have improved lately.

Considering the traumatic events that are soon to occur, that fortnight is a rather idyllic time in Elizabeth's life. As is always the way, though, she will not think of those autumn days like that until after they are gone.

~

A Tuesday. Elizabeth and Lucky have once again come to the pond. The mornings have grown cooler and Lucky is wearing a knitted jersey with a black pea-coat buttoned over the top. Elizabeth thinks he looks like a Scandinavian whaler. She fancies his shoulders and chest have filled out, at least slightly, now that he has resumed eating Mrs Booker's food. His cheeks no longer look so sunken.

He squats by the pond gazing intently at the circling goldfish. His hair hangs down over the collar of his coat. She has broached the idea of cutting it, but he will not entertain the thought. For some reason that he cannot put into words, Lucky is fond of his tangled hair and beard. Elizabeth looks around but cannot see Martin Templeton. The chauffeur has grown casual in his surveillance. She suspects that he is dozing in a patch of sunlight somewhere.

'We could go into the city soon, if you like. I think it might be good for you.'

'Why?'

'Aren't you curious about where you live?'

'I live here.' His gesture takes in the trees, the water, the unseen house beyond.

'There's a wider world,' says Elizabeth.

'I've seen all I want to see of the *wider world*.' He sounds bitter.

'The world isn't the war, Lucky. Anyway, the fighting is over now. The world is far bigger and more beautiful than what you've seen. I think you'd like our little city if you gave it a chance. It's actually quite pretty.' He does not respond. 'Do you remember what it's called?'

He flicks her a hard look. 'Yes. I've been told many times by the woman who says she's my wife.'

'Do you doubt that she really is your wife?'

'I don't even know her.'

'That doesn't necessarily mean that she is not your wife.'

'Then *you* could tell me that we have been married for ten years. That could be true as well.'

'As far as I'm aware, you and I have never been married.'

A faint smile springs up, then blooms among the dark brambles of Lucky's beard. It is the first time Elizabeth has seen him truly smile.

As if embarrassed, Lucky turns his gaze back to the fish. Elizabeth notices that there is something in his right hand, a strip of metal that flashes in the sunlight. It is a knife. Before she can say anything, he lunges at the water and impales the largest of the goldfish on the point of the blade. Lucky flicks the fish out of the pond and up onto the bank. It lands on the grass close to Elizabeth's feet, almost touching the tip of her shoe; a twitching, arching thrash of spraying water and orange skin.

It is all so sudden, so unexpected, that Elizabeth lets out a scream. She is immediately ashamed. After all, it is just a fish.

It is flipping and twisting down the bank towards the water. Lucky springs at it, and holding it down with one hand, pushes the blade into the top of its head, behind its eyes. The fish stiffens and its eyes bulge even wider. One more twitch and it lies still, although blood continues to pump from the crimson spring of the wound.

Martin Templeton has heard Elizabeth's scream. Here he comes running through the trees, shouting at the top of his voice. 'Hey, you! Stop! Get away from her!' He is holding one of the stout walking sticks from the elephant's foot umbrella holder that sits in the foyer of the house.

Lucky swivels towards the approaching man. He steps forward to meet him, the knife held in front of him. The chauffeur sees the bloody knife (but not the silver scales along the blade or the fish on the grass). Here is a wild man, a known danger, standing in front of a distressed woman, a weapon in his hand.

'What have you done, you bastard?'

'Martin, stop!' says Elizabeth.

But it is too late. Raising the heavy walking stick like a club, Martin Templeton charges. He brings the stick down hard, but Lucky steps back and sideways and the blow merely glances off his shoulder. Lucky's eyes are hard and dark, his face a primitive mask.

'Stop it! Both of you!'

Elizabeth is suddenly certain that Lucky will kill Martin as casually as he killed the fish. In a flash of realisation, she — finally, fully — understands. Killing has been Lucky's constant companion since the moment he awoke in that trench in France. He was born to it. War was his midwife and his mother. It was all around him, even in the hospital. Fighting, killing, death, these are everyday things to him. Men shoot and bayonet and blow each other apart with mortars and shells. They die quickly and are left to rot in no-man's-land, or perish slowly on stretchers and hospital beds. He has heard the screams, the death rattles, the silence. Lucky has seen it all.

Martin raises the bulbous head of the walking stick to his shoulder, then turns his body side-on like a softball player waiting for the pitch. Lucky feints in and Martin starts his swing but his opponent is too quick. He takes three steps forward so that he is inside the arc of the bat. It strikes his upper arm with no real force. Lucky plunges the knife into the driver just below his collarbone.

Martin cries out and stumbles backwards, falls. The knife is still in Lucky's hand as he steps in to finish off his enemy.

'No!' Elizabeth has rushed forward. She places herself between Lucky and the moaning figure on the ground. 'Stop! Lucky. It's over.' For a moment she thinks he is going to stab her too. 'Please.' He takes a step back. And then another.

'It's over,' Elizabeth repeats. 'Give me the knife.'

He looks past her to the man on the ground. 'No.'

He does, however, move back to the edge of the pond. Elizabeth turns to Martin and crouches. The left shoulder of his jacket is sodden with blood. 'Let me see. Take your hand away.'

Martin's face is grey with shock. 'Are you all right? Did he cut you?'

'No, I'm fine. He only killed a fish.'

'A fish?'

'I shouldn't have screamed. I was surprised, that was all.'

'He didn't hurt you?' His eyes are still on Lucky.

'Not at all. Now let me see.' She carefully removes his jacket, undoes the buttons on his shirt and peels the bloody material back from the shoulder. 'That's a deep wound but it's missed anything major. We'll get it cleaned up and you'll need some stitches. Here, press your jacket down on it hard. Don't let up on the pressure.'

His eyes are still on Lucky. 'I thought he'd hurt you.'

'Everything's fine. It was just a misunderstanding. Can you stand?'

'Yes.'

Martin gets to his feet but sways. 'Take your time.' Elizabeth looks over at Lucky. 'I need to talk to him. Wait here.'

Lucky is standing by the edge of the pond. There is something of the chastised boy about him. Elizabeth is reminded of Jack, when he thinks he's in the right but also knows that he is in trouble.

'I'm going to take Mr Templeton back to the house. Lucky, look at me. It's going to be all right. He thought you were hurting me. He was just trying to protect me. Do you understand?'

Lucky nods.

'Wait here. I'll come back and get you shortly.'

Lucky turns without a word and crouches over the fish.

'He shouldn't have a knife,' says Martin quietly when she returns. 'Where'd he get it?'

'I don't know. The kitchen probably.'

'I should take it off him before he hurts anyone else.'

'Don't, please.'

'I'm not afraid of him.'

'He could have killed you.' *And not given it another moment's thought.* 'I'll ask him for the knife later. He'll give it to me once he's calmed down, but right now let's get you back to the house.'

'All right.'

Martin grunts in pain as they set off, his bloody jacket pressed to his shoulder.

When he is sure that he is alone, Lucky begins scaling and filleting the dead fish. The silver scales fall onto the green grass and some stick to his hands. It would be wrong to let the fish go to waste. You must gather food and eat while you can. You never know when everything will be taken away from you.

twenty-eight

The next morning, Merry catches Elizabeth before she goes upstairs and tells her that Mrs Blackwell and a man are waiting to see her in the conservatory. Elizabeth hears his laughter even before she enters the room, a high, slightly simpering sound. Mrs Blackwell and the stranger are drinking tea. He rises from his seat and smiles. He is younger than his voice suggested, in his early thirties. A dark tailored suit and waistcoat lend his slightly corpulent frame a veneer of sleek elegance.

'This is my husband's nurse, whom I have told you about. Mrs Whitman, this is Dr Parkinson. He is the head of the Mansfield Psychiatric Hospital.'

Dr Parkinson's smile exposes two rows of small white teeth. 'Better known these days as Sunnyside.'

They exchange greetings before Mrs Blackwell gestures towards the table and they all sit.

'Tea, Mrs Whitman?'

'No, thank you.'

'Dr Parkinson has been kind enough to accept my invitation to visit us at short notice.'

The doctor smiles again. 'As I said, Mrs Blackwell, it is absolutely no inconvenience at all.'

'I have asked Dr Parkinson to give me his opinion of Paul's progress.'

Elizabeth frowns. 'I understood that I alone was to be responsible for your husband's care.'

'In light of yesterday's incident I thought it best to seek professional advice.'

'What happened to Mr Templeton was a misunderstanding.'

The doctor's eyes are fixed on Elizabeth. They are a pale shade of blue and she finds his stare disconcerting. 'Am I right in believing that Mr Blackwell stole a knife from the kitchen?'

'Yes.'

'And that he then used the knife to butcher a goldfish?'

'He did but . . .'

'*And* that soon after that he stabbed Mrs Blackwell's chauffeur?'

'Martin overreacted because he thought I was in danger, when I wasn't. Before he was stabbed, Martin struck Mr Blackwell with a stick.'

'I am told that this is not the first time the patient has been angry and violent?'

Mrs Blackwell sighs. 'No. There have been numerous other incidents.'

'I see. And can I ask you a question, Mrs Whitman?'

'Of course.'

'Is it true, what Mrs Blackwell tells me, that sometimes you refer to Mr Blackwell by the name Lucky?'

'That's the name he was given by the other soldiers after he was wounded.'

'Do you call him this in his presence?'

She hesitates. 'I do.'

A raised eyebrow. 'To his face?'

'Yes.'

The doctor shakes his head slightly. 'The war is over. He is no longer a soldier. Why then do you call him Lucky rather than his true name, which is Paul Blackwell?'

'He doesn't believe that he is Paul Blackwell. He has no memory of his life before he was wounded.'

Dr Parkinson allows a sceptical smile to reach one corner of his mouth. 'Mrs Whitman, I have a very extensive history of treating patients with mental illness, not to mention a doctorate from the University of Cambridge on the subject.'

Although you did manage to mention it, thinks Elizabeth.

'There are several patients I am treating at the moment who believe themselves to be someone else. There is a woman in my care who firmly believes that she is Joan of Arc. She sits at her window and has long and quite involved conversations with God. Only a few days ago she told me quite confidently that it would not be long before she drove the English out of France.' He chuckles. 'Another patient, who incidentally also suffered wounds and considerable trauma during the war, believes he is the prime minister.'

'Mr Blackwell is not the same as those patients.'

'Please, let me finish. The woman who imagines that she is Joan of Arc is actually named Lillian Baxter. She is a bricklayer's wife and the mother of two children who miss her greatly. As you can imagine, her family wish for nothing more than the return of their wife and mother.'

'As I said, I believe that Mr Blackwell's case is different.'

Dr Parkinson holds up a hand. 'It is standard practice at the hospital when treating these patients that neither I nor any of my staff is seen to support their delusions in any way. Otherwise they will persist and even grow stronger. Surely you see that, Mrs Whitman?'

'I must repeat, Doctor, that I believe there are significant differences between those patients you mentioned and Mr Blackwell.'

He frowns and leans back in his chair. 'Really? And what are those differences? In your opinion as a nurse.'

'Paul Blackwell is not suffering from delusions. He has, however, suffered a penetrating head injury and I believe that injury has resulted in a profound loss of memory.'

'Permanent memory loss is very rare, almost unheard of. The fact is that Mr Blackwell believes he is someone else.'

'With no memories he has been forced to form a new identity.'

'That is unprecedented.'

'Just because something is rare or even unique does not make it impossible.'

'Is your background in psychiatric nursing, Mrs Whitman?'

'It is not. Even so, I believe that I am right in my assessment.'

The doctor turns back to Mrs Blackwell. 'I would like to speak to your husband alone. There are some standard questions I can ask him that will give me a very good idea of his mental state. For someone of my experience, it will not take long to make a preliminary diagnosis.'

Mrs Blackwell is obviously relieved. 'I would appreciate that, Doctor. Thank you.'

Dr Parkinson nods towards Elizabeth. 'I will of course take into account any head injury.'

'Shall I have Paul brought here?' asks Mrs Blackwell.

'That won't be necessary. Let Mohammed go to the mountain, shall we?'

Mrs Blackwell smiles and tinkles a small brass bell. Merry appears almost instantly. 'My maid will show you the way to Paul's room.'

'Thank you. If you will excuse me, ladies. I shan't be too long.'

He follows Merry out of the conservatory and Elizabeth and Mrs Blackwell are left together.

'If you will excuse me, I have some matters to attend to,' says Mrs Blackwell, rising to her feet. 'Please ask Merry to inform me when Dr Parkinson returns. I am anxious to hear what he has to say.'

'Of course.'

Elizabeth is left alone. There is nothing to be done except wait.

twenty-nine

Even before Lucky turns from the fireplace, he smells the man's cologne

'Good morning. I am Dr Phillip Parkinson.' The stranger carries himself like a person who is used to being obeyed, an officer or a senior doctor at Shand. He crosses the bedroom and holds out his hand. Lucky is not wearing a shirt and his muscles are tingling pleasurably from the heat.

'Will you not shake my hand?'

'Why should I?'

'To show that you and I are friends.'

'I don't know you, so how can you be my friend?'

'Do you think that I am your enemy?'

'I don't know yet. It's as likely as you being my friend.'

The doctor withdraws his hand. He walks towards the bookcase and glances at the titles. 'Do you often think that people are trying to hurt you?' Lucky does not reply. 'Will you at least tell me your name? I have given you mine.'

'It's Lucky.'

'Actually, isn't it true that your name is Paul, Paul Blackwell?'

Lucky scowls. 'Some people say that.'

'But you do not believe them?'

'My name is Lucky.'

The doctor makes a sweeping gesture with one hand, indicating the room and its contents but also taking in the rest of the house and the grounds. The movement subjects Lucky to a fresh wave of cologne. 'Is this not your own home, where you were raised, and where you now live with your wife?'

'I think you should leave me alone,' says Lucky quietly. He closes his eyes and concentrates on the feeling of the heat on his skin. But the man does not leave. Instead he starts to pace the room, circling and buzzing.

'I have some more questions, only a few. Why do you keep this room so hot?'

Lucky does not open his eyes when he speaks. 'My first memory is of winter. It was so cold that I thought my bones would freeze and shatter.'

'That's very poetic. Did this happen when you were a child?'

Lucky does not reply. The burning logs of macrocarpa crack and pop and an ember is spat out onto the tiles in front of the grate.

'Do you ever hear a voice that tells you what to think or what to do?'

Lucky turns his head to look at him. 'All the time.'

The man's face lights up. 'That's very interesting. Can you tell me more?'

'Yes. I'm hearing a voice like that right now. I hear one every time the woman who calls herself my wife appears.'

'I see.'

'Leave me alone.'

'I have more questions.'

'But I have no more answers.' Lucky takes a step towards the man. He is taller than the doctor by almost a head. 'Leave me. Now.'

The doctor takes two steps back. 'You should not get so excited, Mr Blackwell.'

Lucky bunches his hands into fists and takes another step towards this droning fool. 'Go!'

The man turns and hurries from the room.

~

When Dr Parkinson returns to the conservatory, Mrs Blackwell is informed and comes back to the room within a few minutes. Elizabeth has not moved from her seat at the table.

'I would like to speak to you about your husband alone, if I may,' he says to Mrs Blackwell.

Elizabeth raises her voice. 'If you're going to discuss my patient, I would prefer to stay.'

'Your patient? Really, Mrs Whitman, you are not his doctor, merely his nurse. I must insist on talking to Mrs Blackwell alone.'

'Dr Parkinson,' Elizabeth begins.

Mrs Blackwell interrupts. 'Mrs Whitman, if you wouldn't mind. Please.'

Elizabeth is about to argue her case further but seeing the look on Mrs Blackwell's face she realises that it would be futile. 'Very well.' She turns and leaves the room without another word.

When the door is closed, Mrs Blackwell sits at the table. Dr Parkinson remains standing. He pauses, as though considering how to begin.

'It is only a preliminary impression, but I have seen for myself that your husband is antagonistic and volatile. Obviously, in light of what happened to your driver, he is more than potentially dangerous. By his own confession, he hears voices telling him what to do.'

Mrs Blackwell purses her lips. 'I did not know that.'

'I am sorry to have to tell you, but it is my professional opinion that your husband is suffering from quite a profound psychological illness, most likely a form of what is called schizophrenia.'

'Schizophrenia?' Mrs Blackwell repeats the word slowly, sounding out the syllables one by one. 'What is that?'

'A rather serious condition, I'm afraid. It is a form of mental illness that has recently been identified by Dr Eugen Bleuler. The good doctor was actually a teacher of mine when I studied in Europe before the war.'

'And you think this is what Paul has?'

'Yes. It is likely that his condition was brought on by the traumatic events he experienced during the war, but it is possible that he was always predisposed towards it.'

'But what about his head injury? Mrs Whitman was sure that was the reason he lost his memory.'

'It is an interesting theory but rather fanciful, I'm afraid. In my experience people do not simply *lose* their memories, not entirely and certainly not permanently.'

'Surely it is possible, though.'

'I think it will be fruitful to look for the most scientifically probable explanation. As I noted earlier, it is actually quite common for the mentally ill to claim that they do not remember who they are. They block out their own history in order to more easily adopt a new persona.'

'Why would they do that?'

'It is not a conscious decision. Often it is to protect themselves from remembering what is too painful to recall — events that have scarred the conscious mind, in a figurative sense.'

'Apart from the incident with the knife, Paul has been much calmer since Mrs Whitman took over his care.'

'I have no doubt. She is feeding his delusions, not challenging the false reality that he has spun around himself. But I must tell you quite firmly, this nurse is doing exactly the opposite of what any trained psychiatrist would do. By supporting the idea that your husband is this fictitious character, this Lucky, she is guiding him deeper and deeper into the very state which you one day hope to remedy.'

Mrs Blackwell sighs. Her shoulders slump and for a moment her head droops forward. When she looks up she seems diminished, even frail. 'She came very highly recommended.'

'I'm sure that Mrs Whitman has your husband's best interests at heart. However she is not a doctor, let alone a psychiatrist. She is simply a nurse, and nurses are trained in little more than administering medicine and making beds.'

'I see now that I should have come to you immediately.'

'Not too much harm done, I'm sure, as long as you allow me to act quickly.'

'What would you advise?'

'I strongly believe that Paul would get the best treatment that modern psychiatry can provide if he were under my care at Sunnyside.'

'I had been hoping to avoid having him institutionalised.'

'I cannot adequately treat him here. He needs to be watched twenty-four hours a day.'

'What type of treatment would you give him?'

'Medication is the main weapon in the modern psychiatrist's arsenal. We would have to experiment but I am confident that the new barbiturates will keep your husband's mood swings in check and make him far more receptive to accepting reality.'

'Is that all?'

'To begin with.'

'And how long would Paul have to be . . . to stay with you?'

'It's impossible to say, really. At least a year, perhaps longer.'

'Such a long time? I will have to think about this.'

'Of course if you are concerned about the family's reputation, we could admit your husband under a pseudonym, to save any embarrassment. It would not be the first time that we have treated a member of a prominent family.'

'Thank you.'

'I would, however, urge you to make your decision sooner rather than later — for your husband's sake.'

Mrs Blackwell rises and Dr Parkinson mirrors her. 'Thank you very much for coming today,' she says. 'It has been most illuminating.'

'It was my pleasure, Mrs Blackwell. I look forward to hearing from you very soon. Good day.'

When she is alone, Mrs Blackwell sits and lifts the tea cup to her lips. The tepid liquid trembles and before she can drink a sob escapes her mouth. She is forced to rattle the cup and saucer back down onto the table. She composes herself. 'Big girls don't cry,' her mother used to say. 'Crying solves nothing.'

thirty

That evening, Jack asks for another instalment of *The Balloonist*. He has a chest cold that has come on quickly and his breathing is raspy and uneven in the darkness, acidic on the air.

Elizabeth almost refuses him. Upset by the accident with Martin Templeton and Dr Parkinson's visit to Woodbridge, she has been anxious and distracted all evening. Besides, she has given no thought to how the story will continue. Yet when she sits on the edge of Jack's bed the words tumble from her mouth as if she had carefully planned the next part of the tale. It is not an exaggeration to say that the story has been growing inside her, unbidden.

The first thing the man saw when he crawled out of the wreckage of the balloon was a large male tiger. The Tiger was sitting perfectly still on the edge of the clearing, only 20 feet from where the man was still on all fours amongst the mud and rotting jungle leaves.

'How far is 20 feet?' asks Jack in a thick, nasal voice.

'From the back wall of the house to the hen house.'

Jack makes a snuffling sound which simultaneously indicates that he understands and that his mother should continue.

The great cat raised one paw and licked it thoroughly. When he had finished he looked up and met the man's gaze.

'Excuse me,' said the Tiger, his voice very deep. 'I was wondering if you could help me?'

The man looked around. He was hoping to spy a nearby tree into which he could scramble, but as luck would have it all the trees on his side of the clearing were either too slender or the branches too high.

'The thing is,' continued the Tiger, 'yesterday, or possibly the day before, I'm not really sure, a group of men captured my wife and child.'

It is always *a bad idea to engage in conversation with any of the larger carnivores. As you know, even so much as smiling at a crocodile is unwise. Still, the Balloonist was curious.*

'How is it that you are not sure when this happened?'

'Ahhhhh,' said the Tiger with a sound almost like a purr, 'that is a very good question.'

He turned his massive head so that the man could see a deep graze running across the fur on the Tiger's skull just behind his right ear. 'When I was attempting to protect my family the men shot me and I became unconscious for some time. It was only the storm that woke me.'

The Balloonist got slowly to his feet. He thought it best not to make any sudden movements. Brushing the damp leaves off his trousers, he glanced towards the wreckage of the balloon. It was in a sorry state.

'I don't mean to be rude, but before you go on with your story, can I ask if you know the whereabouts of Mboli and Dougal MacTavish?'

'I take it you are referring to your two companions?'

'I am.'

'The impressively red-headed one in the skirt took one look at me and ran off in that direction.' The Tiger flicked his tail towards the north.

'MacTavish.'

'Indeed? Well, your MacTavish is going to find the jungle a difficult place in which to survive. Not everyone he meets will be as friendly as I am.' And the Tiger smiled, showing a set of teeth that were very white, very large and clearly very sharp.

'And Mboli?' asked the man.

'If my nose serves me well, and it always does, he is still inside your flying contraption.'

The man lifted aside part of the deflated silk balloon that covered the basket and saw that the Tiger was right. Mboli had always been a very sound sleeper and apparently neither the thunder nor the resulting crash had been enough to rouse him from his hammock. He was still lying entangled in it. His neck, however, had been broken and he was dead.

The Balloonist emerged from the wreckage, looking grim. 'So how can I be of help to you?' he asked the Tiger, who had not moved.

'I thought you might be so kind as to negotiate on my behalf with those who have taken my wife and child. I would speak to them myself, but I do not wish to be shot at again.'

The man took a moment to gather his thoughts. 'I have three questions, if you don't mind.'

'You would be a fool if you didn't have questions.'

'Firstly, what would I gain from this bargain?'

'If you help me then I will give my word to lead you out of the jungle. Without my help you could wander in here for weeks and not come close to finding the nearest village.'

'My second question: what do these men want with your wife and son?'

'You will appreciate,' said the Tiger, 'that I had little chance to question them in any depth on the matter, but I do believe that they intend to sell my family to a zoo. I have heard that zoos, particularly ones in America, will pay very well for a female of breeding age, especially with a cub.'

'I see. My final question is this: you said you wish me to negotiate on your behalf, but what will you be offering the kidnappers in exchange for your family's release?'

The Tiger stood up. It was a movement so quick and fluid that it happened in the course of the Balloonist's single blink. 'Come with me and I will show you.'

Without so much as a backward glance, the Tiger stalked majestically to the edge of the clearing and disappeared into the dense foliage. The leaves closed behind him like a curtain. Taking only a minute to throw some supplies into a duffel bag, the Balloonist set out after the Tiger.

She thinks that Jack is asleep and is surprised when he speaks. 'Hugh's father is back from the war.' Hugh is a boy who lives down the road, a friend.

'Is he?'

'He lives in their house with Hugh and his sister and their mother.'

'That's good.'

'And Mrs Wilson's son's back, too.'

'Yes.' Of course she knows what he is going to ask.

'Why isn't Dad home yet?'

'Well, Jack, not everyone has come home so soon. Some of the men have to stay and help in Europe.' That is not, strictly speaking, a lie.

Jack nods. 'When will he be finished helping?'

She puts a hand on his warm head and gently ruffles his hair. 'I'm not sure, but soon, I hope. Now it's time to go to sleep. Goodnight.'

'Goodnight, Mum. I love you.'

'I love you, too.'

thirty-one

'Ah, Mrs Whitman. I'm glad I bumped into you.'

Elizabeth, still unbuttoning her coat, is met by Mrs Blackwell in the hallway. She is certain that her employer has been waiting for her to arrive. Mrs Blackwell looks tired; there are dark bags under her eyes. Elizabeth, too, has had an unsatisfactory night's sleep. Jack developed a cough and a slight fever and he spent most of the night tossing and turning, while in the bed next to his Elizabeth's thoughts kept circling back to Lucky.

'Can we talk for a moment?' asks Mrs Blackwell.

'Of course.'

'Perhaps in the library?'

'Certainly.'

Merry brings tea and the two women wait politely while it

is poured. After a minute, Mrs Blackwell comes to the point. 'Dr Parkinson believes that Paul is suffering from a form of mental illness brought on by his war experiences. Have you heard of a condition called schizophrenia?'

'No, I haven't.'

A look of disappointment flicks across Mrs Blackwell's face. 'That is Dr Parkinson's diagnosis.'

'With all due respect to Dr Parkinson, he spoke to your husband for only a few minutes.'

'Nonetheless, he is very experienced. He was something of a prodigy, I believe, the youngest ever medical school graduate in this country. Afterwards he studied in Europe under some of the top minds in his field.'

'That doesn't necessarily mean that he's right about your husband.'

'And you think that you are?'

'When I was nursing in England, I saw many soldiers whose minds had snapped because of the terrible things that they'd seen and done. God knows how there weren't more, considering. In fact, given the things they had to endure, insanity might well have been the only truly sane response.' Mrs Blackwell looks at her blankly. 'My point is that your husband is not like those men.'

Mrs Blackwell sighs. 'I'm sorry, but I must follow the best medical advice that is available.'

'He simply can't remember. That's the root of everything that's wrong with him. It's not an illness.'

'How can you be so certain?'

'Because I've talked to him. He has convinced me. Your husband is a blank slate just waiting to be written on. He doesn't belong in a mental hospital, any more than a child would. It's experience he lacks, not sanity.'

Mrs Blackwell holds up a hand. 'Please. Dr Parkinson telephoned last evening.'

'He is very persistent.'

'I am certain that he just wants the best for Paul. He proposed a more detailed examination, at Sunnyside this time. I have agreed. I should also tell you that I have decided to follow whatever course of action the doctor thinks best.'

'Including putting your husband in an institution?'

'Yes, if he thinks that is called for.'

'When your husband becomes difficult to manage, and I'm sure he will in a place like that, then they'll undoubtedly give him sedatives.'

'I'm sure the doctors will do nothing unless it is for the best.'

Elizabeth stands. 'I can see you are decided.'

'I am.'

'Is there nothing that I can say to change your mind?'

'I'm afraid not. I apologise for the short term of your employment with us. Don't worry, you will have no trouble being reinstated to your position at the hospital. I will arrange for you to be paid up until the end of next month — to compensate you for any inconvenience.'

Elizabeth shakes her head. 'I believe in being paid for the work that I do, no more, no less.'

'Of course, as you say.'

Elizabeth walks to the door where she pauses and turns back. 'Mrs Blackwell, your husband should not be locked up in Sunnyside.'

'I am sorry, my mind is made up.'

'Then please allow me one last thing. I would be very grateful if I could accompany you to the examination. I would like to be there and perhaps make my case directly to Dr Parkinson.'

Mrs Blackwell nods curtly. 'All right. The appointment is tomorrow afternoon.'

'So soon?'

'Dr Parkinson thinks the case is most urgent.'

'I'm sure he does.'

thirty-two

When it was completed in 1867, the institution was named the Mansfield Lunatic Asylum. I will not tarry over architectural exposition. It would be too easy — fish in a barrel — to describe the building as darkly Neo-Gothic, although technically that is the architectural style. To liken the tall windows to unlidded eyes staring dully out at the Blackwells' car as it pulls up in front of the main building would not be fair. It is probably best to stick to the facts.

The day is dominated by a low sky the colour of dirty concrete from which falls an intermittent drizzle. Martin Templeton holds the car door open for Mrs Blackwell with his good hand. His shoulder is bandaged, the arm supported by a sling. Elizabeth and Lucky leave the other side of the vehicle under their own steam.

'Wait here please, Martin,' says Mrs Blackwell.

‘Yes, ma’am.’ The driver shoots Lucky a dark look (and who can blame him?).

Even though the institution has been renamed the much more felicitous Sunnyside, it still manages to loom over the three figures walking towards the entrance. The large wooden door is flanked by two lanterns, recently electrified. It *may* give a very slight creak as it swings open. Perhaps it does close rather heavily. But to say that the sound echoes down the corridor like hollow laughter, well, that is a bridge too far. Such descriptions belong to a model of mental institution that by 1919 was already antiquated.

Elizabeth, Mrs Blackwell and Paul/Lucky (again, take your pick — you may have changed your mind at this stage) find themselves in a building which, in almost all particulars, is the same as any well-run hospital of the day. They are met at the reception desk by an attractive young nurse. She smiles warmly and, seeing Elizabeth’s uniform, gives a collegial nod.

‘Good morning,’ says Mrs Blackwell. ‘We have an appointment with Dr Parkinson.’

The nurse refers to a typed list that is sitting on her desk. ‘Certainly, you must be the Blackwells. Please follow me.’

She leads the trio along a corridor — neither narrow nor dim — past rooms that are not padlocked and from which come no screams or howls, not so much as a faint moan. They are shown into a waiting room with soft deep chairs and a mahogany coffee table on which sit several recent newspapers and periodicals.

As is his habit, Lucky walks to the window and looks out. The drizzle has temporarily abated and a few patients are strolling in the grounds. None of them seems visibly distressed although one plain, freckled woman with a halo of red hair is sitting very still on a bench, as though listening to her own internal muse.

They wait in silence until Dr Parkinson emerges from his office a few minutes later. He appears suddenly, apparently already smiling broadly before he enters the room.

‘Good morning, everyone.’

Elizabeth almost expects the small group to chorus ‘Good morning, Dr Parkinson’ in the high voices of a class of five year olds.

Mrs Blackwell stands and offers her hand. She seems relieved to see the doctor. 'Good morning. It is very kind of you to take us so soon.'

He beams. 'Not at all.'

Lucky remains by the window and does not acknowledge the doctor at all. Elizabeth confines herself to a small nod. If Dr Parkinson is surprised to see her here he does not show it. He continues to address himself directly to Mrs Blackwell. 'As I said on the telephone, this will be a more detailed assessment. It's really just an interview between Paul and myself. I'll be asking a series of questions, running some tests, nothing too rigorous.'

At the use of the name Paul, Lucky gives the doctor a look of the most intense dislike. Elizabeth catches his eye and shakes her head very slightly.

'If you ladies would like to wait here, it would be best if I saw Paul alone in my office. Mr Blackwell, do you mind?'

Again Lucky makes eye contact with Elizabeth and this time she nods. He follows the doctor into the adjoining office.

thirty-three

Elizabeth has done her best to prepare Lucky for this interview. 'It's very important that you don't lose your temper.'

'Why. Will he beat me?'

They had been together, earlier that day, in the billiard room at Woodbridge. Lucky had been curious about the game and Elizabeth had explained how to play as best she could. They took turns hitting the white ball with the cues, knocking it into the coloured balls, which rolled over the green felt, clinking against one another but seldom falling into the pockets unless by chance.

'No, he's not allowed to beat you. But he could persuade Mrs Blackwell to send you to live at Sunnyside.'

'And if I said that I didn't want to go?'

'You wouldn't have a choice.'

'Why not?'

'It's the law. It's called being committed. You wouldn't like it there.'

'Why not?'

'You wouldn't have any freedom. You certainly couldn't just come and go, not even from your room.'

'This prison or that one, what's the difference?' Lucky struck the white ball with sudden force and it ricocheted around the table.

'Trust me, you would prefer it here.'

'With you?' He looked at her curiously.

'Yes.' Her gaze faltered and broke.

'Good.'

He gave her one of his rare smiles and she was suddenly flustered. It was her turn at the table. She fumbled with her cue and barely managed to hit the white ball into the blue. 'The very worst thing to do would be to get angry.'

'Then this doctor shouldn't insist that I am someone that I am not.' His voice was already rising.

'Listen,' said Elizabeth, 'won't you consider telling him what he wants to hear, that you are Paul Blackwell?'

'No, I can't.'

'But why not? It would be so easy.'

'Who I am, who I believe that I am, is all I have. There is nothing else in the entire world I can call my own. I cannot give that up.'

Elizabeth nodded. 'In that case I want to tell you another story.'

'About what?'

'Just listen. At the start of the war there was a man who was a conscientious objector.'

'What's that?'

'Someone who refuses to fight because he doesn't believe in violence, especially killing, no matter what the circumstances.'

Lucky absorbed this eccentricity without comment.

'When this man refused to join the army he was arrested and locked up in a special prison for a long time. Soldiers forced him and other men like him to dig trenches and then fill them in again. They made him go on long marches in all sorts of weather and perform other pointless but difficult tasks. Some of the guards taunted the man, called him a coward, even struck him.

'A handful of the other men in the prison could not stand the conditions and eventually broke down. They agreed to go to the war to fight, but this man never did.

'After almost a year in the prison he was put on a ship and sent to France anyway. The sailors taunted him even more than the guards at the prison camp. They called him a traitor and a coward and gave him food crawling with weevils. They kept him locked in a small cell far below the deck, even during a violent storm that came close to sinking the ship.

'When the ship arrived in France the man was immediately taken to the front. The soldiers guarding him spat on him and one slapped him hard across the cheek but the man didn't say a word. He was taken into no-man's-land and tied to a special stake. The way he was tied made it painful even to stand. It was winter and there was a bitter wind. But he never complained or condemned the soldiers who tied him. That happened every day for almost two weeks.' Elizabeth paused.

'What happened to him?' asked Lucky

'Even the soldiers realised that the man was going to die before he agreed to fight. He was brought before a major and asked if he would become a stretcher bearer, one of those men who went out under fire and brought back the wounded. The man said he would think about it. The next day he agreed, as long as he did not have to carry a gun.

'That's how he came to eventually help some of the same soldiers who had taunted and tortured him. He would go where no one else dared. Every time a cry of "stretcher bearer" was heard he would risk his life. Everyone agreed that they'd never met a braver man.'

Lucky put his cue down on the billiard table. 'You want me to be more like the man in your story.'

'You can take from it what you want. That's how stories are.'

'That one seems rather obvious. Did you know this man?'

'I heard about him.'

'And what if I take nothing from your story?'

Elizabeth gave a small shrug. 'That's your choice.'

thirty-four

When telling a story, what is left out is just as important as what is included. That sounds nonsensical, but it is true.

Some storytellers make the mistake of including everything. If there is a kitchen in the story, then its sink is a model in 304 grade stainless steel — bought on sale from a well-known plumbing supplies shop in Smith Street, undermounted, with welded double bowls, an overflow and incorporating a rack where dishes can drain.

Tedious.

'But what happens *next*?' becomes the reader's increasingly testy refrain.

Too much of that sort of thing and the book inevitably gets put on the bedside table, never to be reopened. The same can be said of countless digressions from the story. Storytelling is a juggling act.

I mention the subject because the question has arisen of what happens between Lucky and Dr Parkinson during their interview. The historical facts of this meeting have been lost and so it must be decided how much detail is necessary. Would it help or hinder our story to describe the psychiatrist's office as being panelled in dark oak? Or should the room be spartan, with only a desk and a few neatly aligned medical texts on a dusted shelf? Or cluttered with books, papers, files, the accrued stubs of pencils; crammed to the gunwales with psychiatric bric-à-brac lying willy-nilly. A model of a human head could be a nice touch, the regions of the brain labelled like countries on a map.

Although Rorschach's test was formulated two years later, in 1921, and wasn't commonly used for several years after that, psychiatrists had been asking patients to interpret indistinct images for many years. It *might* help with the story to go into some detail about the cards that the doctor holds up in front of Lucky, an ink blot on each one. Or should Lucky's responses to those ambiguous stains be skimmed over as lightly as a flat stone bouncing across the surface of a pond?

'A cat.

'A lizard.

'Two women arguing.

'A muddy field with a broken tree.

'I don't know — it looks like nothing. Well then, I suppose a heart.'

Perhaps there is also a series of questions the answers to which are: 'Yes. Yes. No. Yes. No. Yes. I'm not sure. All right, no. Yes. Yes.'

The important part of this episode, the part that absolutely cannot be left out, is what Dr Parkinson concludes from his interview. After forty minutes, he emerges from his office. Mrs Blackwell and Elizabeth have been sitting still and silent as stumps. Both women rise to their feet at the same time.

'I have asked Paul to wait in my office. Mrs Blackwell, can I speak to you in private?'

'Actually, I would like Mrs Whitman to hear what you have to say, Doctor.'

He frowns and seems on the point of arguing. 'Very well.' The doctor pauses for a moment, either to collect his thoughts or for dramatic effect, it is difficult to be sure. 'I have confirmed my earlier diagnosis of schizophrenia.'

Of course you have, thinks Elizabeth.

'It is my professional opinion that your husband's memory loss is not organic in origin but has come about as a result of the mental trauma that he suffered in the trenches. I am convinced that a period of treatment and convalescence here at Sunnyside will eventually restore Paul's memory.'

Mrs Blackwell looks relieved. 'You determined this by scientific testing?'

'I can assure you that I have employed the most modern scientific methods at my disposal. I am one hundred per cent confident that my diagnosis is the correct one.'

'Do you really think that you can bring back the man that I married?' Her look is imploring.

'I think that there is a good chance, yes, although I make no promises. As I have explained to you already, we have some remarkably effective new methods.'

'Barbiturates.' Elizabeth speaks for the first time. 'Mrs Blackwell has mentioned those.'

'Yes. There have been significant advances in the development of pharmaceuticals in the last few years.'

'And when would you like to start Paul's treatment?' asks Mrs Blackwell.

'Today, immediately. The sooner we begin, the sooner your husband will be restored to you.'

Elizabeth finds that she cannot stay an observer any longer. 'And what if you're mistaken, Doctor? What if Mr Blackwell's memory loss *has* been caused by his wound? What impact will strong sedatives have on him then?'

For a fleeting second Dr Parkinson looks uneasy and then his professional countenance slides back into place. 'I do not believe that I am wrong, Mrs Whitman.'

'But what if you are?' insists Elizabeth.

Dr Parkinson ignores her question. He turns back to Mrs Blackwell, who has been watching the exchange uneasily. 'It is up to you to make the final decision.'

Mrs Blackwell takes a deep breath and draws herself up. 'I have been thinking about this very carefully. Mrs Whitman, you have brought about a great change for the better in Paul in a very short time and I am grateful. But now it seems clear to me that I must trust to a more learned judgement than your own.'

'But I'm sure . . .' begins Elizabeth.

A slender hand is held up. 'No. I'm sorry. Paul will come to Sunnyside.'

For a moment the room is very still.

'Mrs Blackwell,' says Elizabeth, as calmly as she can manage. 'I understand that you've been forced to make a very difficult decision. You must of course side with the most persuasive argument. However, I still don't believe that Sunnyside is the right place for your husband.'

Dr Parkinson can contain himself no longer and his pale eyes flash. 'I am not in the habit of having my diagnoses second-guessed by nurses.'

Elizabeth keeps her eyes fixed on Mrs Blackwell's. 'As a great favour to me, can I please ask that your husband remain under my care at Woodbridge for just a while longer.'

Dr Parkinson is shaking his head. 'No. I do not recommend that, not at all.'

'To what purpose?' asks Mrs Blackwell.

'I believe that given the excellent progress that he has made, even another month will see great changes for the better.'

'He has improved a lot. Do you really think he might remember me soon?'

'It is possible.' *Although I doubt it.* 'Surely another month can't hurt?' says Elizabeth.

'I disagree,' says the doctor churlishly. Both women are forced to look at him. 'In my opinion a month could make a great deal of difference to your husband's recovery. I don't have to remind you, Mrs Blackwell, that it is only a few days since he attacked a man.'

'It was a misunderstanding,' says Elizabeth.

'Nonetheless, a man was stabbed. Mrs Blackwell, please, listen to reason. This woman is well intentioned, I'm sure, but the fact is she is completely unqualified to express any opinion whatsoever in this matter. Sunnyside is the only suitable place for your husband. The sooner he is under my care the better.'

A lesser woman would have crumpled under the man's stern gaze. Mrs Blackwell regards him coolly. 'Did you go to the war, Dr Parkinson?'

He seems surprised by this change in tack. 'No, but I hardly think that is relevant.'

'Mrs Whitman may not be a psychiatrist, but she has dealt extensively with wounded soldiers, both here and overseas. She is greatly respected by those doctors who have worked alongside her. I think you would do well to remember that.'

'I meant no disrespect.'

'I am sure you did not.'

Mrs Blackwell draws herself up to her full height. 'I *will* allow her to tend to Paul, but only for another month, up until his birthday on the 29th of July. Unless there is a radical change, and he remembers who he is, at that date he will come here to you for treatment.'

Dr Parkinson lips are tight and bloodless. 'I think that is a mistake.'

'Possibly,' says Mrs Blackwell firmly. 'But I have made my final decision, and you can be sure, Dr Parkinson, that I will not be changing my mind again.'

thirty-five

The Tiger walked ahead, leading the Balloonist through the jungle. It was dark beneath the high canopy of the trees, and the great cat was just one more shadow among the deeper shadows, slipping easily in and out of view between the tree trunks, solid for a second or two before vanishing into thin air like a ghost.

The man scrambled and pulled himself up, pushed and heaved over fallen trees and through narrow gaps. Sometimes he was forced to wriggle his way on his belly through the mud. He gasped and grunted and sweated. The jungle was nothing like the native bush near his home in Mansfield. Here, the enormous trees were supported by tangles of exposed roots, some as thick as his waist. The ground was always boggy and the air so hot that it felt as if it had come straight from a kitchen kettle. Thickets of bamboo and hanging vines grew everywhere.

It began to rain, but this did not make the air in any way cooler. The man's uniform was soaked through within seconds, so wet that he could very well have been swimming in it. He could hear the raindrops hitting the broad leaves around him. At first there were a few at a time: they made a sound like clap, clap, clap. *Soon the fat, wet claps were coming so hard and so fast that it was as if the jungle were filled with mocking applause.*

He had not seen the Tiger for some time. He stopped and looked around. Warm rain dripped from his eyebrows and nose and from the tips of his fingers. This part of the jungle looked exactly the same as all the other jungle that he had passed through that day.

He called, 'Tiger? Tiger? Where are you?'

There was no reply except for the clapping of the rain. Suddenly the Tiger was standing right beside him. He had not heard his approach at all.

'How slowly you go.'

'Is it much further?' asked the man.

'At this pace everywhere *is much further,' said the Tiger and walked off.*

The Balloonist sighed and followed.

Actually, their destination was not very far. The rain stopped as quickly as it had begun. The trees thinned out slightly, and where sunlight hit the ground the earth steamed. The man found himself walking through a thin mist. The floor of the jungle began to slope upwards and he realised that he was now following the Tiger up what must be the side of a mountain. Stopping to collect his breath, he looked back and through a gap in the trees he saw that he was already quite high up. The jungle stretched as far as he could see in every direction, unbroken green in countless shades.

Turning away, he felt his duffel bag catch on something

tugging at his shoulders. The man was standing beneath a jibjab tree. He could see the famous jibjab thorns protruding from its branches. It was one of these that had snagged his bag. He was just tall enough to reach up and pull down the lowest branch. Very carefully he grasped the nearest thorn and twisted it free. It was 8 inches long and razor sharp along its outer edge and at its vicious tip. Wrapping the thorn in a piece of material ripped from the spare shirt in his bag, the man slipped it into his pocket and resumed walking up the mountain.

The Tiger was waiting for him, twitching his tail impatiently. 'What have you been doing?'

'Nothing,' lied the Balloonist. He could feel the reassuring shape of the jibjab thorn, long and sharp as a dagger, pressed flat against his thigh. 'Shall we carry on?'

'No need, we are here.'

The man looked around, confused. All he could see were more trees, more vines, more bamboo. 'Follow me,' said the Tiger as he went between two trees into a wall of green leaves. The man followed.

He emerged at the entrance to an old mine. Without pausing, the Tiger stalked into the dark mouth of the mountain. Only a few feet in front of the man the darkness became as thick as squid ink. How far the mine shaft extended into the mountain was impossible to say.

'I will be able to see perfectly well in the dark,' said the Tiger, his eyes shining, 'but as your species is inferior in so many ways that count, you may require the use of one of those.' He flicked his tail in the direction of several whale-oil lamps, which were hanging from hooks on the wall.

The Balloonist took down a lamp and lit it, using the matches he had cleverly thought to pack in his bag. He noticed that the Tiger eyed the flame suspiciously.

'Follow me,' said the Tiger.

The shaft ran straight into the heart of the mountain.

They passed several side tunnels but the Tiger never veered either to the left or to the right. When he finally stopped, the man held up his lantern. They were in a natural cavern the size of a small room where shadows twisted over the walls. Scattered around on the uneven ground were picks and shovels.

'What happened to the men who dug this tunnel? It looks as though they left suddenly.'

'They did not leave,' said the Tiger. 'They are still here.'

The man got quite a shock when the Tiger said that. He held his lantern higher and strained his eyes and his ears. Sure enough, the Tiger had been telling the truth and he saw the miners. In the corner was a pile of human bones.

The Tiger licked one paw. 'In his youth, my father developed quite a taste for your kind. I asked him about it once. He said that you taste a lot like chicken. But on the whole, he believed that hunting you was more trouble than it was worth. It was he who told me about this place.'

The man shivered. 'Why have you brought me here?'

'Don't you see?' said the Tiger.

The man looked around the cavern. He saw the white bones and some water that dripped darkly down the walls. 'I see rocks.'

'Look closer.'

It was only then that the Balloonist noticed how the light from his lantern was reflecting in several places off the walls as though dozens of small dusty mirrors were protruding from the rock. He walked over to the nearest one and prised it free with a pickaxe that lay nearby. It was the size of a large marble, rounded and milky.

'Diamonds,' he murmured. 'This is a lost diamond mine.'

'Well done.'

'You want to buy back your wife and cub with diamonds.'

'Precisely,' said the Tiger, 'A few of the larger ones should

be enough. And because there is not much time before my family are put on a boat and lost to me forever, can I suggest that you start digging?'

thirty-six

In the days that follow Mrs Blackwell's decision, Lucky develops a new symptom. There's something amiss with his balance: he teeters on the balls of his feet and begins to stumble from mantelpiece to doorframe, to the edge of the bed and back again like a green cabin boy in a storm. The tremor in his hands returns and for several days he runs a fever and sweat soaks his sheets. Even so, he complains of the cold. At his insistence the fire is built up until the flames cause the bricks at the back of the fireplace to glow.

Elizabeth has no medical explanation beyond the complexity of the human body. She tells Lucky that the unsteadiness and the fever will pass and ensures that he drinks glass after glass of tepid water flavoured with lemon and honey. She asks Mrs Booker to prepare chicken soup.

The days are still fine although it is now after mid-morning before the sun can truly be said to give any warmth. On the fifth morning Elizabeth judges that Lucky is well enough to resume their rambles. She pushes him out the front door in a large wheelchair that was apparently used by his father, although she does not inform Lucky of its provenance. He wears a heavy overcoat and has a woollen blanket draped over his legs.

They wander with no objective in mind. If plotted on a map, their travels would leave a cat's cradle strung between oak and poplar, stretching to the east, to the stand of ash, around the brick chapel, and on to western border of the garden. At last they find themselves beneath the large magnolia growing in the middle of the lawn in front of the house.

'How did you meet your husband?' he asks unexpectedly.

'It was at the hospital in London. I'd only been there about a week. We were understaffed and I didn't know where anything was and it was all a bit daunting. Jonathan had just been admitted with shrapnel wounds to his legs and back. One morning I was blundering around the ward on the verge of tears and then there he was, leaning on his crutches and grinning at me.

'He said to me, "Haven't we met before?" Which sounds like the most terribly silly thing to say, but it turned out that we *had* met. We were both from here, from Mansfield, and we'd been introduced at a dance a couple of years before the war. We'd even had one dance together. We ended up laughing and chatting like old friends. After that I felt right at home at the hospital and had no trouble at all. Jonathan and I talked every day, although I had to be careful not to be seen to be favouring him over the other patients. I was surprised how upset I was when he was discharged but as it turned out he was sent to a training camp just outside the city. The army had redeployed him there as a machine gun instructor.

'Whenever we could arrange for our leave to coincide he would visit me. After about two months he asked me to marry him. I said yes straight away.'

'Because you loved him?'

'Yes, very much. My parents said later that I shouldn't have rushed into it. They don't understand that time moves differently when you're in a war. Six weeks was a lifetime. Married women weren't allowed to continue nursing so we were married secretly by one of the army chaplains, a friend of Johnny's. I had a friend from the hospital, another nurse, as my bridesmaid and Johnny had a sergeant from the training camp for his best man. Both were sworn to secrecy.'

'What was it you liked about him?' asks Lucky. He sounds curious. 'Is he very handsome?'

Elizabeth laughs. 'Oh, heavens no. Johnny's just average-looking, really. I suppose that I liked him at first because he was funny — he made me laugh. And because, even on crutches in the middle of a busy hospital ward, he seemed so relaxed. He always looked as though he were just off on a stroll down a country lane, without a care in the world.'

She picks up a magnolia leaf from the grass and strokes the broad shiny surface. 'Then he was unexpectedly sent back to the fighting in France, to the front. I didn't even get to see him before he shipped out. It was another three months before we saw each other.'

Lucky closes his eyes and turns his face towards the sun. 'Do you think that he is still alive?'

'I still have hope.'

'If the war is finished, why hasn't he come back to you?'

'I've thought of a hundred things that could have kept him. The most likely is that he has been captured and sent east somewhere. Maybe he escaped and is hiding in the mountains, not even knowing that the war is over. It's possible he was badly wounded and is being cared for somewhere. Maybe he has lost his memory.'

Lucky opens his eyes and regards her. 'I understand that does sometimes happen.'

'Yes, apparently it does.'

It is the first time Elizabeth has heard Lucky laugh. She likes his laugh, likes it a lot.

thirty-seven

Elizabeth is cutting Lucky's hair. It falls black and tangled onto the wooden floor of his room. Sitting on a stool with an old bed sheet draped around his shoulders and fastened at the back with a safety pin, he squirms and wriggles.

'Sit still.'

They are to go into Mansfield that afternoon and the haircut is a condition that Elizabeth has imposed; Lucky must let her make him look at least halfway presentable.

It has been a week — a full quarter of her allotted time — since her arrangement with Mrs Blackwell began. Lucky's balance has returned as mysteriously as it departed but other than that he has made no obvious progress. She feels that he has taken two steps back and one step forward. Elizabeth knows that the restoration of his memory is less than unlikely. So what, she wonders as she snips at his heavy locks, is she hoping to achieve? Perhaps she is just delaying the inevitable.

'What's the matter?' he asks.

'Nothing. Keep your head still.'

'Is it almost finished?'

'Soon. If it's any consolation, you're looking better already.'

Elizabeth works slowly and methodically. She asks him to tilt his chin up and snips at his wild beard. At least when she holds the scissors close to his throat Lucky stops wriggling.

'There,' she says at last, stepping back.

'Can I see?'

Lucky tilts the hand mirror she gives him this way and that, a frown upon his face. 'I wouldn't know myself.'

It is only when a fraction of a smile tugs at his lips that she realises that he is making another joke. She laughs and immediately feels better.

After lunch, Martin Templeton drives them into the city, his shoulder still bandaged beneath his jacket. Elizabeth does not know for sure how Mrs Blackwell managed to avoid involving the police after the stabbing. She suspects that some type of financial arrangement has been reached with the driver. Even so, civility does not seem to have been part of the bargain. It is plain that he holds a grudge, and not just against Lucky. He has barely said a word to Elizabeth since that day; in fact he positively bristles in her presence.

Martin Templeton parks the car close to the university and they go on foot towards the central square, Elizabeth and Lucky walking ahead, the driver hanging behind. Lucky moves slowly, drinking in the sights. He is wearing a new suit that his wife has had made for him. It is navy and double-breasted, a very fine cut. Even with his hair shortened and beard trimmed, people look at Lucky uneasily, give him a wide berth. There is still something of the foreigner about him. It is there, in the unguarded way that he stares at everyone, particularly children, and everything as though seeing it for the first time.

One boy of about four meets his gaze and begins to cry. The boy's mother takes her son's hand and hurries him on his way.

'You do know what a child is, don't you?' asks Elizabeth.

'Of course. I just haven't been so close to one before.'

This has never occurred to her. Of course there would have been no children on the hospital wards or aboard the troopship that brought Lucky back from England.

'I should introduce you to Jack.'

Lucky is still staring after the boy. 'Children are very strange.'

'In what way?'

'They are like real people but also not like them.'

'Adults?'

'Yes.'

'I suppose that's true, but every one of us was once a child,' she says and then adds, 'including you.'

Lucky gives her a look but does not contradict her or become angry as she is sure he would have done when they first met. Elizabeth takes this as a sign of progress.

They cross the bridge over the shallow Stratford River and Lucky pauses to watch the ducks bobbing for food. He stares for a while at a young couple sitting hip to hip on a tartan rug on the river bank.

In the Square the shadow of the cathedral spire lies across the cobblestones at their feet. Lucky tilts his head and gazes up at the spire. At the tip is a tarnished copper cross, green against the blue sky.

Elizabeth says, 'When I was a young girl, an earthquake knocked the top of the spire right off. My father took me to see it.'

'Do you remember it?'

'Not really. I remember the ice cream he bought me afterwards.'

'Then how do you know you saw the fallen cross?'

Elizabeth frowns. 'It's something that my family has talked about since then. Would you like to go inside?'

Lucky nods.

The interior of the cathedral is vast and dim and cold, stretching away from the entrance down twin rows of marble columns, which prop up a vaulted ceiling. Martin hangs back by the doors, his mood as cold as the air inside, while Elizabeth follows Lucky down the aisle. Half a dozen people, all women, are kneeling, still and silent as though they had been planted between the pews in wooden furrows and were waiting for sunlight to come through the stained-glass windows to make them grow. Elizabeth is grateful Lucky doesn't ask her questions about the purpose of prayer, or about God. They circle the pulpit with its lectern carved into a wooden eagle, a large Bible resting open on the back of its outstretched wings. The massive pipes of the organ rise above the choir stalls.

'Do you feel up to climbing the tower? There are steps. I haven't done it since I was a girl but you can see most of the city from the top.'

'Yes,' says Lucky, a tourist in his own home town (a tourist in his own life).

Back near the entrance is a small room from which narrow stone stairs corkscrew upwards. They have not climbed far before Lucky is breathing hard. The steps are narrow and he keeps his left hand on the stone outer wall as it curves and curves again, on and on, until even she feels dizzy. Somewhere behind them is Martin Templeton. Elizabeth can hear his footsteps as they echo.

Lucky stops, gasping.

'We can turn back if you want,' says Elizabeth.

'No.'

'I didn't realise it was this far.'

'I'm fine.'

They carry on and finally come to a small doorway beyond which is a ladder they must also climb. The thick ropes of the cathedral's bells hang just out of reach. Near the top of the ladder, they pass the bells themselves. There are four and Elizabeth could stand inside any one of them without stooping.

It is a relief to Elizabeth when they reach the top of the ladder and pass through another door into the open air. The balcony is set halfway up the spire. A wrought-iron balustrade at waist height is the only thing preventing them from stepping out into thin air. Below, Mansfield is spread out to be inspected, the streets lined up in neat rows. To the west is the green swathe of the Botanic Gardens and York Park. To the north is the river and the more affluent suburbs. To the south she can make out the railway station and the dark plumes from the gas works, and beyond that the swell of the hills where the suburbs splash up onto the lower slopes. The only direction she cannot see is east, because of the tower at her back, but she knows that from up here she would see the blue glint of the ocean.

Lucky runs a hand through his freshly cut hair. 'It looks like a nice place to call home.'

Elizabeth smiles. 'Yes, I've always thought so.'

She is surprised to find that she is happy, perhaps for the first time in years, and even more surprised to realise it is because she is with Lucky. He is making her feel this way.

'What's the matter?' he asks. 'You suddenly look worried.'

'Nothing, just a thought. I'm fine.'

Lucky takes her at her word and goes back to admiring the view but Elizabeth has lost interest in the rooftops of Mansfield. She watches Lucky, her emotions eddying between joy and consternation.

~

As they walk back from the cathedral, Lucky once again pauses on the bridge. The young couple on the rug are still there and he watches them as they kiss.

Displays of affection that would have been considered offensive, vulgar — even illegal — five years earlier are now commonplace. Everywhere the young are seizing the day, aware that so many of their generation no longer have that chance.

Lucky leans his elbows on the rails. 'When did you know that you were in love with your husband?'

'I suppose I really knew for certain after we were married.' Elizabeth laughs. 'That must sound strange. But there was a particular day when I knew beyond any doubt.'

'What happened?'

'It was the first time we were able to get leave together since we were married. Johnny took the train up and we met in London. He had four days. I had three. On the first evening we went to a nice restaurant just down the street from our hotel to celebrate. The head waiter looked down his nose at us a bit because we were colonial but Johnny was in his uniform and he was an officer. While we were eating, an Australian private tried to bring his girl in. The head waiter told them that they couldn't. He was quite rude. We could hear the whole thing from our table. The Australian was embarrassed and was all set to leave when Johnny got up and went across. I could tell he was angry although he kept his voice very calm.

'"This man's come halfway round the bloody world to risk his life so that you don't have Fritz marching down that street out there. The least you can do is serve him and his guest a meal."

'The waiter held his ground. "It is a restaurant rule, sir, that we only serve officers."

'I saw Johnny take the man by the elbow and firmly turn him aside. He leaned in and said something quietly into the man's ear. The waiter gave a start and his eyes went wide. After that he sat the private and his girl at a table near the back.'

'What did he say?' asks Lucky.

'Johnny wouldn't tell me. But that was the moment when I was sure that I loved him.'

~

'My mother fell deeply in love with a man who had no memory.' That's what MN first said to me on the telephone.

When did it happen? I mean, when was it clear to Elizabeth that her feelings for Lucky went beyond that of a nurse for her patient? Surely she resisted the idea. She was a nurse known for her professional detachment, living in an age with far stricter moral codes than our own. She was also a married woman with a child. Lucky was also married, even if he did not acknowledge the fact.

There are no accounts of how or when it happened. MN's mother never shared this aspect of her relationship with her son. She did not mention it, not even in passing, and it was not referred to in any detail in her letters to him. It is left to me, as the chronicler of this tale, to decide on when and where and how.

There are many possibilities. Perhaps it was a slow realisation, which came upon Elizabeth gradually every day that she cared for Lucky, like drops into a bucket — drip drip drip — until one day the water overflowed.

Or love can be sudden; a single day, a moment in time where there was a look or a touch, after which it was obvious that her feelings were irrevocable.

At some point I will have to decide.

I must also keep in mind that love between two people seldom happens simultaneously.

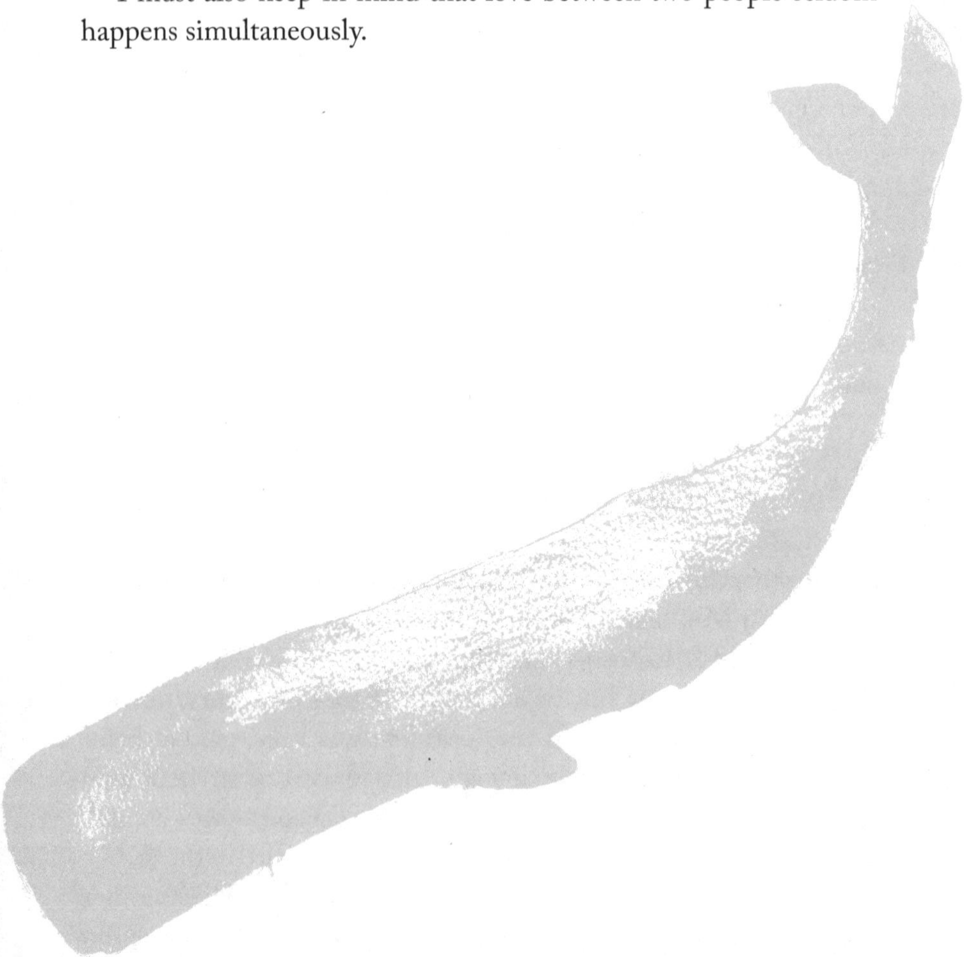

thirty-eight

The next day, they are driven into town again. The night has been clear and cold and the first frost of the year stiffens the grass and steam rises off the surface of the river as they walk along Nelson Avenue. Elizabeth had planned to take Lucky to the university, to show him the new cloisters and the observatory. It seems, however, that he has different ideas.

'I want to go into that building over there.'

'The university is just up the road.'

'No. I want to see that one.'

Lucky crosses the road, oblivious to a swerving bicycle and the angry glare of its rider and Elizabeth hurries after him. She catches up outside the entrance to the museum where he is scrutinising the entranceway with its four Doric columns and carved inscription.

'Does this look familiar?' asks Elizabeth, trying to sound casual.

His frown deepens. 'I'm not sure.'

Surely it can't be coincidence that Lucky is drawn to the building where he once worked. The idea that there is some link, however intangible, between Lucky's past life and his present makes Elizabeth's pulse quicken.

I must be careful not to rush matters. I cannot pressure him.

'I'd like to go inside.' He is already moving towards the entrance and she follows. The door opens directly into a large hall, where the only natural light falls through leadlight windows set high in the south side of the building. A few electric lights are switched on, but even so the atmosphere is at best dim. Large areas are roped off for displays. Glass cases and tall shelves rise up in front of them, every surface taken up with some object or other. The hall is so full of exhibits that Lucky and Elizabeth are forced to navigate a circuitous and uncertain route. Even so, Lucky moves confidently, turning left and right without hesitation and Elizabeth dares to hope that this is another positive sign.

Elizabeth would not have been surprised to learn that the Mansfield Museum had changed little since it was founded in 1865. Its method of presentation is still resolutely Victorian. In one roped-off area alone, measuring no more than 15 square feet, a giant clam shell from Samoa competes for space with a miniature Sumatran rhino. They are both cheek by jowl with an armadillo, itself giving the impression of being about to joust using the horn of a narwhal. Next to the armadillo a teak mask from East Africa leans on a copy of the Rosetta Stone, alongside a juvenile Australian salt-water crocodile, stuffed and grinning broadly at the monstrous horns of an elk.

In 1885 the Mansfield was identified by the British Museum's publication *Museum* as one of the top ten museums in the world. This honour was due largely to some significant bequests of both funds and private collections of bones and fossils. But since those heady days, and despite its record-breaking whale skeleton, the museum has slipped down the rankings like a fading tennis star who is feeling his age, lurching from one injury to the next but gamely hanging on. Better funded museums have stolen the limelight. Now the place has a palpable air of neglect. Dust lies thick on the glass tops of the display cases. The Sumatran rhino and several more of the stuffed animals have been badly chewed by moths.

Lucky seems as interested in a wide drawer full of pinned ants as he does in the African mask which, according to the small handwritten card, was 'used by the priests of Niger in their fertility rituals'. At one point he stops in front of a display of fossilised crabs. The card explains where the crabs were found and on what date. Looking over his shoulder, Elizabeth notes that they were donated to the museum by the Blackwell Family. If Lucky takes in this fact, he does not comment.

He spends most time standing in front of a huge display case, the largest in the hall, containing at least two hundred brightly coloured birds. Birds, birds, birds and more birds crowd together; all the continents and regions of the world have sent delegates to this gathering. Elizabeth finds it difficult for her eyes to settle on one among so many. Sheer size alone finally focuses her attention on a hook-beaked albatross, its wings judiciously folded. Gathered around it like disciples are a dozen canaries of various colours, also a fantail, a German owl and wading bird with red stilts for legs. Birds of Paradise. Birds of prey: falcon, hawk and even a bald eagle. In the far corner are a pair of weaver birds, mated now forever. A nightingale seems to whisper in the ear of a kiwi.

A man in a grey suit appears, seemingly out of nowhere.

'Paul! I thought that was you. I can't believe my eyes.' He seizes Lucky's hand and shakes it warmly. He sports large white sideburns. 'It's me, Teddy.'

Elizabeth steps forward quickly. 'Hello. I'm Mrs Elizabeth Whitman, Mr Blackwell's nurse.'

The man peers at her, uncertain. 'Pleased to meet you. I'm Edward Brown. Paul and I worked together here for several years before the war. Isn't that right, Paul?'

Lucky shakes his head. 'I'm sorry, I don't know you.'

Teddy Brown looks as though he had been slapped. 'Don't be ridiculous. We shared a tent for two weeks on the Grey River dig.'

'Mr Brown, may I speak to you?' says Elizabeth.

She takes him aside and explains the situation but it takes several minutes for her to convince him.

'Nothing at all?'

'I'm afraid not.'

'My God.'

When they return to where Lucky is standing, Teddy Brown looks pale and grim. He seems at a loss for words. 'I'm sorry if I upset you. It's just that Johnstone and Sinclair are gone too, you see. Never came back,' he trails off. 'Anyway, all the best for the future.'

'Thank you,' says Lucky.

'The damn war, eh. Good day, Mrs Whitman.'

With a final glance of the utmost sadness, he vanishes among the displays as quickly as he appeared. As soon as the man is out of sight, Lucky staggers and puts out a hand to the glass of the bird display to support himself.

'Are you all right? What's the matter?'

'I'm feeling dizzy again.'

'This trip has gone on long enough. We'll go back to Woodbridge now.'

Lucky does not protest when she takes him by the arm and leads him back through the maze of exhibits to the door.

thirty-nine

The next morning Lucky is unable to get out of bed without falling and his fever has returned, even higher than before. Elizabeth blames herself for taking him into town two days in a row — it was obviously beyond him. She sits by his bed and encourages him to eat a few spoonfuls of Mrs Booker's soup but he shakes his head and slumps back on the pillow.

'Tell me another story,' he says.

'I wasn't sure if you liked my stories.' He does not reply. 'All right. Actually I thought of one last night.'

'No, something that really happened.'

'Like all stories it's difficult to say how much is true and how much isn't.'

He raises no further objections but settles lower on the pillows and closes his eyes.

'There was a man who was a soldier, although it was not in the war that you fought in.'

'When?' asks Lucky, eyes still shut.

'It doesn't really matter. There have been so many wars. This soldier was fighting in a desert town. He had been badly wounded and was close to death. Everyone knew that the town was only hours away from being overrun. The wounded soldier lay on a dirty wheat sack in the corner of the town square. A shopkeeper ran past clutching what he hoped to save of his wares and the soldier called to him.

'"Please, won't you help me? The enemy will be here soon."

'The shopkeeper shook his head. "I can't. I have to save the goods from my shop otherwise everything I have will be looted by the enemy soldiers and I will be destitute." He left the wounded soldier lying on the wheat sack and ran on.

'After a while another soldier from the same division as the wounded man came hurrying along. He was wide-eyed, pale and trembling with fear.

'"Won't you help me? Take me with you," pleaded the wounded soldier.

'"I can't. The enemy has returned and is outside the gates of the town. You'll slow me down too much and I'll be captured." And he ran away up a cobbled street.

'The town soon fell to the attacking army. The first person to find the soldier still lying on his sack was a captain. He rode into the town square on a large black horse and drew up next to the wounded man. The captain climbed from his horse and inspected the soldier's wounds, then dressed them himself with bandages from his saddlebag. When the captain's men arrived in the square he ordered them to lift the wounded soldier onto a stretcher. The captain himself rode ahead through the streets until they found a doctor, whom he ordered to take care of the soldier as though he were one of their own.'

Elizabeth stops speaking and a blackbird sings from the tree outside the window.

'Is that the end?' asks Lucky.

'Yes.'

'It's a strange story. I don't think it's true.'

'Why not?'

'Why would the soldier's enemy help him?'

'Why do you think that he might?'

Lucky frowns. The fever beads his forehead with sweat. 'Perhaps the captain wanted something from the wounded soldier, maybe information.'

'So his kindness was a type of trick?'

'I think it must have been.'

'And what if I told you that the captain wanted nothing, that it was not a trick in any way?

'Then I would say that it's a very strange story.'

Lucky closes his eyes again and despite his fever it is only a few minutes until he is asleep. Putting the bowl of soup onto a tray, Elizabeth leaves the room as quietly as a mouse. Or a nurse.

forty

Boys will be boys.

That evening when Elizabeth arrives at her parents' cottage in Sydenham Street her mother reports that Jack has been fighting. He has punched the boy who lives in the house three doors down. Apparently there was a dispute over the ownership of a rusted tin can, a stick and a potato. Elizabeth's father saw the whole thing from the kitchen window.

The other boy is Hugh Taylor, whose father recently returned from the war. Jack's balled-up fist struck Hugh in the side of the face and blackened his eye.

'The little bugger went down like a ton of bricks,' chuckles Elizabeth's father.

Her mother frowns. 'Go back to your paper.'

'I think he's got a good career ahead of him as a pugilist.'

'Dad, don't encourage him. I don't want him fighting.'

'He's just a boy. These things happen. Go easy on him.'

Jack is brought out from his room, but after the inevitable round of tears, accusations and explanations he is still unwilling to apologise.

'The potato was mine,' says Jack stubbornly, 'and the stick.'

Elizabeth sighs. 'That's not the point. You don't hit people just to get what you want.'

'Why not? Dad's allowed to *shoot* Germans if they don't do what he wants. He can even *kill* them. All I did was hit Hugh.'

Laying aside for a moment the tricky semantics of the adult world, you have to admit that it's a very good point. Even so he is sent to bed early that evening and with no bread-and-butter pudding for afters.

~

Later that evening there is a knock at the door and Elizabeth finds a man standing on the bottom step clutching his hat in both hands.

'Yes, can I help you?'

'Mrs Whitman?' He rubs the brim of the hat between finger and thumb.

'Yes.'

'I'm Samuel Shepherd. I hope I'm not bothering you at tea time or anything.'

'No, we have finished eating. What's this about?'

'The thing is, I served with your husband. I was with him at Le Quesnoy.'

'Oh.' Elizabeth feels suddenly light-headed, her stomach hollow, as though she might be sick.

'Do you mind if I come in?'

She glances over her shoulder. Jack is asleep but her parents are both in the living room. They will be sure to come out if they hear a strange voice in the house.

'I'd rather stay here if you don't mind. I live with my parents.'

He nods. 'Of course, fine.'

'Please, can you tell me, is Jonathan dead?'

His eyes go wide and he grips his hat harder. 'No, I'm sorry. I don't have any news, nothing like *that*. I was just there that day, before him and the others went on patrol and I don't know, I thought it was the right thing to see you and tell that he was greatly respected. That's all really.'

'Greatly respected?' repeats Elizabeth.

'Yes. Everybody liked him.'

'But you were there when he went missing?'

A shrug. 'We were on the other side of the town. There was shelling into the forest but that's all I know. I just came to pay my respects. You and your son can be proud.'

Elizabeth tries to draw him out, to find out as much as she can, but it is like pulling teeth. Samuel Shepherd weighs his sentences carefully. He gives her the facts without embellishment, description without story. All she can get from him is that there were roughly a hundred soldiers outside the town. They were sheltering in a mixture of forest and barren fields. The walls of the town were stone, 20 feet high and in the end a small group used ladders to get inside. Once the gates were open the Germans surrendered easily.

After ten minutes, where he circles around the same half dozen pieces of information, Elizabeth gives up. 'Thank you for coming, Mr Shepherd. I appreciate it.'

He seems relieved. 'It was the least I could do.'

'The best of luck with your future.'

'Thank you. And with yours.'

Satisfied that he has done his duty, Samuel Shepherd returns his crumpled hat to his head, turns and walks down the path.

Her mother looks up from her knitting when Elizabeth comes into the lounge. She is making a winter jersey for Jack. 'Who were you talking to, Lizzy?'

'Someone who served with Jonathan overseas.'

'Any news?' asks her father anxiously.

'No. Nothing like that. He just wanted to pay his respects.'

'Thank God,' says her mother.

'Actually, I'd settle for any news, good or bad. I just need to know for sure.'

'Don't say that, Lizzy. No news is good news.'

Elizabeth suddenly feels overwhelmed. She wants to scream and rant. Instead, she goes outside, to the back of the house and stands in the middle of the lawn. There are no clouds and the stars are out, the moon a sliver low in the east. A hardy moth is slowly circling the outside light and she can just make out the yellow leaves of the bean plants withered against the fence.

Elizabeth tries to imagine Jonathan's face, not the frozen image from Jack's photographs but Jonathan as he was when she last saw him, when they said goodbye at the train station near the hospital and she held him warm and alive. She wants to be able to call up his smile, which always bloomed so suddenly. And the way that he cocked his head to one side when he was listening, or the habit he had of speaking out of the corner of his mouth.

Although she knows that Johnny did all these things she can no longer see them in her mind's eye. No matter how hard she tries or how long she stands behind her parents' house in the darkness, her husband's face stays just out of reach.

Elizabeth wipes the tears away. She waits a long time before she goes back inside. She does not want her parents to know that she has been crying.

forty-one

‘“Can I suggest that you start digging?” I think that was the last thing that the Tiger said to the Balloonist. Is that right?’ asks Elizabeth. It is the following evening.

Jack nods. He is still upset at the injustice of having been forced to walk down the road before dinner to apologise to Hugh Taylor.

‘What happens next?’

‘Well, this bit is quite sad. Are you sure that you want to hear it?’

‘Yes.’

Through the wall, Elizabeth hears her father cough loudly and at length and imagines that she can hear the coal dust rattling around in his lungs.

‘All right then, if you’re sure.’

The Balloonist quickly gathered up as many diamonds as he could. Wrapping them in a handkerchief, he shoved them into his bag.

'Will that be enough?' asked the Tiger.

'There's a king's ransom here,' said the man.

'What about a tiger's ransom?'

'Believe me, it's enough. Let's go.'

He followed the Tiger out of the mine. When they arrived back at the entrance, however, they found that the dark of the mine had leaked out into the world, which was to say that night had fallen.

'I won't be able to follow you in the dark,' said the man. 'We should camp here tonight.'

The Tiger sighed deeply. 'If you must.'

The man made a fire and the Tiger went off to hunt. When he returned he dropped the remains of what looked like a small deer onto the ground at the man's feet.

'Thank you,' said the man.

The Tiger did not reply but lay down well away from the fire and seemed to sleep. The man cooked the meat over the flames and, to his surprise, found that it was delicious.

At dawn he was woken by the Tiger standing over him. For a moment the sight of the great striped head so close to his face frightened him and the man's hand darted towards the jibjab thorn in his pocket. The Tiger gave a rumbling growl and the man froze.

'We will go now,' said the Tiger.

The jungle birds were singing the dawn chorus from the treetops so loudly that the noise was almost deafening as the Balloonist followed the Tiger back down the side of the mountain. They travelled as quickly as the man was able, which, as the Tiger pointed out several times, was not particularly fast. Even so, within a few hours they arrived at a wide brown river. There was a ramshackle jetty and a hut with mud walls. But they were too late.

'What do you mean, too late?' asks Jack, sitting up in bed. 'They can't be too late.'

Elizabeth shakes her head. 'But they were. The kidnappers were gone.'

'Gone?'

'Yes, and they had taken the Tiger's wife and cub with them.'

'Gone where?'

'You'll have to wait and see.'

With a sigh of frustration Jack lies back on his pillow and stares up expectantly at his mother.

The Tiger sniffed at the warm embers where someone had recently roasted a mudfish. He walked out onto the jetty and tasted the air with his thick pink tongue.

'My wife and cub were here only minutes ago. They have been taken downriver in a boat.' He growled sadly. 'They are gone forever.'

But the Balloonist had seen something that even the Tiger's keen eyes had not. A native canoe was half hidden among the bushes on the bank.

'We can follow them in this,' he said, dragging what was little more than a hollowed-out log into the shallow water. Lying in the bottom was a wide paddle.

The Tiger shook his head. 'Their boat is much larger and has an engine.'

'Then I will just have to paddle hard,' said the man.

The Tiger gave him a look that was as close to gratitude as tigers allow themselves.

If you have ever seen a fully grown male tiger trying to get from a rickety jetty into a narrow and precarious canoe without tipping it over, you will know exactly how awkward the next few minutes were. But eventually the Tiger was settled safely in the rear of the canoe and the man sat in front of him facing forward and began to paddle. It was fortunate that they were heading towards the sea because out near the middle of the river the current was strong.

The man paddled for many hours.

Sometimes he thought that he heard the chug of a boat's engine just around the next bend and he would dig the blade of his paddle deeper into the brown water and force his aching shoulders to pull harder. But when they came around the bend there was never anything to see except another stretch of river hemmed in between tree- and vine-covered banks.

That is how the chase went on all through that day until the sun sank in the west. Dragonflies began to skim low over the river and countless fish rose to feed on them, making a sound like raindrops on water and leaving ripples that spread out and touched and melted into each other.

'We must stop for the night,' said the man.

'Just a little longer,' said the Tiger.

'If it is too dark for us to carry on then it will also be too dark for them. They will not want to risk hitting a sandbank or a floating log. Trust me, they will stop.'

So that night the Tiger and the man camped on the river bank. The man made a fire and ate food from his bag. The Tiger went off to hunt and returned in the night with the fur around his jaws black and matted with blood.

At first light they set out again.

The man paddled all that morning, until the sun was directly above them and his shoulders ached and arm muscles burned. He was just about to tell the Tiger that he couldn't go on when the banks of the river widened and they came suddenly to the place where the river spilled out into the ocean, staining the indigo water the colour of milky coffee. The kidnappers' boat was already out to sea, less than half a mile ahead of them. Black smoke rose from its funnel. The man and the Tiger were close enough to see the kidnappers standing looking back. They could also see the two cages on the deck containing the Tiger's wife and his cub.

They both knew that they had failed. They could not hope to catch the kidnappers now, not in a canoe, in open water. It was impossible.

The man slowly paddled to the beach and they got out onto the white sand. The Tiger stood and stared at the boat as it headed towards the horizon, getting smaller and smaller. He let out a great roar of despair and rage.

Faintly in the distance he heard his wife roar back.

He roared again but there was no reply.

~

A good place for that instalment of *The Balloonist* to finish. As the old showbiz adage says, you should always leave an audience wanting more.

It is worth noting that bedtime stories have a way of creeping out from their allotted time. It is not unreasonable to think that Jack requested parts of the story during daylight hours and that, if it was convenient, Elizabeth obliged him.

Imagine, for example, a sunny Sunday. Elizabeth and her mother, along with Jack, have packed a simple picnic lunch, sandwiches and homemade biscuits, and caught the tram to the sandy beach on the east of Mansfield. It would have to be unusually warm for that time of year; perhaps the last good day before dreary winter settles in, the final chance they will have to go to the beach. Elizabeth's father has chosen to stay at home. Just lately his coughing has been worse, aggravated by the smoke billowing from chimneys all over the city. Now that the nights are cold every home in Mansfield has a fire burning in the grate. The air outside 22 Sydenham Street is visible in the evening, as bitter as corked wine on the tongue. Even in his retirement, the coal dust is still out to get him.

Even though the water is cold Jack has been playing in the

waves under his mother's watchful eye. When he is finally too tired and goose-bumped to carry on, he sits next to Elizabeth on the sand, lips blue. She drapes a towel around his thin shoulders. His grandmother has gone for a walk up towards the pier that points like a wooden finger towards the curved horizon.

'They can't just give up,' says Jack.

'Who?' asks Elizabeth, staring out to sea, although she knows very well.

'The Balloonist and the Tiger. You said that they've given up.'

She looks at him. 'Did I?'

'Yes.'

'What else could they do?' asks Elizabeth. 'It is impossible to catch a boat with an engine, not in that little canoe.'

'Then they need to find another boat!'

'It's a remote beach. There *was* no boat.'

'Then that's the end of the story. It's over,' says Jack. He kicks out with one bare foot, threatening to spray sand onto the remains of their lunch.

'Jack, don't do that.'

He stops kicking and they sit and stare at the foaming water and the driftwood and the seagulls.

'I suppose you're right,' says Elizabeth at last, 'the story is over. Unless . . .'

Jack turns his face towards her. 'Unless what?'

'They *could*, just maybe, meet someone who can help them.'

'Who?'

'You're right, there's probably no one.'

'Who? Tell me, please.'

'Listen and you'll find out.'

The Tiger's sensitive ears heard footsteps on the sand behind him. First the Tiger and then the Balloonist turned and saw a most unusual sight. Just a few paces away stood a young woman. Although it was not her true name, everyone called her the Moon Virgin. She was called that because the people of the village she was from were all born with coal-black hair and skin the colour of the darkest, brownest chestnuts. But when the Moon Virgin had come into the world, her skin and her hair and even her eyes were as pale as the face of the full moon.

As a child she had been tolerated by the villagers; however, when she had turned fifteen and had become a woman, the people became frightened by her. Some said that she must be a witch, and no man would marry her. After a flood and the death of one of the chief's wives from the bite of a black snake, the Moon Virgin was unfairly blamed. She had been banished from her village and now lived alone on the beach in a hut made of bleached driftwood and banana leaves.

The Moon Virgin spoke to the Tiger in his own language. 'Good afternoon to you, o Most Beautiful Emperor of the Green Shadows and Most Feared of All.' This of course is the proper way to address a fully grown male tiger. She bowed her head low.

The Tiger bowed his head, but ever so slightly. 'And to you, Female Ape with Very Little Hair.' That is the politest way that tigers have of referring to human animals. The less polite ways are very rude indeed.

The Balloonist did not understand what the Moon Virgin and the Tiger were saying to each other. To him it was just a series of soft growls and deep throaty grunts.

'Excuse me,' he said, 'but you don't happen to have a boat, do you?'

The Moon Virgin regarded the man with her pale eyes. 'Why do you need a boat?' She said this in English learned from a missionary's daughter.

The man quickly told her about the Tiger's wife and his cub and their mission to rescue them from the kidnappers. As he spoke the Moon Virgin looked towards the horizon where the boat was by now just a dark speck.

'If I help you, how do I know that you are wise enough to do the right thing?'

'What is the right thing?' asked the man.

'Exactly,' said the Moon Virgin. 'That is my point.' She thought for a moment. 'Listen and answer a question. Then we will see how wise you are.'

'All right,' said the man.

With the music of the waves playing beneath her words the Moon Virgin told the man a story.

'Once there were two men. They had been great friends as children but were now bitter enemies. Both had sworn to kill the other on sight. They agreed to meet on a certain day, on the east side of a bridge over a ravine near the town where they had been born, and fight until one of them was dead. One of the men travelled very far to get to the bridge. He had no horse, so he walked for many weeks. His path took him through a great desert with no roads, only baking rocks and shifting sand. There was no water in the desert except for the little he could carry. The sun threw its heat down on his head day after day without a cloud ever shading him, even for a moment. Three times he had to fight off bandits who would have stolen everything he had and then taken him in chains for a slave. One night, while sleeping in a shallow cave he was stung by a black scorpion and lay for a week full of fever and only a wish away from death. Finally, exhausted, hungry and weak, he arrived at the place where his enemy was waiting, ready to attack him on sight.'

The Moon Virgin looked at the Balloonist. 'Tell me, what is the first thing that you would make sure of?'

The man stared out over the ocean. At last he smiled

slightly. 'I would make sure which of the two men I was.'

The Moon Virgin also smiled, showing teeth even whiter than her skin. 'That is a good answer. I think you are perhaps wise enough to do the right thing. I will help you.'

'How?' asked the man.

She did not reply but walked down to the edge of the ocean and waded in so that the waves were caressing the tops of her pale legs. She began to sing. It was singing but not as we sing in church on Sunday. At times the notes rose so high that there were parts of the song that the Balloonist could not hear (although the Tiger could). There were other parts where her voice seemed to dip as deep as the ocean itself.

'What is she doing?' whispered the man.

'I do not know,' the Tiger responded, 'but it is more than either of us so I suggest we do not interrupt her.'

The singing went on and on, until the black speck that was the boat disappeared over the bright curve of the horizon and even the dirty trail of smoke it left behind thinned and vanished. The Balloonist hung his head and turned away.

'Wait,' said the Tiger. 'Look.'

Beyond the breakers the ocean was beginning to boil. A great shape rose, lifting higher and higher. Water cascaded down its sides as if a dark and dripping island were being thrust out of the ocean.

The word big *did not begin to describe what the Balloonist saw. Neither did* large *or even* huge. *The word* enormous *did not come near to describing its size.* Colossal *comes slightly closer. Or perhaps* gigantic.

'Mum,' protests Jack, wriggling on the sand. His hair is dry by now and stiff with salt. 'Stop it. Just tell me what it was. Please.'

'All right, Impatient Boy,' says Elizabeth.

It took the man a moment to realise that what he was looking at was a whale. It was the largest type of whale — a blue whale. And this particular blue whale was the largest of its kind, perhaps even the largest whale that had ever lived. He was the king of all the whales.

The Balloonist and the Tiger stood open-mouthed on the beach, although the Tiger composed himself sooner than the man, and after that tried hard not to seem at all impressed by the Whale. A series of deep echoing calls floated up to them from the great creature.

'He says that he will allow us to ride on his back,' said the Moon Virgin, still standing in the white foam of the waves.

'Really?' said the Balloonist. 'That's very kind of him.'

'You said us,' said the Tiger. 'Are you coming?'

'You will need someone to translate.'

Again, the Tiger bowed his head to the Moon Virgin but more deeply than before. 'Thank you.'

'How are we to get up there?' asked the man.

'We must swim.'

And without hesitation she turned back to the ocean and, giving a short cry to the Whale, dived in and began swimming away from the beach, over and under the waves, nimble as a dolphin.

The Tiger followed. The man took the diamonds from his bag, stuffed them into his pocket next to the jibjab thorn and, leaving everything else on the sand, waded into the warm water.

The waves were bigger than they had looked from the beach. They jostled and shoved and poked salty fingers into his eyes. When at last the Balloonist managed to get out beyond the breakers, he looked around but could not see the Whale. It has changed its mind and swum away, he thought. He was having trouble staying afloat. This was not because he was a poor swimmer but because of the diamonds in his pockets. It is difficult to swim when *weighed down by rocks, regardless of how valuable they are. Common schist or greywacke will pull you down to your death as easily as rubies or diamonds.*

The man swallowed a gulp of seawater and then another and began to sink into the blue depths. Looking up through the clear water, he saw the Tiger swimming above him, the great paws stroking rhythmically.

It was then that he felt ground beneath his feet. Not as deep as I thought, but still deep enough to drown.

But miraculously the ground was moving, rising beneath him, lifting him through the water and then, into the air. He took a deep gasping breath and looked down. It was not coral or sand he had felt beneath his feet but the great black back — as big as a football field — of the Whale.

With the Tiger, the Moon Virgin and the Balloonist safely on his back, the Whale turned his great body west and set off in pursuit of the kidnappers' boat.

forty-two

What type of story is this?

At the very beginning I cast around for words strong enough to carry the burden of everything that would follow. If the opening salvo had been 'Once upon a time', from which all else would have flowed true to form, then perhaps around this point in our story Lucky would have undergone a miraculous transformation. The stories that Elizabeth fed to him like spoonfuls of malt in the weeks leading up to his birthday would have nourished him in body, mind and spirit.

Imagine the scene. The day of his birthday would make an excellent occasion for him to show his wife just how much he had improved. Mrs Blackwell has organised a party to mark the occasion and the ballroom at Woodbridge is decorated with lights and streamers; a string quartet claims one corner. Everyone is present:

the host and hostess, assorted relatives and family friends, members of Mansfield's high society. Of course Elizabeth is there. Perhaps Elizabeth's parents and Jack have also been invited. Even Booker the Cooker and little Merry are present, although they are flat out seeing to the needs of the guests.

At some time during the evening, Lucky taps a fork against the rim of a glass and makes a speech. Everyone is moved by his eloquence and sincerity. It would be obvious to them all that even if his memory has not returned, he has acquired a level of wisdom and tolerance that he had previously not possessed. Above all, it is obvious that Sunnyside is not the place for him.

Only Dr Parkinson remains unconvinced. He has arrived late and has brought with him two large male orderlies who stand ready to bundle Lucky away if he offers any resistance. Elizabeth accuses the doctor of not having Lucky's best interests at heart. In a firm, clear voice she informs the entire gathering that Dr Parkinson is interested in Lucky only because of the large bequest he believes the Blackwell estate is sure to give to the hospital if he treats the heir to the family fortune.

Lucky becomes angry and threatens Dr Parkinson with bodily harm. Who can blame him? Such relentless persecution would test the patience of a saint.

'Proof!' cries the doctor. 'He is a danger to himself and others. Seize him.'

The two orderlies rush forward and, grabbing Lucky, they begin to drag him out the door towards the van with the barred back window that is waiting in the driveway.

Surprisingly, it is Martin Templeton who reacts first. He has become aware that a great injustice is about to be done. Shaping his remaining finger and thumb into the approximation of a fist, he punches the largest of the orderlies squarely on the jaw. A fierce fist fight ensues between Martin, Lucky and the two orderlies.

In the chaos Lucky stumbles against a shelf. A fossilised trilobite teeters and then falls. Mrs Blackwell screams. Elizabeth springs forward but she is too late. Lucky is struck on the head, a heavy blow that leaves him bloody and unconscious.

For a moment all is still. Lucky lies splayed on the floor of the ballroom, the guests gathered around in a shocked circle. They believe that he has been killed.

'No, look, he's breathing,' says Mrs Blackwell, kneeling beside him.

When Paul opens his eyes he sees his wife looking down at him anxiously. Everything comes flooding back — a lifetime of memories, first in a trickle, then in a tsunami.

'Darling,' he says, 'where am I? What happened?'

Just how much tolerance do you have for improbable occurrences if they bring about a satisfying resolution? Perhaps I am pushing matters too for if a telegram arrives a short time later — that very evening — with the news that Captain Jonathan Whitman has finally been found. It turns out he *was* badly wounded, languishing in a prisoner-of-war camp high in the Swiss mountains, in an area that has been cut off for several months by unseasonable snow. The telegram confirms that he is now safe and well and will be coming home to Elizabeth and Jack as soon as possible.

Would *that* story tick all the boxes for you?

forty-three

There are only four days left before Paul Blackwell's birthday. It is obvious to Elizabeth that Lucky has made no progress, certainly nothing that Mrs Blackwell is going to be satisfied with. He has remembered nothing that is going to earn him a reprieve from incarceration at Sunnyside.

Knowing this, Elizabeth has devised a plan. To say that she is proud of it would be untrue. In fact she is torn between her loyalty to her employer and her duty to her patient. She even doubts her own motivation. Is she really putting her patient first or have her own feelings towards Lucky clouded her view of what is right?

That morning she informs Lucky that they are going back to the museum. He does not object and Martin drives them into town and pulls the car up outside the building on Nelson Avenue. Elizabeth leans forward and gently touches the driver's shoulder.

'Why don't you stay here, in the car. We're only going to be inside the main hall.'

'Mrs Blackwell said that I should keep an eye on him.'

'There's not going to be any problem. He's been fine for weeks.'

It's true. Since the incident with the fish and the knife, Lucky has been nothing but compliant. Even so, Martin looks doubtful. 'Well, it'll be warmer in here with the engine running. That hall will be like ice on a day like this.'

The sunny days have been replaced by persistently low clouds and biting winds from the south and Elizabeth and Lucky are both wearing heavy coats. Lucky also has a scarf and gloves and has managed to scrape up from somewhere a black woollen hat, of the type favoured by working men like Elizabeth's father. Elizabeth has not asked him where he found it but she is grateful that Mrs Blackwell has not seen him in it.

'We'll be fine,' says Elizabeth.

Martin sniffs. 'Right then, but I'll be here if you need me.'

Elizabeth is already getting out of the car. 'I'm sure we won't. We'll be an hour.'

She leads Lucky into the museum. Martin was right, the main hall *is* extremely cold.

Elizabeth takes Lucky's gloved hand in hers. 'Come on, this way.'

He looks at her curiously. 'Where are we going?'

'There's something we have to do. Don't ask questions, please. Just follow me.'

She guides him through the cabinets and roped-off areas and then into another room set aside for items relating to Antarctic exploration. They pass a sled on iron runners; a preserved husky waiting patiently; an almost round egg in an Adelie penguin's nest of stones. Down a short corridor and out a door.

Lucky finds himself in the open air. He is standing in the part of the Botanic Gardens at the rear of the museum.

Elizabeth does not stop. 'This way.'

They must pass by the skeleton of the blue whale hanging from its chains beneath the tin roof. This is the first time that Lucky has seen it and he gazes at the bones like a child.

‘What is it?’

‘A whale.’

‘Is it real?’

‘Yes.’

‘It’s hard to believe that a creature so huge can really exist.’

‘Yes, remarkable.’ Elizabeth sounds impatient. She is in a hurry; they only have an hour.

But Lucky still hangs back. He runs a gloved hand along the curving jawbone. There is nothing to stop people from touching the skeleton: not a barricade, a rope or even a sign. It was not unknown for children to swing from the jaw, or actually to climb, balancing on the ribs in the cavity where the great heart used to beat.

Heart size: 9 feet.

Weight: 2000 pounds.

But on such a cold day there are no children. There is no one; the space where the heart once was is empty.

‘Come with me, please.’

‘I’m coming.’

They walk past barren flowerbeds until they come to the furthest gate from the museum. They leave the gardens out of sight of the car, not that Elizabeth believes Martin Templeton would notice them anyway. He is undoubtedly engrossed in his newspaper. But ‘better to be safe than sorry’, as her mother often says.

The legal firm of Burfoot, Clarke and Small is only a five-minute walk from the gardens. Elizabeth has selected them after a number of discreet enquiries. The firm occupies all three levels of Dalgety Chambers, a large brick building overlooking Victoria Park and a pleasant stretch of the Stratford River. They are met in the reception area by a middle-aged woman with a hawkish countenance who leads them down a panelled hallway to a lift. She silently accompanies them inside and pulls back the heavy metal grille. The cage rattles and judders up to the third floor.

Mr Burfoot squats behind an enormous desk, his tailored belly jammed against the wood. As they enter the office he places two hands on the rosewood desktop and with a deep grunt thrusts himself laboriously to his feet. The room reeks of cigar smoke and human flatulence and Elizabeth finds it difficult to decide which odour is the more offensive.

'Come in, come in,' he rumbles. His voice is so deep that each word seems to echo within the cavity of his wide and fleshy mouth. Emerging from behind the desk, the lawyer offers Lucky his hand. 'Ah yes, Mr Blackwell, welcome. It is good to see you again. It has been several years since we last met, before the war, I believe. A dinner party at the McKellar-Smiths' home.'

'I don't remember you at all,' says Lucky.

Mr Burfoot blinks his small pale eyes. 'Quite right. It's refreshingly honest of you to say so. I myself don't remember half the people I've met.'

Elizabeth's hand disappears completely inside the lawyer's grasp. His skin is dry and soft. 'I am Mrs Elizabeth Whitman, Mr Blackwell's private nurse.'

'I see. It is nice to meet you, Mrs Whitman. Please, won't you both take a seat.'

Mr Burfoot retreats back behind his desk. He sinks with a sigh into his leather chair, which gives a surprised squeak.

'Now, what can I do for you both?'

Elizabeth tells a version of Lucky's story.

Mr Burfoot is a good listener. Only occasionally does he speak, and even then he simply repeats one word: 'truly?' It is clear, however, from the growing emphasis that he puts on this single word, combined with the way in which he leans forward as the story unfolds, pressing his girth towards Elizabeth as much as the meeting of the desk and his belly will allow, that his interest is piqued.

When Elizabeth can think of nothing further to add she sits back in her chair.

'Truly?'

Mr Burfoot's final utterance is a loud full stop to her tale and for a moment there is silence in the office. A tram can be heard rattling along the street below. The lawyer's head turns slowly on his shoulders (seemingly without the aid of anything resembling a neck) so that he is now staring at Lucky.

'Let me be quite clear about this. You say that you have absolutely no memory of your former life? None whatsoever? You don't remember your childhood, your parents, your home or even your own wife?'

Lucky nods solemnly. 'That's right. I remember none of those things.'

'At all?'

'Nothing.'

Mr Burfoot emits a loud grunt of astonishment. 'How extraordinary. May I inspect your wound?'

Without waiting for an answer, the lawyer once more comes out from behind his desk and with surprisingly deft fingers parts Lucky's hair. Leaning in, he peers at the scar. The white latticework left by the stiches is plain to see, and a lump the size of a shilling where the bone has been replaced by steel.

'May I touch it?'

'All right.'

Lucky feels the light caress of the man's corpulent finger.

'Extraordinary.' Mr Burfoot steps back and Lucky unconsciously rearranges his hair. 'And just to clarify, it is solely because you have no memory that your wife intends to have you institutionalised?'

Elizabeth interrupts. 'His behaviour *was* quite erratic when he first came home but he was confused and anxious.'

'As you would be if you didn't remember a thing and people kept on insisting that you must remember,' says Mr Burfoot.

'Exactly.' Elizabeth smiles gratefully.

'Yes, yes, yes. Well, it is undeniably a fascinating case. In fact, it is undoubtedly unique. One minute, please.'

Now that Mr Burfoot's interest is aroused the lawyer's whole demeanour has changed. He moves almost swiftly across the room and throws open the door. His secretary, sitting at her desk in the outer office, looks up in surprise.

'Miss Sellers, I want you to go to the first-floor library. I need all the case notes relating to grounds for involuntary committal to a mental institution.'

'A mental institution?' she repeats.

'That's right, everything you can find from here and the United

Kingdom. I will also require the relevant statutes. Well, don't just sit there with your mouth open, I need them immediately.'

When the woman does not leap to her feet, Mr Burfoot grunts. 'I'll come and help you find them myself.' He turns back to Lucky and Elizabeth. 'Make yourselves at home. Someone will bring you a cup of tea if you ask.'

And then he is gone, huffing down the corridor like a steam train in a tunnel, Miss Sellers trailing behind him.

Elizabeth closes the door. 'I like him.'

'How long will this take?'

'I don't know. We'll just have to wait. Not long, I hope.'

There is a grandfather clock in the office that loudly ticks away the minutes. Elizabeth opens a window to expel some of the fug from the room, then sits down again. She fiddles anxiously with the edge of the chair. It has been forty minutes since they left the museum. Martin Templeton will probably check on them when their allotted hour expires. She will have to think up a plausible lie as to why they have left the museum.

It is another twenty minutes before Mr Burfoot returns, balancing a stack of half a dozen leather-bound books, which he awkwardly deposits on his desk.

'I've got Miss Sellers and two of the juniors looking for other cases that might be relevant, but here are a few things to be going on with. I doubt we'll ever find a case that's exactly the same, but there are bound to be some broadly similar precedents in case law.'

'Are there many families who try to have someone committed?' asks Elizabeth.

'Oh yes. It is remarkable how many families are keen to institutionalise at least one of their members. I myself have an older sister who would be a lot less bothersome if she were in a lunatic asylum.' He opens the largest of the books and turns to a page marked with a strip of paper. 'Here is the relevant act: the Mental Deficiency Act of 1913. As it stands, the law is quite simple. Your wife can certainly have you institutionalised on grounds of diminished mental responsibility as long' — and at this point he reads from the book — 'as three suitably qualified and independent medical professionals of good character unanimously agree on a diagnosis of significantly diminished responsibility attributable to a recognised mental illness.' He replaces the book on the desk. 'The signature of a justice of the peace is also required, however I imagine that is merely a formality in a case like this. So there you have it.'

'How do they define mental illness?' asks Elizabeth.

'An excellent question, Mrs Whitman. We will make a lawyer of you yet. The answer is that the lawmakers have not defined it, not in any detail. They have left that for the judiciary to decide, in the context of specific cases. Although the Act does mention in a later paragraph that being a threat to other people's or your own safety is of particular interest.'

Elizabeth frowns. 'As I said, Lucky did stab someone.'

'That is undoubtedly a point against him.'

'Mrs Blackwell has consulted with only *one* professional that I'm aware of. That was Dr Parkinson.'

'The director of Sunnyside?'

'Yes. Do you know him?'

'Only by reputation. I don't imagine that the good doctor will have any trouble producing a further two signatures on his paperwork seeking Mr Blackwell's committal. He may already have them.'

'But no one else has actually assessed Lucky.'

'I doubt they will bother. I'm sure that two of Dr Parkinson's colleagues at Sunnyside will be more than happy to sign the forms with virtually no questions asked.'

'But that doesn't seem fair.'

'They will perhaps glance over Dr Parkinson's notes before signing.'

'Can't we do anything?'

Mr Burfoot scratches one of his chins. 'I think we can. Off the top of my head, there are at least two legal arguments I believe we could make. However, first things first. If Lucky is sent to Sunnyside, and from what you say that is in all likelihood going to happen, then I will immediately petition the Magistrate's Court for a writ of habeas corpus.'

'Which is what exactly?' asks Elizabeth.

'In short, the law states that no one can be held against their will without being brought before a judge. It is a basic tenet of English law dating back to the Magna Carta. Normally it is used by people who are in prison but I have found several instances where those who have been institutionalised have sought such a writ. I believe it will serve us very well.'

They talk for another fifteen minutes. When Elizabeth says that they really must go Mr Burfoot escorts them to the lift, still animatedly talking. He shakes both their hands again and promises to be in touch shortly.

It is not surprising that when Elizabeth and Lucky emerge into the street some eighty minutes after they entered the building they are feeling optimistic. Perhaps their mood would be less jovial if they had chanced to notice Martin Templeton standing in a doorway on the other side of the street, watching them. When Elizabeth and Lucky hurry back toward the museum, the Blackwells' driver crosses to Dalgety Chambers. He takes careful note of the bronze plaque on the side of the building bearing the name of the law firm, even going so far as to scribble down the details on a piece of paper that he pulls from his coat pocket. When he is finished he all but runs back to the car. People he passes turn and look after him strangely.

Five minutes later Lucky and Elizabeth find the driver sitting behind the wheel, perusing the racing section of the newspaper.

'You were gone a while,' he says, folding the paper. 'I was just about to come and see how you were getting on. Must have been some interesting stuff in there.'

Elizabeth struggles to control her breathing. 'Yes, we learned a lot. I hope you weren't too bored.'

'No, I was fine. Actually, I learned quite a lot myself — in the paper, I mean.'

~

Later that same day, Martin finds Mrs Blackwell in the glasshouse, watering the orchids.

'Are you sure?' she asks, when he has finished. She carefully puts down the watering can.

'I'm sure, all right. She took him to a lawyer. Here.' He hands her his scrap of paper.

'Thank you, Martin. That will be all. You've done the right thing.'

forty-four

It is just after ten o'clock that evening when Elizabeth's mother hears the letterbox rattle. She pulls back the curtain above the kitchen sink and is just in time to see a tall man wearing some type of uniform walking briskly off down the street.

The letter is addressed to Mrs E. Whitman. Elizabeth immediately recognises the heavy paper and the firm rounded handwriting.

> **It has been brought to my attention that you have broken trust with me in the most grievous and calculated manner possible. By seeking legal advice regarding my husband's situation, you have not only gone behind my back but challenged the agreement**

> that I have entered into in all good faith with Dr Parkinson.
>
> I can only assume that you believe you have my husband's best interests at heart. However, it is inconceivable to me how you can possibly imagine that it is in any way your place to not only go against the wishes of his family, but also against the best advice of the medical establishment.
>
> You have acted far outside your role as my employee and as a nurse. I have no alternative but to terminate your employment immediately. I trust that you have the good sense to end further contact with any member of the Blackwell family.

The letter is signed Mrs Paul Blackwell. Within the envelope is a £10 note and six shillings — the exact wages owed to her.

'What is it, Lizzy?' asks her mother. 'You've gone pale. What's the matter?'

Elizabeth is sitting at the kitchen table. 'The Blackwells have let me go.'

'Whatever for?'

'I think I made a mistake.'

'You'll be able to get your old job back at the hospital, won't you?'

'I think so.'

Her mother looks relieved. 'Well then, no real harm done. You said at the start you'd just see how things went with that lot. People with money aren't like the rest of us. You're best off out of it.'

Her mother has more to say on the subject but Elizabeth isn't listening. She is thinking about Lucky and wondering what will happen to him now.

forty-five

The next day, without any fuss, the man they call Paul Blackwell is driven to Sunnyside Mental Hospital where he is committed under the Mental Deficiency Act on the grounds of reduced mental capacity.

forty-six

The Whale swam through the warm blue ocean. High on its back stood the Tiger, peering anxiously ahead, his eyes narrowed against the glare of the sunlight off the water. They had been travelling for over an hour, the great tail fanning the ocean behind them, a bow wave surging in front of the Whale's mountainous head. About a mile in front of them lay the kidnappers' boat and the Tiger could make out the two cages on the deck. He could also see that several of the kidnappers were standing in the stern staring back at the Whale. Every one of them was holding a rifle.

The Balloonist came to stand by the Tiger's side. His

clothes had dried quickly in the sun and his pockets still bulged with diamonds.

'I'm worried that if we get too close they will start shooting.'

'My thought exactly,' said the Tiger. 'They would have to be very poor shots indeed to miss our fishy friend.'

'Actually Balaenoptera musculus *is a type of mammal.'*

The Tiger growled deeply and the man stopped talking.

At that moment, the engine noise from the kidnappers' boat faded to a low rumble and then died. The boat bobbed ahead of them. At a word from the Moon Virgin, the Whale also came to a halt, just out of range of the rifles.

'I need to talk to them face to face,' said the man. 'I'll swim the rest of the way.'

'Are you sure you can swim that far?' said the Tiger.

The man was already taking off his shoes. 'I was swimming champion at my grammar school three years in a row.'

'I'm assuming that you did not race with your pockets full of stones.'

'A good point,' said the man, remembering how he had almost drowned earlier. 'A few of the larger ones should be all I need.'

He emptied his pockets of all but the three biggest diamonds. The rest he handed to the Moon Virgin for safekeeping.

'Good luck,' she said in her sing-song voice.

'Thank you.'

It was too high to safely dive from the Whale's back so the man slid down the curving flank, tall as a cliff, until he hit the water with a large splash. When his head reappeared he set off towards the boat, using a strong crawl.

'Watch out for sharks,' called the Tiger mischievously, but the man's ears were full of water and he did not hear.

The kidnappers were waiting for him when he reached the boat. Two of them hauled him roughly out of the water and dropped him like a large fish onto the deck. They all stood over him with the muzzles of their rifles pointed at his chest. The Balloonist stood slowly.

The leader of the kidnappers was a burly German with a shaved head and a scar that writhed across one cheek. His name was Karl Kruger and he was famous across three continents both for his cruelty and his overwhelming love of money. In his hand he held a pearl-handled revolver. Kruger had murdered a quite famous cowboy in order to steal that gun. Now he pointed it at the Balloonist.

'What brings you to my boat?' he asked in his thick German accent.

'I think that we can do business,' said the man. 'It will be to both our advantages.'

'What type of business could I do with a dripping rat pulled from the ocean?' A nasty smile made Kruger's scar twitch like a tortured snake.

'I represent a mutual acquaintance, the Tiger who you may already have observed.' He gestured towards the Whale. The Tiger could clearly be seen standing at the front of the beast's great head. 'He would like the safe return of his wife and cub.'

'He can't have them,' snarled Kruger.

'He is willing to pay.'

Kruger gave a mocking laugh and was joined by several of his men. 'What could a mangy house cat like that possibly have of any value?'

The man reached into his pocket. Every rifle that was pointed at him was raised a little higher and fingers twitched on hair triggers.

The Balloonist froze. 'If I may?'

Kruger nodded. 'Slowly.'

Carefully the man removed the three precious stones

from his pocket and held them out on his palm. Several of the kidnappers gasped. 'Diamonds!'

Kruger snatched the diamonds from the man's hand and inspected them closely.

'Would you look at that,' muttered one of the crew, an African with a gold earring in each ear. 'They're as big as hen's eggs.'

'I think those should more than match what any zoo would give you for the female and the cub,' said the Balloonist.

Kruger raised his eyes from the diamonds. 'The price is ten diamonds.'

The man frowned. 'That's too many.'

'I see you're not denying that you've got more.'

The man knew that Kruger had him at a disadvantage. 'We will give you five.'

Karl Kruger raised his revolver and shot three times. The first bullet splintered the deck between the Balloonist's bare feet. The other two droned past his head like angry flies.

'Ten diamonds,' repeated Kruger.

'Agreed,' said the man.

Kruger laughed. 'Actually, I've changed my mind. I've a better idea.' He turned and yelled up at the wheelhouse. 'You up there, start the engine. Turn this floating bucket of rust around.'

'What are you doing?' said the man. 'We had a deal, ten diamonds.'

'The deal's off.' Kruger gestured and two of his men grabbed the Balloonist. 'Throw him in the cage with the cub!' said Kruger.

The Balloonist struggled but the kidnappers were too strong. 'The diamonds would've made you rich,' he shouted, as he was dragged away.

'I know what will make me richer. First we kill the male tiger. Second we convince you and your pale female

friend back there to tell us where these came from. Then we'll have all the diamonds we want.'

The engines spluttered into life and the boat swung slowly around to face the Whale.

'Full steam ahead!' yelled Kruger. 'All guns to the bow!' His revolver flashed in the sun as he raised it and let off another shot. His men raced to get into position.

As the boat picked up speed, the Balloonist was thrown into the cage with the young tiger. The padlock snapped shut as the cub whimpered and backed away from him into the corner.

'It's all right,' said the man. 'I'm a friend of your father. Everything is going to be fine.'

But the Balloonist didn't believe his own words. Even as he spoke, he could feel the boat gathering speed, the deck vibrating beneath his feet. The engines roared, black smoke billowed into the sky. Through the thick bars of the cage he could see the kidnappers lining up along the bow, their rifles loaded and at the ready.

forty-seven

For several days after she is dismissed from the Blackwells' service, Elizabeth does little except haunt her parents' house. She makes no effort to contact the hospital about returning to her work on the wards. It is possible that she now believes she did the wrong thing in championing Lucky's cause. Perhaps she slips into a brief depression, overwhelmed by her circumstances and the seeming hopelessness of her situation. Or maybe she just needs time and space to think.

Jack is delighted that his mother is available to take him to the park and read books but even he is aware that she is strangely distant; sometimes it is as though she were speaking to him through glass. When Elizabeth's mother begins to grumble and snap, Elizabeth takes to going for rambling walks through the city. She does not choose her path in advance, but turns left or right or moves straight ahead as the mood takes her. After almost a week of such random perambulation, she finds herself standing in the foyer of Dalgety Chambers.

She is informed by the woman at the front desk that Mr Burfoot is out of the office on business.

'When is he expected back?'

'Not until tomorrow morning. Do you wish to make an appointment?'

'Perhaps. Actually, I'm not sure. Thank you anyway.'

Back on the steps of the building she is at a loss about where to go next. She stands in the sunshine, turning her head slowly this way and that as though searching for inspiration.

'Mrs Whitman?'

She recognises Mr Burfoot's secretary and recalls that the young woman's name is Miss Sellers.

'Oh, hello.'

'Are you coming to see Mr Burfoot? I'm sorry but he's out today.'

'I know. The woman in the foyer just told me.'

'Are you all right? You look a bit lost.'

'Do I? I suppose I am. I was really hoping to see Mr Burfoot. It took quite a bit of courage to come here and I'm not sure I can muster it again tomorrow.'

'Is it very urgent?'

'Yes, I think it is.'

Miss Sellers takes Elizabeth by the arm and leads her down the steps. 'Look, I really shouldn't say anything but I know that Mr Burfoot's quite excited about your case. He's been talking about it a lot with the other partners ever since you first saw him. Today's his day for having lunch at the Mansfield Club. He'll be there all afternoon. But they won't let you in. It's for men only.'

'I can try. Thank you, Miss Sellers.'

'Just please don't say that I told you where to find him.'

'My lips are sealed.'

The Mansfield Club is a large brick building located down a quiet street adjoining Latimer Square. The club is frequented by wealthy farmers in town for a few days, and also by urban professionals seeking an oasis from both work and domestic obligations. At the door Elizabeth stretches the truth by telling the doorman that there is an emergency. He disappears inside and returns a few minutes later with Mr Burfoot in tow. He shows no surprise at her unexpected appearance.

'Mrs Whitman, welcome. It is good to see you again.'

'It is terribly impolite of me to interrupt you like this.'

'Actually, I was just ruminating on your Mr Blackwell's case. Shall we walk?'

'Certainly.'

They cross the road and sit on a bench in the park. Mr Burfoot listens to the latest instalment of Lucky's story, leaning forward with his elbows on his knees, his fingers forming a plump steeple.

'I can't help thinking that I did the wrong thing by bringing Lucky to you,' concludes Elizabeth.

'So you think he belongs in Sunnyside?'

'No. But I am, after all, just his nurse. Mrs Blackwell was perfectly justified in dismissing me.'

'There are higher principles than obligation to an employer, Mrs Whitman. Do you wish to abandon the case? Is that what you have come here to tell me?'

'No. I have been doing a lot of thinking and I would like you to continue on Lucky's behalf.'

'I'm glad. It is unusual that someone outside the family should try to prevent a person being institutionalised, but I see no reason why we shouldn't proceed.'

'Thank you.'

'As it happens, I've taken the liberty of drawing up the petition to the court seeking a writ of habeas corpus. I'll have it sent this afternoon, if you are quite sure that you want to proceed?'

'I am.'

'Mrs Whitman, can I ask you if you've given any consideration to what will happen to Lucky if we succeed and he is *not* kept at Sunnyside? What then?'

Elizabeth frowns. 'I hadn't really thought that far ahead. I suppose that he will be free to do as he chooses.'

The lawyer emits a disapproving drone from deep in his throat, like a bagpipe as it inflates. 'Hmmmmm. I have been thinking about Lucky's plight quite a lot since our first meeting. It seems to me that making choices for your future is almost impossible if you have no past. Don't you agree?'

'I will have to give that some thought,' says Elizabeth.

They continue to talk for a few minutes and then she accompanies him back to the entrance to the club.

'One last thing. I hope you don't mind if I ask who will be paying for my services?'

'I will. I have some savings from my time overseas.' Elizabeth does not say that the legal fees will be coming from the money she has put aside to secure a down-payment on a home for herself and Jack — and Jonathan, of course. Neither does she explain that, in all likelihood, if the case drags on her money will barely be adequate.

'Good day to you, Mrs Whitman.'

'And to you, Mr Burfoot.'

As she rides the shaky tram back through the city, Elizabeth ponders the lawyer's words about past and future. She had been telling the truth when she said that she hadn't considered what would happen to Lucky if the legal challenge were successful, but now that the matter has been raised it is all she can think about. Somehow she had imagined that Lucky would simply stay in his room at Woodbridge, having daily baths and eating the meals that Mrs Booker prepared for him. The thought had been in the back of her mind that he would eventually develop interests, cultivate friendships, perhaps even find some type of employment. But as the tram rattles and bumps, stopping and starting with unpredictable shudders, she now realises that this is all a fairytale; one of those stories we tell ourselves about the future to act as both compass and map through uncharted waters.

It is only five days later that Elizabeth receives a hand-delivered letter informing her that Mr Burfoot's petition to the Magistrate's Court has been accepted. A writ of habeas corpus has been issued to Sunnyside, and Lucky has been called to appear before a judge in two days' time.

forty-eight

Lucky is brought before the Mansfield Magistrate's Court at 11 a.m. on Friday the 8th of August 1919. Elizabeth is not permitted to be present, as the session is not open to the general public. Although Lucky has been at Sunnyside for only thirteen days, he appears to have lost weight. He sways slightly as he is led into the courtroom, which is unsurprising as the doctors have been giving him lithium almost since the moment he passed through the doors of the institution.

The magistrate is, appropriately, named Laws. He slowly enters the court from a door behind the bench. Magistrate Laws appears much older than his sixty-two years. As he sits down his bones click and pop loudly enough to be heard by everyone in the room. Laws peers over the top of his spectacles at Lucky before looking down at his notes and the small group waits patiently while he shuffles through the paperwork. Eventually he looks up.

'So, Mr Burfoot, I take it that you are to represent Mr Blackwell?'

'Yes, Your Worship. We believe that he has been incarcerated illegally.'

'Clearly. That after all is why we are here.' Magistrate Laws swings his head around to the other lawyer in the room. 'And you, Mr Fisk, you are here on behalf of Mr Blackwell's wife, who I understand is the signatory to his committal paper and his undisputed closest living relative.'

'Yes, Your Worship. I am also authorised to discuss with you the details of the reports on Mr Blackwell's mental state written by Drs Parkinson, Buck and Judkins.'

'Whose signatures I also see on the committal papers I have in front of me.'

'That is correct, Your Worship.'

'Well then, let us begin with you, Mr Burfoot.'

Legal arguments are fired around the court room like artillery shells. Mr Burfoot argues that three doctors from the same institution, two of whom he has ascertained are reliant for their employment on the one whose assessment they are supporting, cannot be said to be 'independent' in the sense that the Act intends. His argument also has a second front, that memory loss is not a recognised mental illness. It is, however, a harder case to make. After ten minutes of his deep voice echoing around the court, Mr Burfoot concludes his arguments.

Mr Robert Fisk of Mitcham and Fisk is everything that Mr Burfoot is not: young, slim, handsome. He smiles charmingly as he addresses Magistrate Laws. Mr Fisk can see no legal reason whatsoever why the two highly qualified and thoroughly professional experts nominated by Dr Parkinson should not have been used to assess Mr Blackwell's mental health. The fact that the two men work alongside Dr Parkinson at Sunnyside is irrelevant. Their professional standards and personal ethics, which are above reproach, ensure that the good doctors are entirely independent in the sense that the lawmakers obviously intended. To suggest otherwise is an attack of the gravest kind upon both doctors' professional integrity and their reputations. It is insinuated that separate legal proceedings on behalf of the good doctors may be forthcoming.

Magistrate Laws eventually interrupts. 'Thank you, Mr Fisk. I think I have the gist of your argument. How do you respond to Mr Burfoot's claim that memory loss is not a mental illness?'

'Quite simply, Your Worship. As the assessment from Dr Parkinson, which you have in front of you, shows, it is a fallacy that Mr Blackwell has had any true memory loss at all. Regrettably he is suffering from the easily identified illness of schizophrenia and as a result is delusional. As are many patients already receiving excellent treatment at Sunnyside.'

'I see. Thank you, Mr Fisk. You may sit down. Mr Blackwell, I should like to ask you a few questions.'

Lucky stands. He appears to be exhausted, his arms hanging by his sides. 'Yes, sir.'

'Your Worship, please. You're not in the army now.'

'Your Worship.'

'Mr Burfoot has stated that as a result of a head wound received in France you cannot remember anything of your past. Is that true?'

'I believe so, yes.'

'You don't sound very sure.'

'It's impossible to know exactly what you don't know.'

The magistrate nods his head. 'Yes, I suppose it would be. Tell me about your first memory.'

We have covered this ground before. Lucky tells the man as much as he can, although the questions are a lot more incisive and probing than those Elizabeth asked. After almost half an hour the magistrate concludes the session by thanking everyone present. He promises to deliver his decision within forty-eight hours.

~

Three days later Elizabeth telephones Mr Burfoot at his office, as they had arranged. The lawyer's voice booms down the line, forcing her to hold the receiver at a safer distance from her ear.

'Good news, Mrs Whitman. The magistrate has ordered that Lucky be reassessed.'

'But not released?'

'No, but this is a very positive step. His Worship concluded that the three doctors *were* independent in a legal sense, but he also felt there was enough doubt as to the diagnosis of schizophrenia that Lucky should face a panel which will make the final decision about his mental health.'

'Who will sit on this panel?'

'Parkinson, unfortunately, and two others, but not doctors this time, and they are to be of the magistrate's own choosing. He specifically states in his decision that neither will be connected to Sunnyside, nor are to be in any way beholden to the others.' He chuckles. 'That will be a bit of a slap in the face for young Mr Fisk. The new panel will convene in a month, on the 8th of September. It's a Monday.'

'So long? Will Lucky have to remain at Sunnyside?'

'Unfortunately yes, in the meantime.'

'We won then.' She sounds uncertain.

'The first round. You don't sound very pleased.'

'I suppose I am. It seems a lot of time and effort, and nothing's really been achieved. They still might decide that Lucky should stay at Sunnyside.'

'At least now he'll get a fair hearing.'

When Elizabeth hangs up, she looks blankly at the wall of the train station where she has come to use the public telephone. People move past her, their footsteps loud on the tiled floor. Even if these two new men do listen to Lucky with open minds it is hard for Elizabeth to see how he is going to avoid spending a long time locked up. After all, he is undeniably a man who has lost, if not all, then at least a significant part of his mind.

forty-nine

And what becomes of Lucky in the month while he waits for his future to be decided?

He sits in his locked room at Sunnyside. It is a good room, as far as rooms in mental institutions go, on the north side of the main building with a view of the grounds. He wishes that he had an open fire but there is a large radiator mounted on the wall that runs all day and night. Lucky lies on his bed listening to the sounds it makes, clicks and creaks and deep metallic groans.

He swallows the pills that the nurses give him every evening and again in the morning. They are white and red, two of each. They make his thoughts distant and as hard to catch as clouds.

The only time he protests is when they try to shave his face.

'Now, now, what's all this fuss?' asks Dr Parkinson, arriving slightly out of breath in Lucky's room. He gestures to the two straining orderlies and they step away. Lucky is not even sure why he does not want them to shave him. He just knows that somehow it will diminish him.

In the end, the doctor decides that it is not worth the fuss and allows Lucky to keep his beard. As the days pass it once again grows thick, eventually filling the gap between chin and throat. His hair reaches for his shoulders.

He meets with Dr Parkinson every second day. These sessions follow a predictable pattern. The doctor asks him many seemingly different questions but the aim of each is the same: to persuade Lucky that he is someone he is not.

As the days drag on, Lucky answers less and less often. He can see no point. Eventually he does nothing at these meetings except sit still, staring blankly at the floor. To anyone seeing him for the first time he might look like a ragged mystic searching for meaning in the patterns on the rug. Or a crazy man.

The woman who calls herself his wife visits on several occasions. Lucky does not explode into shouts and curses in the way that he did at woodbridge. He cannot, however, see any point in her small talk. In the face of his lengthening silences, Mrs Blackwell inevitably stumbles and leans on the past for support. She cannot help herself.

'Do you remember the time,' she begins. Or, during another visit, reaching into her handbag, 'I just happened to find this photograph in the library. Look, it's of the day when you and I drove to the mountains to go ice skating.'

The woman talks and talks, but it becomes clear, even to her, that Lucky is not listening. She perseveres but after a week her visits dwindle and eventually she ceases to visit him altogether. By then Lucky hardly notices.

The hospital has a policy of allowing only immediate family to visit the patients. Elizabeth would not have been allowed to see Lucky even if Mrs Blackwell had not issued written instructions explicitly excluding her.

One day — Lucky couldn't say whether it was a Monday or a Sunday or any day in between — he hears a scraping sound and sees an envelope slipping beneath the door of his room. It is a letter from Elizabeth.

We can only surmise, but it is likely that Elizabeth asked a favour of one of the nurses, perhaps someone she knew from another hospital. It is even possible that she bribed an orderly. Delivering a letter would involve only a small risk.

Lucky opens the envelope and smooths out the single sheet of paper. Elizabeth writes to say that a date has been set to reassess his committal. She hopes that when his case is reviewed he will be released.

Halfway down the page she begins a story:

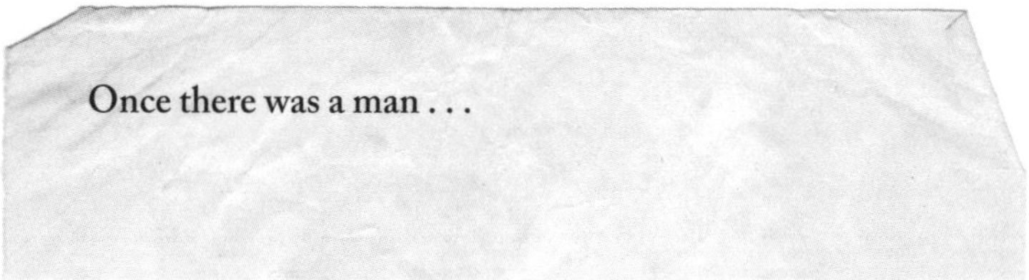
Once there was a man . . .

Lucky reads the story several times. As he reads he can hear Elizabeth's voice and see her face. For the first time in a long while there is something solid that his mind can latch onto.

For the rest of the month, every morning after the orderly inspects his mouth to make sure that Lucky has swallowed his pills and then left, Lucky fumbles under the mattress and retrieves the hidden letter from Elizabeth.

He reads the story again and again. It becomes his anchor.

fifty

Let's jump ahead to the day of Lucky's competency hearing. Do not imagine a crowded courtroom. Having ordered a new psychological assessment of Lucky and made the decision regarding the composition of the panel, the judiciary's involvement is almost at an end. The hearing is convened in a nondescript meeting room at the Mansfield Town Hall. Lucky and Mr Burfoot sit on one side of a wide table facing the three men who are to decide Lucky's future. An elderly female stenographer hunches at the end of the table focusing on the chattering keys of her machine.

Mrs Blackwell is the only observer. She sits in one of the dozen chairs arranged in two rows close to the door, wearing a hat and a heavy woollen coat, which she does not remove. A fox stole is draped around her neck.

Lucky stares across the table at the three men. On the face of it, they are a somewhat odd, even unpromising assortment. On the left is a layperson selected by the magistrate, a Professor Duvauchelle, a Frenchman who came to Mansfield four years earlier to escape the horrors of the war. Although only thirty-six, he is well known in the new field of art theory. Now he is lecturing at the Mansfield University. Monsieur Duvauchelle is, however, by this time regretting his decision to travel so far from the Old World. In fact, on the day of the hearing he is awaiting written word from several European universities to which he has applied for teaching positions. He will be profoundly relieved to return to a country where wine is not an exotic drink, horse racing is not considered high culture and vegetables are prepared in ways other than by boiling.

The man seated in the middle of the three is a lawyer, Mr Pottinger, who has come down specially from the capital by train. He is sixty-three, and completely bald. There is a patch of dried egg yolk on the collar of his jacket, acquired in the dining room of the boarding house where he is staying. Mr Pottinger is prone to motion sickness and the combination the previous day of the rocking of the carriage and the sight of the ocean slopping backwards and forwards outside the window as the train hugged the coast had been enough to make him sick to his stomach. Even after a night's sleep he is still feeling somewhat queasy. Occasionally he will grimace and pinch the bridge of his nose between finger and thumb and peer over the top of his spectacles at whoever is speaking, as though they had suddenly materialised in front of him in the most alarming and impolite way.

The third member of the panel is, of course, Dr Parkinson.

~

For obvious reasons, Elizabeth has stayed away from the hearing. Not the least of these is that Mrs Blackwell will be present. Elizabeth fears that there would be a scene if she were to appear.

She is not very far way, however. She has taken the day off work. (By this time Elizabeth has returned to the hospital, much to her mother's relief.) Mr Burfoot has told her where and when the hearing is to be held. She knows the route that someone leaving Sunnyside would most likely travel to get into the centre of the city. That is how she comes to be standing on the footpath on the corner of Lincoln and Queen streets as the black car carrying Lucky and Mrs Blackwell sweeps past.

Years later, in her letter to her son, Elizabeth will write that she had to guess which side of the intersection would give her the best chance of catching Lucky's eye. As the car approached she saw his face in profile and knew that she had guessed correctly.

She did not shout or wave but willed him to turn his head, to see her.

Perhaps it was that sense which tells us when we are being watched. Maybe Lucky was turning away from someone who was speaking to him from inside the car. Or was it the most unlikable of narrative devices, coincidence? The fact is that Lucky *did* turn his head towards her at that moment. He *did* see her.

Their eyes met and Elizabeth smiled.

And then the car moved on and they were once again parted.

'My mother fell deeply in love with a man who had no memory.'

If I must choose, than I will say that it was at *that* moment, when Lucky turned and looked at her, just for a few seconds, when their eyes met, that Elizabeth finally and irrevocably fell in love with him. It was then, despite everything, all the obstacles and doubts, that the cogs of her feelings clicked into place. The story of her life, the story she told to herself in her heart, changed forever as she stood on the footpath and watched the car disappear, Lucky's face still as clear in her mind as if he were in front of her.

During the hearing she waits on a park bench, in the weak sunshine of early spring, across the road from the town hall. Despite the complications her love will create, and her anxiety about the outcome of the hearing, despite a part of herself that is grieving for Jonathan and will always grieve as long as she is alive, Elizabeth is happy. No one said that love was easy. And if they did they were fools.

~

Inside the room where the hearing is being held, the three men take it in turns to ask Lucky questions.

'Do you deny that you are Paul Edward Blackwell?'

And 'Why is it that you call yourself by the name . . .' Mr Pottinger checks his notes, '*Lucky*?'

'What is your earliest memory?' The Frenchman.

'Isn't it true that you hear voices?' (That was Dr Parkinson. Lucky denies hearing anything beyond the usual babble.)

'Why did you viciously attack and stab a man?' (Parkinson again.)

From the sublime: 'How would you define love?'

To the ridiculous: 'Why do you wear a beard?' and 'How regular are your bowel movements?' Both of these come from the Frenchman, who considers himself a budding Freudian.

If the lethargy of the past month had remained, if Lucky had given monosyllabic answers or, worse, none at all, then his continuing incarceration would have been guaranteed. The only account of his responses comes second-hand through Elizabeth, who claimed in her letter to her son that Lucky knew what was at stake. She wrote that he rallied in an effort to save himself. The story that she had sent him in her smuggled letter may have provided inspiration; that was obviously its intention. Or maybe the sight of a smile glimpsed through a car window was enough. Sometimes small kindnesses can make all the difference. We will never know for certain.

When all the questions are exhausted, the lawyer with the egg-stained lapel asks if Lucky has anything he would like to say.

Lucky stands. 'Yes. I'd like to tell you a story.'

Apart from a few clarifications and interjections Mr Burfoot has been largely silent up until this point. Now he looks as though he has accidentally swallowed a spider. This is not what he and Lucky had talked about earlier. He clears his throat in warning, and then once again, but his client continues talking.

'Once there was a man who could not remember who he was. He really did want to remember. He tried very hard because he wanted more than anything else to know who he really was. But no matter how hard he tried, he just couldn't remember. It was simply impossible.

'People kept on telling the man who *they* thought he was. They told him that he had a name and a house and a wife. They told him how he should behave and what he should be like. All the time they pointed out things and places they believed he should be familiar with and showed him photographs of people that they said he should know. Eventually they became frustrated with him and began to insist that he remember. The man felt as though he were letting them down. He also became frustrated and angry. In the end he just wanted to be left alone.'

Lucky pauses. He looks the three men in the eye one at a time. Only Dr Parkinson cannot hold his gaze.

'Everybody wants me to return to being who I was. It is impossible. That person is as dead as if he had been killed in the war. The only hope that I have is if I am allowed to start again, to become somebody new. Thank you for listening to my story.'

fifty-one

In a story less faithful to the historical facts the members of the panel would have made an immediate decision. Perhaps they would have adjourned to another room close by. Imagine the palpable tension while everyone waited for the outcome.

But it can be a banal world, unsuited to gripping narration.

The three men shake hands outside the town hall and agree to have their written conclusions submitted within two weeks. The lawyer with the tempera lapel catches the evening train north. The French professor of art theory returns to his lodgings close to the university where the first thing he does is check with his landlady if any mail has arrived. Apart from a shrill telegram from his estranged mother, who lives in Biarritz with her third husband, there is nothing.

Among their many other professional and personal duties, both find the time to prepare written reports. These — and the report of Dr Parkinson — are duly typed up by secretaries beneath the official letterheads of their respective institutions and mailed to Magistrate Laws. He in turn forwards copies of the letters to Burfoot, Clarke and Small and to the Blackwell family solicitors.

It is not a unanimous decision. There is no prize for guessing that it is Dr Parkinson who continues to argue that Paul Blackwell is suffering from a severe form of mental illness brought about by his wartime experiences. The doctor repeats his earlier diagnosis of schizophrenia. At fifteen pages, his report is more than twice as long as the other two combined. Dr Parkinson concludes by stating that it is his professional opinion that Mr Blackwell would benefit greatly from the continuation of his treatment at Sunnyside, the positive therapeutic results of which are, according to the good doctor, already much in evidence.

Perhaps a factor in Lucky's favour was that both Mr Pottinger and Professor Duvauchelle had witnessed the results of war. The Frenchman had a brother who for six months in early 1915 had been a patient in a Paris hospital set aside entirely for the treatment of wounded soldiers. It had been that traumatic experience which had, in great part, led to his decision to emigrate to Mansfield.

In the days when he still had a head of dark curly hair, Mr Pottinger spent eighteen months as an army scout in South Africa during the Boer War.

They say that travel broadens the mind. Perhaps it is true that it also broadens the definition of mind.

The final score: two to one in Lucky's favour.

In his brief summary of the panel's decision, Magistrate Laws writes that he believes its members have come to the right decision. Lucky is to be released from Sunnyside that very day.

I quote from that summary:

> **Beyond his possibly irreversible loss of memory, a majority of the panel have concluded that they have neither seen nor heard any evidence Mr Blackwell,**

or 'Lucky' as he now prefers to be called, suffers from any known mental illness beyond the considerable emotional strain that a person finding himself in such an unprecedented situation could reasonably be expected to experience. As a returned serviceman and one who has been badly wounded in the course of his duty, we must acknowledge that we all owe him a collective debt of gratitude and wish him well for his future.

fifty-two

Let us select a day at random; say, for the sake of symmetry, one in the month of May. It is 1925, six years after our story began with Elizabeth walking to work.

Mid-afternoon, and a family of five stroll through the Botanic Gardens: a man, a woman and their three children.

Lucky walks slowly. He has been having a little trouble with his balance again. Sometimes he feels as if the ground were shifting beneath his feet, as though he were walking on an active fault line. His hair is still slightly longer than is fashionable but his beard is neatly trimmed. For the rest of his life Lucky will be slim but his face could no longer be described as gaunt. He has developed a keen interest in new styles of architecture and is attending lectures on the subject at the university. He is fascinated by the recent work of the Frenchman known as Le Corbusier. He reads widely: politics, economics, psychology, photography and modern art.

Elizabeth walks next to him. Watch as he makes a joke and she laughs.

Jack runs ahead. He is ten now, an active and inquisitive boy who enjoys science and loves watching the airplanes that occasionally fly over Mansfield going to and from the new aerodrome in the west of town.

'Come on, Mickey,' calls Jack good-naturedly as he starts to run towards the pond. 'First one to touch the water is the winner.'

Jack's half-brother Michael is only four. Of course, he worships every hair on Jack's head. The younger boy squeals and sets off in pursuit. It is uncertain whether his reaction is because of the excitement of the race itself or the injustice of his older brother's head start. Most likely it is a combination of both. 'Wait for me!' he yells.

Elizabeth is pushing a black perambulator in which sleeps her and Lucky's daughter. They have named her Katherine and she is eight months old; plump, as if butter fed.

If we cast our gaze wider than this small group, over the gardens, the winding rivers, the roofs and the spires, nothing major seems to have changed in Mansfield. But scratch below that surface and it is evident that the mortar that has held together the old order for so long has begun to crumble. They do say that it takes a great fire to forge metal into something new. It is the 1920s, the post-war years, the modern era. You can see signs of change everywhere if you look hard enough. It is there, in the unrestrained drape of the changing fashions, the women's short hairstyles. New businesses are springing up. New inventions. New social movements and endeavours. There has been a decisive change of government. Optimism hangs in the air, almost as tangible as the swing and jazz coming out of the wirelesses. The people of Mansfield have embraced fresh ways of thinking about themselves, their city and even their nation's place in this rearranged world.

The Blackwells' divorce was just another change among many. Even so, the dissolution of a marriage was still a novelty, especially among those families who were wealthy and well connected. There's no denying that for at least a time tongues wagged.

Although Lucky may consider himself a different person from Paul Blackwell, it is fortunate that the law does not; he is still heir to the Blackwell fortune. This is despite the fact that he has officially changed his name. He is now Lucky Newman. His little joke.

Mr and Mrs Newman do not live at Woodbridge. At the time of the divorce settlement Lucky said that the house had too many bad memories for him. (No one present missed the irony of that.) He said that he wanted to make what he called 'a fresh start'. Lucky and Elizabeth have had a villa built on the hills in the south of Mansfield, at the end of the tram line. They could have afforded something much grander, but the scale of their wishes is modest. Neither of them feels the need for a mansion or servants. The house faces north and is sunny, warm and homely. When Elizabeth stands beneath the purple wisteria that she planted herself and which by 1925 has grown up along the front of the verandah, she can see all the way from the ocean in the east to the mountain range in the west. There is a wide lawn on which the children play. The local schools are considered very good.

Throughout their life together neither Lucky nor Elizabeth falls into the trap of ever wanting more than this.

And so they live together happily.

fifty-three

I almost wrote **ever after**.

As if by ending the story at that point the moment would be preserved forever and their happiness stretch out day after day, unchanged for the rest of Lucky and Elizabeth's lives. In the worst offending stories, this moment where everything seems perfect often comes just after the first kiss, but before the wedding (this makes perfect sense for anyone who's ever had to plan a wedding).

The truth is that *ever after* is just another storyteller's device.

Life goes on and everything changes. We are constantly being dealt new cards. They can bring fortune or, just as easily, misfortune. Comedy or tragedy, either — or both — can appear with the flick of the dealer's wrist, in the blink of an eye.

In the interests of telling the truth, here's what happened in the years that followed that happy May day in 1925.

Lucky's first wife kept both the name Blackwell and a lifetime interest in Woodbridge. Lucky was certainly more generous than was required by the marriage laws of the day and bore his forgotten wife no ill will. Mrs Blackwell relinquished the family name only when, in the summer of 1931, she married an admiral whose name was Toogood. He was a widower and brought with him to the marriage four daughters, all as pretty and as reserved as china dolls. The girls spoke quietly and respectfully and knew which fork to use for a shrimp entrée.

The admiral and his daughters moved into Woodbridge's empty rooms. Their light footsteps and the sound of piano and cello practice hung in the hallways, along with the tobacco smoke from the pipe that Admiral Toogood habitually had clamped between his teeth. In time a family portrait was commissioned for the now barren foyer. All in all, Mrs Blackwell found her new life very satisfactory.

Not unexpectedly, Jack grew up. At high school he was a bright and conscientious student. He gained his pilot's licence at the age of nineteen and began working for a small airline that specialised in scenic flights over the mountains and fiords of the deep south. Mathematics, however, was against Jack.

1915 + 24 = 1939

At the first opportunity Jack enlisted in the air force. He served in the Pacific as a pilot, flying spotting missions. His job was to look for Japanese ships, or for submarines resting on the surface like slim grey whales. Jack was last seen climbing into his Sunderland flying boat with his co-pilot and lifting off from the flat blue of a lagoon on the east side of Stirling Island, which is part of the Solomons group. It was 22 December 1943. The plane rose into the air, water dripping from its pontoons and banked sharply back over the beach and the tangled jungle beyond. The shirtless soldiers on the sand saw Jack give a cheery wave before the plane levelled out and headed north-east.

The wreckage was found two weeks later, and even then only by chance. Jack's Sunderland had crashed and broken in two in shallow water close to a tiny unnamed atoll about 30 miles from where he had taken off. The two halves of the plane lay among the coral, beneath 10 feet of water so clear you could call it invisible.

Both Jack's body and that of his co-pilot were retrieved and buried in the sandy soil of the island, their graves marked by crosses of faded driftwood. It was never determined if the plane was shot down or if it simply succumbed to mechanical failure.

Katherine (the baby in the perambulator) grew up to become a nurse just like her mother. She specialised in theatre work, assisting during operations with such skill that she often had the right piece of equipment ready before the surgeon even realised that he needed it. Katherine was known for her good nature, her hard work and her brand of pragmatic compassion.

Not surprisingly, Katherine Newman married a surgeon, a man she met for the first time, perhaps inauspiciously, over an open bowel. They were a good match. She had her first child in 1953, at the then relatively late age of twenty-nine. Three more babies followed. In keeping with Katherine's methodical nature, her children arrived — boy, girl, boy, girl — with no more than fifteen months between any of them.

And what of Michael Newman — MN? Perhaps you have already deduced that he was the man who, in his last years, decided that he did not want his parents' story to be forgotten. He contacted a local writer, a novelist and a playwright, and said, 'My mother fell deeply in love with a man who had no memory.'

Michael turned twenty in 1941. If mathematics was also against him, improvements in the science of cardiology were not. When being assessed for suitability as a possible offering to the gods of velocity (now more worshipped and stronger than ever), it was discovered that Michael suffered from arrhythmia. That fortunate/unfortunate heart condition meant that he served the remaining years of the war behind a desk at the Defence Department in the capital.

In 1947, still mourning the death of his beloved older brother, Michael enrolled to study engineering at the Mansfield University. He chose that discipline, he said, because he wanted to make a practical contribution. In his own words, 'After so many years of things being destroyed, I wanted to help build something.' He graduated with honours and spent most of his life employed by the Mansfield City Council designing bridges and roads.

The army doctor who had diagnosed his heart condition in 1939 told Michael confidently that his heart would not allow him to live beyond middle age.

'Fifty, tops,' the man had said breezily. 'If I were you, I'd make the most of things while you still can.'

As it was, Michael not only outlived the doctor by twenty-seven years but also lived longer than most other people of his generation. He died within a month of his wife, in 2011, aged ninety-three. They had been married for sixty-three years. He had enjoyed his professional life and had been much respected by others in his field. There is even a small suburban park named after him: a patch of green with swings and a slide.

Michael Newman is survived by three children, seven grandchildren and one great-granddaughter. It can truthfully be said that he took that army doctor's advice — he 'made the most of things'.

fifty-four

By the age of fifty-three Elizabeth has lost a husband and a son in two separate wars. You may not want to know this, but by the time Jack died she had also buried Lucky. His health had always been subject to inexplicable ups and downs. He bore these stoically, rarely complaining. On the whole Lucky was thankful for his life, for Elizabeth, the children, the years spent in the sun-filled house on the hill. A tremble in his hand or an unexplained fever, bouts of fatigue, even the headaches that came later, well, he considered these a small price to pay for everything that he had been given. Swings and roundabouts.

Lucky died in his own bed after a short illness in 1936. He was forty-nine. Whether his relatively early death was caused by his head injury is impossible to say, although we can speculate that, like Phineas Gage's demise at the age of only thirty-seven, it was most likely a factor. His death certificate gave the official cause of death as pneumonia.

In the week before he died, Lucky often lay with his head turned to look out the window. He had a view of the frilled top of the jacaranda tree that grew on the edge of the lawn, and beyond to the sky above Mansfield. It was January, and warm enough to leave the window in his room open.

Elizabeth tended him day and night; once a nurse always a nurse. Often she simply sat holding his hand. Of course she told him stories.

'Do you remember the time that Jack . . .?'

'Michael came home from school that December and said . . .'

'The first time that I saw you, you were crouching by a roaring fire. You looked so wild.'

~

I have reconsidered.

I *do* want to finish this story on that bright autumn day in 1925 when Elizabeth and Lucky and their children are walking through the Mansfield Botanic Gardens. On a day they are all together, happy and relatively healthy.

See them as they pass along an avenue of tall trees. The leaves are orange and yellow and red but very few have yet fallen; the air is still as glass. Lucky is strong enough to make a father's sudden grab and swing Michael high into the air. The boy squeals gleefully. When Lucky lowers him to the ground the two brothers run ahead through shafts and patches of sunlight and shadow.

The family walks on: past the enormous glass dome of the conservatory, which to Jack's dismay is shut for minor repairs; through the rose garden, laid out like a labyrinth with a bronze sundial at its centre; over the wide lawn to stand beneath a tall purple beech. Hundreds of discarded, brittle and transparent cicada shells cling to the bark on the trunk. For ten minutes the children delight in pulling them free. The group moves on in a ragged line and finally arrives at the museum and the skeleton of the blue whale. Of course, the two boys have seen the whale before but they are still young enough that the bones make them ooh and aah.

Let us make our ending right here and now.

With Lucky and Elizabeth standing shoulder to shoulder in front of the Mansfield whale. They watch as the boys run their hands along the sweeping jawbone, and clamber beneath the rail to swing off the great ribs. Katherine wakes. Elizabeth scoops her up and holds her against her shoulder. Her husband watches and smiles.

'I'm lucky,' he says and takes Elizabeth's free hand in his.

'Yes, I know you are.' She leans over and kisses him lightly on the lips.

What better place than here to end our story.

fifty-five

A loose end?

The story that Elizabeth told to Jack, *The Balloonist*, has been left up in the air — as it were. To see how that story concludes we must return to the papers that Michael Newman showed me at our second meeting. You may recall that among the official documents and photographs were the first two pages of a manuscript for a children's book. What happened to the other pages is a mystery.

It was most likely in the late 1950s or early 1960s when Elizabeth wrote down the story that she had begun to tell to Jack nearly forty years earlier. She recorded it in longhand, using a fountain pen. The title of the story is written on the top of the first page: *The Balloonist*. Underneath this, written in faded pencil, can still be read, *Or the Story of the Virgin and the Whale*.

Upon inspection, it seems to me that those pages are more than a first draft. There are only relatively minor crossings out and just a single note in the right-hand margin. The story is full and detailed and the sentences flow easily. For these reasons, I suggest that this version of the story is a copy of an earlier draft that has since been lost.

Late draft or not, it's difficult to say exactly how closely the story on these two yellowed pages resembles the story told to Jack in the dark of their shared bedroom in Sydenham Street. By the time she came to commit the story to paper, Elizabeth must have been a different person. The birth of two further children, Lucky's continuing bouts of ill health and then his unexpected death, not to mention losing Jack, all that must have changed her. It's impossible to say how Elizabeth grew (or diminished) over the years, as a person and as a storyteller, what new emphasis or insights the years had given her by the time she came to write *The Balloonist*.

We do know, however, that by that time she had begun telling *The Balloonist* to her grandchildren. Both Michael's and Katherine's children recall hearing at least parts of the story from their grandmother.

Tucked alongside the two pages of manuscript was a letter from a local publisher. The company was most active in the 1950s and 1960s but, in a sign of the times, has since been swallowed up by an international publishing conglomerate. The letter is of the standard type sent by publishers to would-be authors.

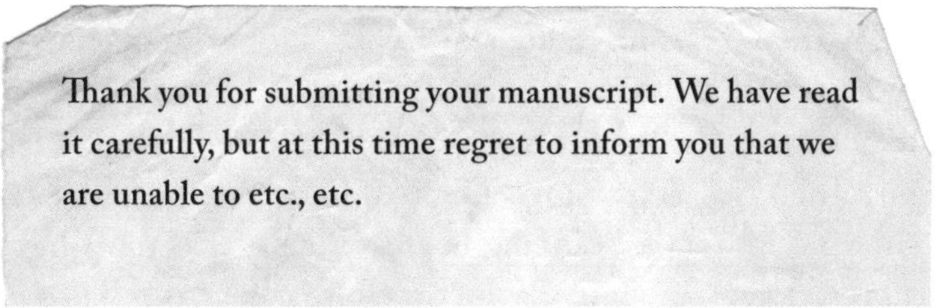
Thank you for submitting your manuscript. We have read it carefully, but at this time regret to inform you that we are unable to etc., etc.

There is, however, a personal touch. Scrawled in pen at the bottom of the letter is a brief note. It is written in blue ink and the handwriting is so tight and tangled that before it can be read it has to be unravelled by the eyes like a ball of twine:

> **An interesting story but far too frightening for young readers. Also, we could never publish a children's book containing the words [sic] 'virgin'.**

The signature is illegible but definitely differs from that on the bottom of the form letter.

In those days, it was still standard practice that submissions to publishers be typed. One of Elizabeth's grandchildren, Michael's second son, recalls his grandmother owning a typewriter of the old-fashioned jab-and-push variety, so it is doubtful whether the incomplete handwritten copy we still have is exactly the same as the one that Elizabeth sent to the publisher and had rejected. What happened to that typed copy of *The Balloonist* is unfortunately also unknown.

One last point. There was an illustration among the papers that I was shown. Neither Michael, nor any other member of the family, could remember who drew it. In a mixture of crayon and paint a child has depicted the Whale, the Virgin, the Tiger and the Balloonist. The drawing seems to show the point in the story when the unlikely band set off from the beach in pursuit of the kidnappers' boat. The crayon Whale is cobalt blue, faded only a little by the years. The Balloonist is a stick figure, made up of four grey lines and a circle. In what seems to be a particularly boyish embellishment, he is holding what appears to be a club or possibly a gun. The black and orange Tiger is disproportionately large. He is showing his teeth. Standing next to the Tiger is the Virgin. She has been drawn in white crayon on white paper so is harder to see than the other characters. Around her body, however, is a yellow outline, as though she were glowing or perhaps she is reflecting the huge yellow crayon sun set up in the right-hand corner of the page.

fifty-six

'Where are we up to in the story?' Elizabeth asks Jack.

It has been a week since Lucky was declared a free man. He has not returned to Woodbridge but is staying at a pleasant hotel near the centre of Mansfield, in the lee of the cathedral. Elizabeth visits him every day and they go for long walks. They talk about the future. That very morning, while strolling along the banks of the river, she held his hand for the first time.

Jack is in his pyjamas. He has requested that the bedside light stay on tonight. 'You remember,' he says. 'The boat is attacking the Whale. All the kidnappers have guns and the man is locked up in the cage with the baby tiger.'

'Oh yes. The man could see the kidnappers lining up along the bow of the boat with their rifles ready.'

'*At* the ready.'

'With their rifles at the ready.'

The Moon Virgin had been watching the kidnappers' boat as it swung around to face them and she saw that is was picking up speed. Beside her, the Tiger paced nervously.

'It seems that the negotiations have failed. Perhaps you should instruct our large friend to swim away.'

The Moon Virgin did not reply. Instead she began to sing again, in a language of her own devising. Although the Tiger did not know what the words meant, he thought it a very beautiful song, particularly for one of the hairless apes, who normally made noises more like the grunting of warthogs. He would, however, have preferred to hear her under less stressful circumstances.

The boat steamed towards them, black smoke pouring from its funnel, until the Whale was almost within range of the men's rifles. One or two of the more overeager kidnappers began shooting but their bullets fell harmlessly into the ocean in front of the Whale.

'I really do think that we should go now,' said the Tiger.

The Moon Virgin continued to sing. And a strange thing happened. A thin mist, barely perceptible on such a bright, cloudless day, appeared in the air above the surface of the ocean. The mist quickly thickened into a haze and then into fog. In less than a minute, the Whale had faded into white and all the kidnappers could see were swirling, shifting walls of heavy fog. The men muttered to each other uneasily.

'Quarter speed and straight ahead,' bellowed Kruger to the helmsman. The boat's engine immediately slowed. The fog had now become so thick that the kidnappers could barely see beyond their own noses.

Crouching in the cage with the tiger cub, the Balloonist saw his opportunity. No one was watching him. They were all too busy staring out into the fog that had sprung up as if by magic. Reaching into his trouser pocket, he pulled out the long, razor-sharp thorn of the jibjab tree. He unwound the piece of cloth that he had wrapped around it and, reaching through the bars, he pushed the end of the thorn into the padlock. The man began to twist it to and fro while the tiger cub watched him with large eyes.

At last the lock gave a click and sprang open.

'Come with me,' whispered the man. 'Stay close as a shadow.'

The cub had been taught well by his parents and did as he was told. Together the man and the cub crossed the deck to the cage holding the cub's mother. The man repeated the trick with the thorn and within seconds that door was also open.

When she emerged, the tigress was almost as big as her husband. Her cub immediately moved to a spot just behind her.

'Do you understand me?' asked the man. She nodded.

'Can you and your cub both swim?'

The Tigress gave him a disdainful look. 'Of course we can swim. We are tigers.'

'Then take your cub and go over the side. Your husband and our friends are waiting. Swim away from the boat. They will find you.'

The Tigress's eyes searched the deck. 'I would rather stay and revenge myself on these reeking hairless apes.'

'They are well armed. Think of your cub.'

The Tigress stared into the man's eyes and then, lifting her cub in her mouth, turned and in three bounds had leapt over the starboard side and into the ocean.

'What was that splash?' Kruger's shout came from somewhere near the bow.

'I can't see a thing!' yelled another kidnapper.

'Sounded like something falling overboard,' called someone else.

The Balloonist was about to follow the Tigress into

the ocean when he heard a terrified scream. It had come from near the stern. He ducked behind a pile of crates just as Kruger appeared out of the fog, waving his pearl-handled revolver.

'What's happening back there?' bellowed Kruger.

What neither Kruger nor the Balloonist knew was that the Tiger was onboard the boat. A few minutes earlier, the Whale had submerged and swum silently up close to the stern. He was so low in the water that the Tiger and the Moon Virgin appeared to be walking on top of the ocean. In the fog no one had seen the magnificent leap which carried the Tiger aboard.

There was a very good reason why the Moon Virgin had earlier addressed the Tiger as 'Emperor of the Green Shadows and Most Feared of All'. The Tiger hunted among them, moving as even less than a shadow through the fog, taking the kidnappers one by one. He killed the first without a sound. The man barely had time to blink.

A sudden blur.

A flash of white teeth.

A slash of claws.

Men who were standing only a few feet away from their companions disappeared without anyone seeing a thing.

The helmsman, sensing something behind him, turned towards the open door of the wheelhouse, but he was too late to save himself. After that, the boat steered itself in large circles through the fog.

Within minutes, there was only Kruger and two others left alive. By now they knew that they were not alone. The African with the gold earrings stood with the hairs on the back of his neck stiff as needles, his rifle lowered, the barrel moving from side to side.

A scream. And he was gone.

The next to die was called Fisheye by his former companions. He had his back to the ship's funnel. Sweat glistened on his face and his rifle shook. He saw movement out of the corner of his left eye and managed to swing around and squeeze off a wild shot. It was the last thing he ever did.

'Fisheye!' yelled Kruger. 'Answer me!'

But Fisheye was as dead as all the rest.

Running to the cages, Kruger saw that they were empty and let out a terrible string of curses in German. He called his men, yelling out their names, but of course none replied.

The Balloonist was watching Kruger from his hiding place behind the pile of crates when he saw the Tiger. The great cat was slinking low across the roof of the wheelhouse. Kruger had his back to the Tiger and had not seen him. The kidnapper ranted and raved and swung his revolver this way and that. The Balloonist watched as the Tiger positioned himself for the killing leap.

Two things happened at the same time. A random eddy of air meant that the fog cleared, just for a split second. In that moment the Balloonist saw every detail of the Tiger: the twitch of his mighty shoulders, the stony black of his eyes, the fresh blood around his jaws.

The second thing that happened was that Kruger somehow sensed movement behind him. At the very same moment that the Tiger sprang, Kruger spun and fired his revolver.

The Tiger gave a roar of pain and fell to the deck at Kruger's feet.

The Balloonist had to stifle a cry. For a terrible moment he thought that his friend had been killed. But the great eyes opened and the Tiger struggled painfully to his feet. The Balloonist could see that the bullet had hit the Tiger in his front leg, where the fur was now dark and matted. Kruger took a step forward and pointed his gun between the Tiger's eyes.

'How terrible it must feel to almost *succeed,' he said.*

The Tiger looked over at the empty cages. 'You are wrong. I have *succeeded.'*

Kruger scowled. 'At least this trip will not have been a total waste. I still have the diamonds and after I have shot you I will sell your body. Your skin will become a rug for rich people to walk on. Your bones will be ground up for old Chinamen to drink.'

'Oh, do stop babbling and shoot me,' said the Tiger bravely.

The kidnapper smirked. 'Very well. I will.'

'Stop!'

The Balloonist stepped out from behind the crates and advanced on the kidnapper. He held the thorn of the jibjab tree in front of him like a dagger.

Kruger was now in a difficult position. He had the wounded Tiger on one side of him and the Balloonist advancing on the other. He could not cover both of them with his gun. He swung the revolver around to the man.

'Come any closer and I will kill you.'

'I've no doubt. The interesting thing, though, is that your pretty revolver only takes six bullets. I've been counting and by my reckoning you've got only one shot left.'

The Tiger growled deeply and took a step towards Kruger. The needle-sharp tips of his claws scrapped the hardwood deck.

Kruger swung the gun back towards the Tiger.

The man took another step forward.

Now Kruger was forced to point the gun back at him. 'The next one to move dies!'

The Balloonist spoke calmly. 'If you shoot one of us, I promise you that the other will finish you off. I suggest that the only sane thing you can do is surrender.'

'Never!' snarled Kruger.

From the look in his eye it was clear that the German was not sane. It was also clear that he had decided his next move. He feared the Tiger more than the man and swung his gun back onto the great cat. 'I choose you.'

'No!' yelled the Balloonist. Raising the jibjab thorn above his head, he charged. Now Kruger had no choice. There was a shot. The Balloonist staggered backwards and the jibjab thorn clattered to the deck.

In a blur, the Tiger sprang. Kruger's shaved head was big, yet it still fitted into the great jaws. With a crunch, like the sound of an ostrich shell breaking, the leader of the kidnappers died.

The Tiger let the limp body fall and walked over to where the Balloonist lay on the deck. There was a small hole close to his heart that leaked crimson blood in a steady trickle.

'Why did you do it?' asked the Tiger gently.

The man managed a smile. 'In a battle some people must die so that their friends may live.'

The Tiger stared down into the Balloonist's face. 'Every year on this day I swear to you I will tell your story to my family. And when I have hunted my last hunt, my children will tell their children. In this way, we will never forget you. It has been a great honour to know you.'

'And you, my friend.'

The Tiger bowed his head low. The Balloonist closed his eyes and took his last breath.

fifty-seven

There are tears on Jack's cheeks. Elizabeth brushes them away with the edge of her finger.

'What happened after he died?' asks Jack.

'The fog cleared and the Whale carried his body back to the beach. The Moon Virgin washed him in the warm ocean and then she dressed him in his uniform again. The Moon Virgin, the Tiger, the Tigress and the cub buried him at the foot of a tree in a clearing close to the beach.'

'Was it a jibjab tree?'

Elizabeth smiles. 'Yes, it was.'

'It's not fair. He had a son too.'

'His family were very proud of how brave he had been.'

'But what will they do now?'

'That's a different story.' Elizabeth stands. 'I think they'll be all right. They'll look after each other.'

Jack has no more questions. He lays his head back on the pillow. Elizabeth switches off the lamp. A strip of yellow light from the hallway falls through the half-open door into the room.

'I didn't know him very well but I'll still miss him,' says Jack quietly.

'So will I,' says Elizabeth. 'I'll miss him every day and very, very much. Goodnight, my love.'

'Goodnight.'

fifty-eight

Enough.

All endings are arbitrary. After all, how can you know when a story is *truly* finished?